D0915992

LIKE
THUNDER

DAW Books proudly presents
the novels of Nnedi Okorafor

WHO FEARS DEATH
THE BOOK OF PHOENIX

NOOR

BINTI: THE COMPLETE TRILOGY
(Binti | Binti: Home | Binti: The Night Masquerade
with Binti: Sacred Fire)

The Desert Magician's Duology
SHADOW SPEAKER
LIKE THUNDER

LIKE THUNDER

THE DESERT MAGICIAN'S DUOLOGY: BOOK TWO

NNEDI OKORAFOR

DAW BOOKS
New York

Jacket illustration by Greg Ruth

Jacket design by Jim Tierney

Edited by Betsy Wollheim

DAW Book Collectors No. 1951

DAW Books
An imprint of Astra Publishing House
dawbooks.com
DAW Books and its logo are registered trademarks of Astra Publishing House

Printed in the United States of America

Library of Congress Cataloging-in-Publication Data

Names: Okorafor, Nnedi, author. | Okorafor, Nnedi.
Desert magician's duology ; 2.
Title: Like thunder : the Desert magician's duology:
book two / Nnedi Okorafor.
Other titles: DAW book collectors ; no. 1953.
Description: First edition. | New York : DAW Books, 2023. |
Series: The desert magician's duology ; 2
Identifiers: LCCN 2023028146 (print) | LCCN 2023028147 (ebook) |
ISBN 9780756418793 (hardcover) | ISBN 9780756418809 (ebook)
Subjects: LCSH: Sahara--Fiction. | LCGFT: Fantasy fiction. | Novels.
Classification: LCC PS3615.K67 L55 2023 (print) |
LCC PS3615.K67 (ebook) | DDC 813/.6--dc23/eng/20230718
LC record available at https://lccn.loc.gov/2023028146
LC ebook record available at https://lccn.loc.gov/2023028147

First edition: November 2023
10 9 8 7 6 5 4 3 2 1

Dedicated to my mother, Dr. Helen Okorafor

Africa breathes stories.

—*Ben Okri,* Birds of Heaven

Translating . . .

Dikéogu Audio File Series
begun April 8, 2074
Current Location: *Unknown Region, Niger*
Weather: *36° C (98° F), N.I.U.F. (Not Including Unpredictable Factors)*

This audio file has been automatically translated from the Igbo language.

Rainmaker

My name is Dikéogu Obidimkpa. I am a rainmaker. Born in Nigeria but *made* elsewhere. The tattoo on my face is red and white, the colors of Shango, god of thunder and lightning. My tattoo turned those colors on its own. It used to be blue. Shango's colors suit me better.

I dictate this account of all that happened after everything has happened. But it's all still happening. You'll understand as you listen. For me, stories never end. I recorded these specific files that I titled "Rainmaker" when I was or *am* having an especially camelshit type of day. When it's hard to think, when I feel like I'll just blow apart or blow away. Making these files help. Sort of. In a blood-letting kind of way. So if I sound different in "rainmaker" files, you'll understand why.

A storm came today. It blew in out of nowhere, but I knew it was coming. I always know when a storm is coming. It snapped palm trees like matchsticks. Threw a scooter like a sack of stockfish. It soaked the sand and grass like Noah's flood. It washed rooftops. It was noisy and glorious.

But I spent that half hour on the dirt floor of this small house with all the lizards, spiders, and centipedes. No one could speak to me. No one could touch me. Only Gambo would have understood.

When I closed my eyes, I saw huge rolling gray clouds. I could smell the land's fragrance rise up just before the rain came. I could smell the clouds as lightning ionized water vapor. I could feel the air pressure drop and then rise.

I was splashed with millions of raindrops. I could feel what could have been. The destruction. The power. I could hear the rain and thunder, outside. First the patter of sand on grass and leaves, and then the splash of mud. The howl of wind.

And when I opened my eyes, I wanted to flee. But I couldn't. Not anymore. I am in fear's chasm. Okay, maybe Ejii would understand, too.

My hands tremble just thinking about it.

I can't change what I am.

I am a rainmaker, but mostly it rained on me.

Don't wish to be me. Or to be able to do what I do. What I can do can be done to me when the sky merely wills it.

CHAPTER 1

Better Told Than Written

I've seen so much.

I want you to imagine it.

So, as I said, I'm recording my words as an audio file on this damn near indestructible e-legba, a piece of portable tech so strong it outlasted the apocalypse. Sure, it looks pretty beaten up. That's because it's taken quite a beating. But no other personal device could do all that this one does, trust me. Recording something doesn't even raise its processor-usage level, not even by a fraction. And it's both solar *and* lunar. This recording will last.

Some things are better told than written. Maybe the old Africans had it right in initially making their traditions oral. Plus I'm more of a talker than a writer. I don't have the patience to spend hours tapping on keys. Plus out here in the middle of the desert, I kind of like the sound of my voice.

And I'm an honest guy, not some *mumu* guy. Of all people, *I* don't believe in gossip. Gossip is what got me in this mess in the first place. You can trust me. It's okay to let your guard down. I'll tell you no lies. No exaggerations. Fear no ego. No need for suspension of disbelief. This all happened and God help me now.

My friend Ejii liked to laugh about how I barely trusted

anyone. She liked to exist in the naïve-nice-person-land where all humans, deep down, are good. I wonder what she thinks now, after so many have proven themselves to be cowards, liars, cheats, murderers, and lackadaisical pacifists who are happy to sit and watch innocent people die terrible deaths. Yeah, I said it. Someone has to. I know what I've seen. I know what I've had to do. And yeah, this thing is recording.

The Great Change was this weird combination of a nuclear apocalypse and the explosion of powerful juju called "Peace Bombs." This messed up many of Earth's laws of physics and brought down the wall between worlds. Then there was a pact of peace. It was written by noble genius baboons with black hands and soft brown fur that smelled like mint and grass. They wrote the pact in a magical language called nsibidi. This pact forced a truce between the evil inflated Chief Ette of Ginen's Ooni Kingdom and the insanely heroic Jaa the Red One of the Sahara Desert. It stopped a war of the worlds, especially between Earth and the jungle planet Ginen. I'm damn proud to say that I was there and a part of why the pact was successful. So was Ejii, of course. She was a big deal that day.

That pact was some serious, deep, *old* mysticism. Even after all I've seen, I still find it amazing. That it happened at all is unbelievable. That it lasted for so long was nothing short of a miracle. For a few months it kept the monster of war still, and for three years it held it at bay. But the pact eventually disintegrated, as it had to. But so did a lot of other things.

How do I explain all that happened? I'll make it simple: eventually, all hell broke loose . . .

CHAPTER 2

Chocolate Factory

Right after the historic pact was made, I had important business to take care of. One problem solved (temporarily, at least), so on to the next one. I was focused, as was my owl Kola. And so was my mentor Gambo.

We all had reasons for going on this mission. For Gambo and me, it was because we'd both actually experienced slavery firsthand. Buji, Gambo's co-husband, was just a guy who revered justice. When he saw injustice, he *had* to do something about it. The Nigérien Bureau of Investigation, a.k.a. the N.B.I., came with us because they were trying to cover their asses and not *look* like asses. As if they could prevent that. All these years and they knew nothing about what was happening in the northern part of what used to be Niger? Camelshit. They knew. And now they knew that if they didn't do something they'd suffer hard-core sanctions and boycotts.

Gambo, Buji, Kola, and I had just left Ejii and Jaa in Kwàmfà. I was so excited to be going north with these people. After all that had happened. Toward this specific place. A place I hated.

Assamakka.

This place used to be a small innocent desert city with mazes of mud-brick homes, camels, goats, desert birds, scurrying lizards, women pounding millet, and men kneeling in prayer. But after the Great Change, when nuclear and Peace bombs fell and huge swaths of land here shifted from dead sand to lively sand and soil, opportunists made it the central headquarters of the cocoa industry. Most of the world's cocoa used to make chocolate came from Assamakka and the farming towns around it. And all these places used cheap labor. *Really* cheap labor. Cheap *young* labor. Child slaves.

There is definitely a reason I hate chocolate. I'll always hate it. I'd rather die than eat it. Chocolate was mixed with blood, sweat, and tears of children. It was a haunted confection. Way way back in 2003, Niger passed a law making slavery illegal. And even before that there were laws against child labor. These did nothing to stop it, though.

Even with all the spontaneous forests and new worlds and people and creatures dying and changing all over the place . . . you could *still* get chocolate. Anytime, anywhere. Common brown blocks of smooth delicious pleasure. Melted or solid. But no one wondered where it came from. How surprised you all would have been, *o*.

All I have to say about the land along the way is that it was dry, cracked, and full of nasty aggressive red beetles that tried to burrow into our tents at night. And they stained whatever you crushed them on. That didn't stop me, though. I had garments stained with red dots to prove it.

This was just before we met up with the N.B.I. We didn't see

any spontaneous forests and the weather was acceptable—
meaning it was harsh and hot during the day but cool at night.
Gambo and I wouldn't have meddled with the weather regardless, even if we came across a severe storm. Even before we'd set
out for Assamakka, he'd made sure to teach me that one should
alter the weather sparingly or work with the will of nature.

"It's irresponsible to do otherwise," he said in his usual
low rumbly voice. "A rainmaker who thinks he owns the sky
is a rainmaker soon painfully killed by rain, snow, lightning,
hail, or all of the above."

About two days later, we stopped at a market for supplies—
a second capture station for water, some new tents (those vile
red beetles had eaten through two of ours), green tea, dried
meat (a group of desert foxes had stolen much of ours), salt
for the camels, a bag of millet to make *tuagella* (those thick
crêpes that you eat with butter or sauce).

I remember all this because this turned out to be the last
time we were in civilization for months. It was also where I
bought this e-legba that I'm using to record my voice. Ejii had
one that she liked to use to check the weather, play games,
read books, and listen to music. I believe she lost it on the
way to Ginen, though.

I used to have an expensive one back in my old life, before my parents sold me out. This new one that I got at the
market wasn't nearly as pricey, but I wasn't complaining. It
did what it needed to do. Of course, the e-legba I bought was
nothing like the souped-up device it is now. Not yet.

We continued on our way, and what would happen next
would shape everything that led me to where I am today.

═══

About a day after leaving the market, we met up with a man named Ali Mamami. He was the head of the Nigérien Bureau of Investigation. He was a pretty intense guy. Ali liked to wear flowing garments that were so voluminous that you couldn't tell if he was skinny or fat. He never smiled. He didn't add sugar to his mint tea or use salt with his meals. He didn't listen to music. The man was like petrified wood. You wonder what someone like that has seen to make him that way. But I didn't think he was so impressive. He'd missed what was going on in the north, for Christ's sake. Still, I kept out of his way.

With him came twenty N.B.I. agents—men *and* women specially trained for this kind of thing. Before the Great Change, they'd have all carried big guns. These people, however, carried machetes, Tuareg-style swords called *takoba*, and high-tech bows and arrows, and were trained in hand-to-hand combat and wore weather gel–treated uniforms and army boots (you did *not* want to be near any of their feet when they took those boots off). Two women even had a pair of those Ginen weapons called seed shooters.

My friend Ejii had told me about these, but I'd never seen one until one of these women showed me. They look like hand-sized greenish brown disks with a notch on the side for your fingers. And they were very light. The woman, her name was Nusrat, clasped it in her hand as she faced the desert, the end of her brown veil over her head fluttering in the breeze. The other woman, Hira, wore a veil over her head, too. I assume they were both Muslim. Or maybe they just liked the attire; you never know.

Nusrat grinned, obviously enjoying demonstrating.

"It feels hard but it's alive, a plant," she said. Her voice was kind of low. If it weren't for the enormous size of her chest (you couldn't miss it, even with the uniform) and her face (okay, she was quite attractive), I'd have speculated that she might have been a man. She had an intensity that reminded me of Gambo, and there's *nothing* remotely feminine about Gambo.

Nusrat took my hand and held it to the seed shooter. As soon as my hand touched it, it changed from greenish brown to dark brown as if it were some sort of plant chameleon. "It responds to touch," she said, laughing. "It doesn't like you. For some reason, seed shooters prefer women. The accuracy is always better when they are used by them. Be very afraid if you come across a man with one, especially if you're *not* his target."

I frowned, thinking of those giant flightless birds Ejii had ridden in Ginen. They supposedly didn't let boys or men ride on them, either. Maybe things from Ginen preferred female humans to male ones.

"You stroke the side and it hums," Nusrat said, rubbing the seed shooter. It made this sound that was oddly like the purr of a cat. You could feel it, too. Like it was more animal than plant. I'd have thrown the thing away, but I wanted to know what it felt like when it shot. "When you squeeze it," she said, "your four fingers have to be touching this smooth patch on the front."

She pointed the seed shooter at the ground, aiming a few yards away, and squeezed my hand. I barely felt or heard a thing. Just a soft *phht* as something reddish orange blasted into the sand. Then there was a sort of oatmeally smell. *POW!* There was a small explosion in the sand as the seed popped like a large popcorn kernel. Some big green beetles emerged from the sand nearby and frantically scrambled away. Imagine what that seed would have done if the seed were embedded in someone's chest, leg, arm, or . . . head.

She strapped the thing against the bare skin of her side, pulling her uniform over it. Seed shooters produce more seeds by feeding on body heat. Needless to say, those two women were probably the most lethal N.B.I. agents in the Sahara because of their skill and those weapons.

I smiled. Lethal was what I wanted.

———

Long ago, people used to talk about Blood Oil and Blood Diamonds. They should have been talking about Blood *Chocolate*, too. All those children. All branded with those tattoos their first day there. Applied by some hairy motherless man who reeked of alcohol and chocolate, with his cruel relentless dirty needle.

A blue line from the center of the forehead, down the bridge of the nose. All the way to the nose tip. Blue dots on the side of the line, like some weird railroad track. Imagine it. You're ten years old or nine or fourteen or sixteen. And this is happening to you. On your face! To always be the first thing people see. And no one will come to stop it. No one cares.

I was one of those cocoa farm slaves. I have the facial tattoos to prove it.

We were all friends because we had to be. When you're in

a bad situation, you stick together. Well, at least until it is time
to get the hell out. I'd still be there if I hadn't thought like this.
The only person who would have come with me was dead.

When I returned to those farms with Buji, Gambo, and
the N.B.I., it had been a year since my escape. Just seeing the
place made my stomach growl with hunger and my heart
clench with rage.

===

When I was a slave, I knew all the children around me. Asibi
was about thirteen years old, like me. We used to bicker a lot
because she never wanted to ever cross the masters, and I
did . . . well, my close friend Adam did and his ideas were
contagious to me. Asibi just wanted to survive. This always
annoyed the hell out of me. One doesn't survive by just surviving.

When Asibi was ten, she was walking home one day when
a man approached her. He was all smiles and compliments,
as those kinds of guys always are to those kinds of girls. He
promised her that if she worked on the farms for a week, he'd
pay her nine hundred dollars and give her a bicycle. She told
me that that would have fed her family for three years and
the bicycle would have allowed her to start her own business.

Asibi dreamed of selling dried butterflies. You know,
those large yellow and red ones that cure colds when ground
into a tea? That man didn't tell her that she'd have to travel
ten hours north in a sweltering empty old oil tanker infested
with biting flies to get to the farm. Nor did her tell her that
she'd almost die from heat stroke and dehydration on the

way. And, naturally, he didn't tell her that he was lying and that she'd *never* be going home.

Now, Tunde, Yemi, and Abiola were what we call "area boys." They were about fifteen years old. They came all the way from Lagos, Nigeria. They'd sold drugs, stolen e-legbas, pacemakers, and hundreds of other electronic devices, extorted money from passersby, dabbled in the illegal trade of human organs, you get the picture. They were trouble and their stupid parents knew it. So, instead of being good parents and taking responsibility for Tunde, Yemi, and Abiola, their parents sold them to slave buyers.

Halima, she was sold by her father for less than fifty dollars. Fiddausi was kidnapped, snatched right off the side of the road as she sold boiled eggs. Bako, Dauda, and Dogonyaro were the children of one of the slave masters! And the three of them worked as hard as anyone else and lived as hard, too! You can see how twisted the minds of the slave masters were. Hell, they made their own *children* slaves! It's a cultural disease and it runs deep.

As we traveled back to the slave plantation, I remembered so many names. I remembered backs with wet festering sores and ugly scabs from whippings. Bent from heavy sacks of cocoa beans taller than them. Cracked lips. Bleeding fingers. Blank emotionless faces. My own story was a little more complicated. Actually, it wasn't . . . like so many others, my parents sold me, too. They couldn't deal with a son who kept getting struck by lightning and having the nerve to keep living through it. I embarrassed and humiliated them. Imagine that.

Oddly, I think I was the only Changed One there. The buyers stupidly didn't notice my abilities. My uncle Segun who brought me there obviously kept that little fact quiet. He wanted his money, I guess.

Normally, the farm owners were smart to avoid buying and taking Changed children. Think of the trouble a wind-seeker, metalworker, sidewinder, sorter, or a shadow speaker could cause. Especially one who manifests strongly at a young age. Of course, one didn't have to be Changed to shake things up. Look at my friend Adam. They feared him so much that they killed him.

Many of the slave children had never even tasted chocolate. There was a busybody girl named Zuumi. She was about nine years old. Really really smart but mischievous. We called her Zoom because she liked to keep a close eye on the masters. She could tell what they were up to even from far away. One day she saw one of the masters drop a candy bar in the sand. Those sick bastards enjoyed eating them in front of us. With their chocolaty breath, sticky hands, and violent tempers. I won't call them what they really were.

They never saw Zoom creep up and snatch up the candy bar. We usually ate burned bananas and thin rice porridge and beans riddled with black beetles. That night in the shed that they always locked us in, she shared the melted chocolate bar. Everyone who wanted one got a fingertip full. Fifty children had their first taste of chocolate that night. For this reason, the shed was noisier than usual. Those who'd tasted it whispered, snickered, giggled, and chatted for hours. I couldn't care less. I'd tasted chocolate plenty of times. Heck, I was well versed in the taste of far more exquisite cuisine. But I was happy for the others. They deserved to taste what they were suffering to make.

Unfortunately, some kid leaked information about the chocolate bar to the masters. The next day, Zoom was dragged out and beaten unconscious. The Masters were so afraid we'd develop a taste for the stuff; that the chocolate would spark ideas of rebellion and freedom in our mouths that would travel to our souls. They had nothing to worry about. We were a broken bunch.

Except for Adam. And me, I guess. They killed Adam by letting him die when he got sick. I escaped. By the skin of my teeth.

━━━━

The place had changed since my time there.

Earth's lands rarely stay the same for long. It's so alive and twisted. Desert can become ocean overnight. Mountain can become flatland. Jungle tends to just get bigger and wilder; rarely does it become desert. But desert certainly becomes jungle. And there is more of everything. More land. More worlds. The Great Merge made sure of that.

The miles of desert that once surrounded the farms, the deserts that had nearly killed me when I escaped, were now grassy savanna. It was populated with bony long-eared hares and small edible yams. Between the small pools of water, the hares, and the yams, a resourceful kid could easily survive an escape from the farms . . . well, if it weren't for one thing. Something lived out there, in the dark. It tried to attack us that night. Some roaring, sniveling thing that no light could catch.

The ground shook as it moved. That's what woke us all up. There was a lot of scrambling, as it was the dead of night.

No moon. The stars blocked by thin clouds. I don't sleep in tents, so I merely had to stand up. Kola, my owl, flew onto my shoulder.

The air was calm. Dead. And the night air was suddenly very very warm and dry. Night in the desert has *never* been warm in places like this. You could hear the clang of *takoba* swords, bows and arrows, machetes, as people snatched for them. I heard Agent Ali bark out orders in his unsmiling voice. But I was looking into the night, past our camp. Like any rainmaker, I could feel it more than see it. About a half mile away, the air wasn't right. It wasn't right at all.

"A man at that market told us about this," Gambo said, stepping up beside me. He smelled of sandalwood and his white garments were swirling around him. "I didn't believe him."

"I did," Buji said, calmly.

I think both Gambo and Buji were smiling. But it was dark and so were they, so I couldn't be sure. Those two always had a thirst for a good fight. Not me, though. No warrior blood in my veins.

"Told you about what?" I whispered. The ground shook again.

"Follow my lead," was all Gambo said. "The others can't do anything about this. Just you and me, Dikéogu." God, sometimes he could be so cryptic.

He quickly moved forward. Instinct told me to run backward. I grabbed his flowing garments, otherwise I'd have lost him in seconds. A thousand things and nothing flew through my mind. I'd seen much by this time. Almost died a few times, too. But, oh Allah, I was scared. My God, I was terrified beyond belief.

We were moving past panicky and excited agents. Buji
was shouting, "Get back. Get back!" as he herded people in
the opposite direction. Gambo didn't even glance back at me.
Then the roaring started. It vibrated in my head. I thought
it was going to blow out my eardrums, or shake my body to
death, or crack my skin open. At some point, Kola launched
herself up and flew away. Gambo's voice sounded muffled as
he shouted, "Bring Shango's wrath, Dikéogu! Lightning!
Rain! Call it with me!"

I didn't need to be told twice. The slightest threat to my
being and the skies rumbled with thunder. It was like nature
didn't like seeing me upset. I was full of adrenaline. I swear I
was looking at death. The darkness before us was infinitely
deep. Absolute nothingness. But it was *alive*. And it was loping
toward us. Hungry. Starved. It would swallow us forever.

I brought lightning and rain and wind like my soul de-
pended on it. Between Gambo and me, the sky happily responded with great force. It broiled and folded on itself, heavy
with gray clouds, even as it thrust down rain and lightning.

Whatever the living darkness was, it hated light and water.
The very things that inspire life, when you think about it. As the
Tuareg like to say, "Water is life." And the Bible says, "Let there
be light." And so on. The lightning crashed and the rain came.
You smelled ozone and you could see the thing's darkness re-
pulsed by each violent flash of the deep blue, purple, yellow.

Gambo and I were soaked to the bone by the deluge.
Even in the flashes of bright lightning, the thing was nothing
more than a shadow, a big big shadow, standing maybe a
half-mile high! We dealt with it. That's all I'll say. Such things
are best not spoken of for too long.

Come morning, the grasses all around us were crushed flat and browning in giant circles. And everything was dry. I hadn't slept a wink. How the hell could I sleep after seeing something like that?!

We packed up and headed for the cocoa farms.

=====

They never saw us coming. The cocoa-farm masters and guards were clueless.

There were about sixty of them. Arrogant bastards. They didn't notice over twenty people approach their farms on flatland in broad daylight. Maybe they didn't expect anyone to get past the miles and miles of monster-harboring savanna. Or maybe they were thrown off by the sudden rainstorm. Gambo did the winds; I brought down the rain, adding a few lighting strikes for . . . dramatics. Dramatics that burned down the lookout point on the north side. I'd only been in there once and it was to receive the worst beating of my life for mouthing off to one of the masters. I burned that place to nothing.

Here's the lay of the land in Assamakka:

Miles and miles of dry savanna, then the cocoa-growing zone starts. I think this place used to be a giant spontaneous forest, because I don't know how all those tall trees and bushes could have grown in a matter of thirty years. I mean, that place, before the Great Change, would have been dry dry dead desert. Now it's humid foresty farmland with tall trees and mistletoe, mixed with well-spaced cocoa trees and a million blood-sucking midges, mosquitoes, and ants. Other things live there, too, I guess. Butterflies, these huge grass-hoppers, sunbirds, rodents, things of that nature.

The cocoa tree is an ugly thing. It's short with white, waxy, poisonous-looking flowers and limp wide green leaves. And it produces a leathery-skinned pod that's green, orange, or red. You open one up sideways and the cocoa beans inside look like a bunch of crooked discolored teeth. And not sur-prisingly, the trees are pollinated by those biting midges . . . and the slaves are bitten by them.

When I was there, most of the cocoa trees were pretty healthy. But you had to watch for plant problems like capsid bugs, blackpod fungus, and swollen shoot virus disease. Why the hell do I know this insignificant information? All the kids did. We were beaten if any of these things were found on our watch.

So you had about two miles of farm forest with raised mud-brick lookout points on the north, south, east, and west sides. Then the headquarters in the center where they'd cleared away all the trees except for a palm tree or two. Here, there was a big house made of bricks and mortar.

We moved quickly down the main path that led into the trees, slogging through the rich soily mud as the rain came down in heavy sheets. This path eventually led to the head-quarters. What a change from the dry sand. It slumped and sucked nastily at my sandals. For once I envied the thick boots the agents wore. After a while, I just took off my san-dals and shoved them in the waistband of my pants. I was soaked and muddy anyway. Kola sat on my shoulder. Her feathers were like a natural raincoat, so rain never both-ered her.

Suddenly, two men came walking out of the trees right in front of us! Four agents grabbed them, but not before one of the men raised the alarm, a shrill whistle that carried over the noise of the rainstorm. Then I heard the whistle repeated in the trees. It was repeated farther and farther. So much for the element of surprise. Those stupid sloppy farm guys got really lucky.

Gambo cursed. Buji and Agent Ali started barking orders. Then Buji disappeared with ten agents into the trees. He had his machete in hand.

Moments later, in the same direction, someone screamed with pain.

"Tell your bird to fly to safety," Gambo snapped at me, looking around.

"Kola, go!" I said. "Find me when it's safe." She took off.

Two agents were grappling with the two captured men, knocking them on their heads and tying their arms.

Phht! An agent beside me fell, holding his neck and gasping. Nusrat dragged him off the path. She dropped him, snatched up her seed shooter and shot into the tree.

Another screech of pain.

"Stay close," Gambo said, grabbing my upper arm and pulling me low.

My heart was smashing against my chest. It was raining too hard for me to see well. *I'm electrocuting anyone who touches me,* I thought frantically. There were twice as many of them as us. Maybe they didn't know *when* we were coming, but it seemed they knew we were coming. There was no other explanation for the swell in their numbers.

The next several minutes were absolute hell. I've never

been in a war before, but I'm certain this was what it was like
back in the days before guns and nuclear bombs . . . minus
those two women with the seed shooters. Running, fighting,
screaming, shouting, cursing, bleeding, some dying. Poison
darts, machetes, daggers, various other types of blades, sling-
shots, bows and arrows, human beings will always find ways
to maim and kill each other. And they will always find reasons. And sometimes there are good reasons.

Some people ran back, some ran forward, some hid. Like
me. I stayed with Gambo for a while. Under the trees, our
weather-manipulating abilities weren't so useful. Our rain
was slowed by the trees and our lightning, which I was best
at, was too dangerous for the agents around us. All we could
use was the wind to blow people away, and this was exhaust-
ing. Doing so required heavy doses of concentration and
heavy breathing. It makes you dizzy after a while. Plus I
wasn't very good yet.

"Keep moving!" Gambo shouted. "Toward the headquarters! You know the way."

"Yeah," I said.

We ran together until I spotted a man running at an agent.
Gambo ran ahead, unaware that I had stopped. That's how we
got separated. The man I had stopped to stare at was very tall,
broad shouldered, arms like tree trunks. The agent was average height but well built, also. They clashed in a spatter of
water and mud. The agent doubled over and gasped. The man
had buried a dagger in the left side of the agent's chest. He
shoved the dagger deeper and the agent gasped again, his eyes
wide with shock. Then he fell, oozing blood into the mud.

I felt nauseous.

The victorious man looked at the dying agent. Then he looked right at me.

I gagged.

I knew this man. He was heads taller than me, many pounds heavier, decades older. We called him Big Blokkus. If you don't know the vulgar meaning of this name, don't ask me for it. Just know that it fit him well. The man was powerful. The man was cruel. And he was a murderer. A filthy bastard who liked to beat on the older boy slaves. He was the one who had given me that terrible beating for mouthing off. My lip had split, my left eye had swollen shut, my shoulder had been bruised, and my right ear rang for days. That had been the day after I found Adam dead in that goddamn shed.

Then a more vivid memory blasted into my mind. Big Blokkus was the last person to see Adam alive. He'd closed the door to the shed where Adam lay on a mildewy bed of hay. He'd had a smirk on his face and Adam had had no expression at all because he was sleeping. The sound of the lock as he shut the door was etched deep in my soul. Who knows what Big Blokkus did to Adam behind that door? Smothered him, injected him with poison, simply did nothing and let Adam's fever finish him off.

My left eye twitched. "You remember me?" I asked, raising my chin.

Water ran down his face as Big Blokkus blinked and squinted at me through the rain. He grinned a savage grin and pointed, rain and blood dripping from his index finger. "*Na* boy who escape," he said in pidgin English. "Long time. Now see peppah. I kill you now, eh? I murdah you like I murdah your little boyfriend."

I didn't know where Gambo was. The noise and wetness of my rainstorm faded. The squishy mud beneath my feet retreated. All my focus was on him. So he *had* killed Adam. It felt so fresh; he could have done it just yesterday. I focused on Big Blokkus. His grinned widened. I must have been out of my mind.

Tears flew from my eyes as I ran at him. Big Blokkus got low, readying himself. I didn't care.

He knocked me hard in the chest. I grunted, flying back and landing in the mud, wheezing.

I got up. Metallic red and blue stars twinkled in the corners of my vision. I ran at him again. I was smarter this time. I lunged low at his legs, wrapping my arms around them as he laughed and looked down at me.

"I missed you too," he said, guffawing like the idiot he was. He was about to raise his foot and slam it down on my head. I looked up at him. I grinned. He stopped laughing as his muscles began to lock up. Slowly, he fell to the ground.

I didn't let go of him.

Think of an electric eel. It can produce a current of hundreds of volts. That amount can kill a human being. Me, I can produce the voltage of lightning, which is closer to a billion volts. Yeah.

I let him suffer. I let him burn. I don't think I could have stopped if I had wanted to. I didn't want to. I'm ashamed of myself for this now. But back then, my mind just went black. You know how when sharks are eating, their pupils dilate really wide? Like they are seeing everything, taking in everything at the same time? It was like that for me. I saw all this man had done in the grand scheme of things. I couldn't help myself. In that moment, I became merciless.

His eyes were locked on mine. First his clothes burned. Then his medium-length Afro burned. His eyebrows. His bushy beard. The hair all over his body. It stank horribly. His skin crisped. His breathing grew ragged.

Finally, I let go of him. I stood up and stared down. He looked up at me. He was a dead man breathing. His lips were wet and bleeding. Smoke rose from his raw body as the rain put out his burning flesh with a soft sizzle. The smell of charred meat.

I shuddered, realization washing over me like hot water. My brain was beginning to work again. This was not a dream, a game, or a story, this was real. There was a near-dead, fried man at my feet. *I* had made him that way. Me.

Again, I felt a wave of nausea.

Tears ran from my eyes, mixing with the rain. He was just a man. How would this have ended if I were not a Changed One?

"Move aside, boy." Her voice startled me and I yelped, jumping back. It was Nusrat.

"I . . ."

"No need," she said. She pointed her seed shooter at the man's head. I shut my eyes just in time. But even over the drip of water and squelch of mud I heard the sound of his last ragged breath. I turned to the side and vomited. It was the first time I'd killed someone. And I had done it brutally with my ability. It wasn't the last time. As I said, you don't want to be able to do what I can do.

======

"We've got this under control," Gambo said. He was breathing heavily and his eyes were the color of mud, as they always were when he used the wind. During these times, he also always seemed taller and, well, less there. To use the wind is to be used by it, too.

At this moment, he was using it to trap three men. A small cyclone of mud whirled around them as they dropped to their knees, their hands over their heads, mud smacking against them. "Go find the children," Gambo said, barely glancing at me.

His words couldn't have been sweeter. I needed to do something before I spontaneously imploded from shock, guilt, and disgust with myself. I knew exactly where they'd be. Even in the humid heat, they'd be locked in the shed. A hundred kids packed inside, sweating, wheezing, and fainting. As I ran there, overhead the sky cleared. I hadn't asked it to. The sky does what it will do. I ran about a mile. The sun's rays heated the sand and soon a heavy mist rose up like a giant ghost. I didn't need to see to know where I was going.

Locks are not a problem for me. I can turn them to rust. I turned this one to ash. The door swung open with a loud creak. The kids could have kicked it down if they wanted to, lock or no lock. But as I said, they were a broken bunch.

A tall girl stood in front of the others, her arms protectively out. Behind her the other children stared, nothing but wide white eyes. In the dark of the shed their sun-blackened skin made them shadows.

The girl wore old white plastic sandals and a tattered

sackcloth dress. She smelled vaguely of sweat, barely of dust. Her hair was a dull orange from malnutrition. The sides of her mouth were cracked and she had a mad look in her eye. She held a sharpened stick in her left hand.

I looked her in the eye. She blinked. Then she frowned. "Dikéogu?" she whispered. Her voice was parched like baked cocoa leaves. She didn't drop her sharpened stick. I swear I will never forget seeing her in such a depleted state.

I smiled despite myself. "Told you I'd come back." Kola swooped down, dropping a large mango at the girl's feet. Then Kola flew onto my shoulder. Kola had been the one to save me from the desert when I escaped. And here she was present to save more children. This was Kola.

The girl was Asibi, the girl who'd wanted to sell dried butterflies. This was what a year of "surviving" did. "You all are free," I said.

Asibi knelt down in the mud and speared the mango with her stick, tears in her eyes. Half of the kids rushed forth; the other half stayed behind, cowering in the shed. Slave mentality. Even when the gates are open, they will not run out, afraid of what will happen. As I stood watching Asibi bite into the mango, waiting for the shouting and capturing to end, there was a fresh rumble of thunder. It was my opinion that this place could use another cleansing rainstorm.

———

Ejii once told me that writing things down is a good way to bleed out the poison. The rage. The anger. I don't know about that. I spent a year with Gambo, Buji, and the N.B.I. going from cocoa farm to cocoa farm, freeing enslaved children. What I saw made me want to curse and spit and strangle. What I'd see later . . . I'll get to that.

I've since read up on the chocolate industry and child slaves. It's nothing new. They used to use child slaves *decades* ago in the late 1900s and well into the 2000s! So it was happening even before the Great Change. But the plantations were in West Africa, particularly the Ivory Coast. This was when it was unheard of for there to be fertile soil in northern Niger.

But after the Great Change, the land in the Ivory Coast grew so wild that there were floods of plants and trees that sprouted sideways. People say they hear the laughter of children in the places where those old cocoa farms used to be. They say that there are more than a few ghosts there and some of the children still live there, too. Still children. The place is not right.

In Assamakka, I dare say we did a lot. We kicked ass, as I told Ejii we would. All the masters were either dead or arrested. We did the same thing all over Northern Niger and Libya. I swear those lands went bitter by the time we were through with them. And the children were sweet with joy and freedom. Some of them were taken by N.B.I. agents to Kwàmfà, Agadez, Bilma, Ghat, even as far as Tripoli. Safe places with safe people and school books and food. Some of them ran away in the night. I understand.

Most of the cocoa for chocolate for the entire Earth, or what used to be the Earth, was produced on those farms. We have ruined the world's chocolate industry. Good.

CHAPTER 3

Lessons

I felt like a hero.

I was making a difference. I felt like I had freed the world. In a way, I had, for aren't children supposed to be our future? My grandmother used to sing a song from a long long time ago that started with the line, "I believe the children are our future." Is this not true? What is there to life when you are not free? So many people take freedom for granted. You probably do. Try not to.

Freeing the children was therapeutic. It felt so good. Though I saw people shot, stabbed, beaten up. Though I saw a man trampled by a camel and children so malnourished that they were covered with sores and their hair was falling out. Though I had brutally killed a man and was forced to injure several more. Regardless of it all, my nightmares about my dead best friend Adam and my experience of slavery began to fade and then disappear. There is something about doing good that undoes terror.

Still, the night we left the last liberated cocoa farm, the day we parted with the N.B.I., I ran away. It was a full moon, but I was sure that Gambo and Buji were asleep in their tents. Kola circled high above me as I fled.

Let me explain. Earlier that day, as Gambo, Buji, and I

had ridden our camels toward Kwàmfà, Gambo had said something that turned my head upside down.

"We should pass Kwàmfà and go right to Arondizuogu," he said.

Buji nodded in agreement. "You should see your parents. You can always return to Kwàmfà later. And your friend Ejii isn't there, anyway." I didn't say a word, though I wanted to know why Ejii wasn't in Kwàmfà. *Where is she, then?* I wondered. But I had bigger problems.

I didn't have much to pack. Slipping away was easy. I took my satchel of things, some dried meat, dates, two yams, and one of the capture stations for water—the old one, of course. I had all I needed. I left my camel. It would have made too much noise when it stood up.

Ah ah, imagine, I thought. *Why would I "reunite" with two people who sold me down the river, or better yet, down the desert? Biko, tell me! My freedom meant nothing to them and their reputations meant everything.*

As I snuck away, my thoughts were solely on my parents. I wasn't really being rational. *So you're famous and rich and own the huge news services called Nigerian Net and the Old Naija Times that preach idiotic irrational adherence to the old ways,* I thought. *So you're both egomaniacs who love to plaster your faces and ideas on the newsfeeds. So your damn son is a Changed One. Big deal! How ignorant can you be to think that the Great Change doesn't change anything? And how dumb must you be to deny the Great Merge?!*

I should travel down there and bring down a terrible storm and flood all of Arondizuogu, especially my parent's goddamn monster house. That will teach them about "change."

Let me make a confession here. I left, but . . . I was heading to Nigeria. To Arondizuogu, my parents' village. Another confession: part of why I bought that e-legba was so that I could watch my annoying mother.

You could watch all sorts of news stories, shows, and interviews with local celebrities, musicians, priests, imams, politicians, and businessmen on e-legbas. Especially when you were in a city with good reception. But the two publication networks that were reliable almost anywhere you went were *Old Naija Times* and *Naija News*. My mother was the anchorwoman on an irritating popular biweekly program on Naija News called *Felecia at Large*. Okay, fine, this was *the* reason I bought this e-legba.

Felecia at Large was a tabloid-like show that featured my mother interviewing people involved in strange incidents all over Nigeria. No matter the situation, she always viewed mysterious incidents from a negative slant. The idea was that the old ways were good and the new ways, the post–Great Change ways, were weird and unstable and bad. As if we could ever go back to the way things were before the nuclear bombs and Peace Bombs were dropped.

In the first episode I saw on my new e-legba, my mother interviewed this guy whose van was occupied by a sparkling lizard. He therefore didn't need gas to run his car. He was using it as a taxi service. My mother stood with the guy next to his beat-up van. The camera kept going staticky and the guy looked a little crazy, I'll admit. But that could have been because the camera was zoomed way in to his mustache and bearded face. He showed his teeth to the camera—I think he was supposed to be smiling. He was obviously not comfortable being digitized for millions of people.

"So show us how it works," my mother said.

The man spoke in English with a strong accent. "You just put key into ignition like this."

He barely touched the ignition before the car jumped and sparked and started. A blue-white spark that looked vaguely like a lizard zipped over the car's hood. My mother squealed, laughed, and stepped away. The image jumped, too. She looked at the camera with wide eyes. "You can feel the charge in the air."

But the man seemed pretty pleased. "I don' have to buy a drop of fuel for this car. I feed my family, buy some land, have new . . ."

"Yes, but how many people have died in your automobile?" my mother asked.

"Oh, none," he said with a laugh, looking a little surprised.

"But you never know."

"Well . . ."

My mother turned to the camera. It focused on her head and I could have sworn I saw the guy get yanked off camera by some other man. Her eyes were wide with drama. "Women can suffer from barrenness, men become impotent, hair loss, electrocution, all results of an electrical current! And as you could see, madness is also a result. Beware, people." She moved closer to the camera. "Beware. This is Felecia on at large."

As we went from farm to farm, freeing the children, in between we'd have a day or two of rest. I'd lie awake at night watching my mother's program. She was always energetic and excitable, as if everything she encountered was new and crazy. And she had a syrupy voice that guys always went crazy for. And she spoke with a somewhat British accent that people loved so much. My mother had been born in London. She returned to Nigeria with her parents just before the Great Change when she was about eight, but she worked hard to never lose her British accent.

That accent had gotten her far. Nigerians are such victims of Western ways of thinking and doing things that it makes me sick. As if to sound, look, behave like a European makes you superior. Ridiculous.

Her hair was getting long. But not one dreadlock looked out of place or unkempt. I wondered how she'd react to my hair. I'd decided to grow dreadlocks too. But mine were bushy and uneven, just the way I liked them. She'd hate them and my father would probably try to tie me down and cut them. Let him try. I'd give him a nice zap.

The more I watched her program, the more I missed both my parents. I never said a word to anyone about it. My own feelings were humiliating. These two people sold me into slavery. How could I miss them? Crave to see their faces in real life? Well, only my mother's. My father could go to hell. Selling me was probably his idea. And my uncle Segun, the idiot who put me on the truck that took me to the farms, was *his* brother.

When we finished freeing the children, and Gambo and Buji brought up the possibility of going home, it jarred me. I didn't want to talk about it. But I wanted to go home, if only to ask, "Why did you do it?" But I didn't want Gambo or Buji to know that. *How pathetic would I look?* I thought. *Like such a baby.* I didn't want them to come along. That's why I ran away.

I didn't get far. About two miles. Then there was a rush of

wind and sand so strong it knocked me to the ground. As I sputtered and coughed and cursed, Gambo strode up to me, his white garments making him look like some sort of demon. I squinted in the moonlight. He looked angry as hell, which was fine, because I was angry as hell, too.

He started shouting at me in Arabic, which I don't understand. He always went back to Arabic when he was mad.

"Why don't you just let me go?!" I shouted over him. "You can't hold me prisoner! I can go wherever I want!" I threw my satchel at him. It was too heavy and hit my feet instead. Gambo spat what could only have been curses at me. And I spat some of my more creative ones at him. Then we both just stood there glaring at each other.

"It would be stupid," he said after a while.

"You can't make me stay," I said.

He laughed bitterly and rolled his eyes. "Dikéogu is free as the wind. I know." As if my ideas were so silly.

"I *am* free," I said.

"After all we've done, you'd—"

"I have business to take care of. On my own."

"What business?"

I refused to respond.

"Your parents?" he asked.

I said nothing.

"You don't want—"

"No," I said.

He stood thinking for a minute. I got up and turned my back to him. It's always easier to leave people without telling them. Now what was I going to do?

I heard him step closer to me. "Don't you want to learn more first?" he asked.

"What?"

"On the way, I planned to train you," he said. I bristled at the word. I'd never liked the word "train." I wasn't a dog. I wasn't a slave. "To teach you," he said, correcting himself.

I frowned. He'd mentioned this before, but I hadn't really trusted him to live up to his word.

"I'm not a rainmaker, but my abilities are very similar to yours," Gambo said. "It comes from a similar place. I can teach you much of what I know."

I sucked my teeth loudly, my back still turned, feeling a flush of anger at how easily Gambo had caught me. Now he was presenting me with annoying hard choices.

"Consider it," he said.

I didn't want to consider anything. I just wanted to *go*. I wanted to be free of answering to anyone. But then Ejii popped into my mind. She'd evolved her shadow-speaker skill by leaving home and traveling. She'd bravely faced the hardest question of all—the question of death. Then I thought of what I'd done to Big Blokkus. How I couldn't stop. I didn't want to do that again, but I knew I would if it came down to it. I had so little control over my abilities.

And I knew I had potential; I could *feel* it. It scared me a little. And Gambo didn't have to convince me that he could do the impossible. The man could fly, shoot into the sky like a rocket, hold the wind in his hand. He was centuries old. I cursed under my breath, mentally admitting to myself if he could teach me all that, I wanted to learn it—if only to make sure I had enough control to properly wash away my parents' damn monster house. Control of my abilities would be very good indeed.

I shook my head, despite my thoughts. "I don't want you or Buji to come with me to Nigeria. That's my own issue."

"It's a dangerous world, Dikéogu."

"I'm a dangerous person," I said.

"You might end up somewhere else," Gambo said. "Maps don't . . ."

"I know," I said. "But I'll get there."

He stared hard at me. Analyzing me. I stepped back. Gambo knew the sky so well. And he'd been a slave, too. Being a slave had filled him with such fury that at the age of nine, he became an Aejej, a living storm. Then he'd lost his family. After hundreds of years passed, all those he knew had died. Slavery ruined his life. And other things too. On top of all this, like his wife, Jaa the Red One, the man was really scary. You didn't want to cross him.

"Let me teach you," he insisted. "Then you go find your parents."

Silence.

"All right," I finally said. *The better to handle my parents when the time comes,* I thought.

Gambo smiled. "Good."

━━━━

That night as I lay on my mat looking up at the stars, Kola flew down to me. She hooted softly, landing beside me without making even a whisper. Then, *WHAM!* The image burst into my head. It was so strong that I jumped up.

The biggest trees ever. Nighttime. But everything was in sight. From the large white owls soaring around the top of a purple sky-scraper to a large green caterpillar munching on a leaf far far be-low. A giant white ant trudged up to the caterpillar and clipped it in half with its mandibles.

Ginen. Kola was showing me Ginen. The skyscraper was a giant plant, the Ooni Palace where Chief Ette resided. The white ants and owls were the protectors of the palace.

Then Kola took to the sky and flew off. I knelt down, so shocked that my belly hurt. I shut my eyes, calling to her. She didn't respond, though I know she heard me.

I knew everything in that moment. She was going to Ginen. She was meeting with the owls. She would be gone for a long long time. Kola. My *chi*. More than my soulmate. A part of me, me a part of her. You can't imagine what separating from her was like.

I curled into a ball. As Kola flew on, I felt stretched. Yet at the same time I felt like retreating. Into myself. I didn't sleep at all that night.

Rainmaker

Let me pause here.

I'm still suffering from this fever. I wonder if it's one that only rainmakers get. Heat, sweat, a pounding in my head like thunder. Sometimes I rub ice crystals off my skin. And sometimes mist rises from it.

I don't remember when it started. Two days ago. A week. I can't recall. Maybe it's from something they are giving me. I probably shouldn't drink the tea they give me. It's easy to hide things in tea. Especially the bitter kind. Though I like the bitter kind. Bitter like the kola nut I used to eat back home in Arondizuogu.

I gave Kola a kola nut once. It's the only time I've seen her dance in the sky. Afterward, it was the only time she's slept during the day. Now they keep Kola and me prisoner here. For now. No one can hold us for long.

I flush hot. See the mist rise from my skin. It's like I'm burning in hell. Out here in the desert, this is not so far from the truth.

As long as my fever doesn't affect my e-legba, I'm fine and I can continue telling this story . . .

CHAPTER 4

The Aïr Mountains

We split up. Buji went on to Kwàmfà to see Jaa. And Gambo took me up to the Aïr Mountains. It was rough, rugged terrain made of a lot of black volcanic rock interrupted with the occasional stunted tree, shrub, or plant. Our camels were not happy. They roared their complaints and would often refuse to move. They were generally irritable and skittish as hell. Their behavior made me wonder if there was something . . . unpredictable living in the mountains.

The place was crumbly and the air was thin. We passed a few small villages where people raised camels and goats and tended half-dead gardens of tomatoes, tobacco, spices, and the bitter flowers used to attract the medicinal butterflies Asibi always talked about. The people here were a mix of dark-skinned Africans of the Ikelan tribe and equally dark but more Arab-looking Tuaregs. But the only "people" who we saw with any regularity were angry nosy baboons who kept trying to steal our food. We finally settled in a deserted cave that sat before a flat area of a few hundred feet. The flat area ended in a steep cliff that I eventually would call Desire's Drop.

"We stay here until you're ready," Gambo said, climbing off his camel.

"How do you know this place?" I asked. My camel moaned and groaned like an old man as he sat down. I climbed off and patted his cheek. He grunted and turned his head away. What a grumpy beast.

"I spent a few months here with Buji just after Jaa saved me from being an Aejej," he said. He looked around and chuckled. "I went mad here."

I frowned and shivered, wondering if I'd made a mistake coming up here with a man who had spent centuries as a giant homicidal sandstorm. Then I thought about calling down rains to wash away my parents' house, again. *I'll take my chances*, I thought with a small smile.

———

Gambo was indeed somewhat crazy. But I soon found out that I was, too. It quickly became about far more than seeking revenge against my parents. I mean, come on, when I realized my potential, I even forgot about them . . . for a while.

I won't go into the details of my rainmaker teachings. Just know that I was good enough to do much of what he taught me. Over those months, I bruised ribs, broke a finger, got a mild concussion, suffered from dehydration, exhaustion, depression, windburn and sunburn, and broke out in a strange rash for two weeks.

I learned how to let the wind catch me. Twice I saw something that might have been God or *a* god. One of them looked like a giant fish woman coiling about in the clouds. She was all bony angles, cracking and snapping as she moved. She was about the size of ten trucks and she spoke in bubbles.

No, I wasn't drunk or hallucinating from starvation or anything like that. It was all real.

It was early morning and I was sitting at the edge of Desire's Drop. I'd just finished breakfast. I was still nursing a cup of tea. Gambo had gone off somewhere for the day and I was glad. I needed the time to be alone with my thoughts. This was not long after I'd tried to end my life by throwing myself over Desire's Drop. I think Gambo was testing me to see if I could be alone and not kill myself. He had nothing to worry about. That impulse was the result of very temporary madness and fear and it was long gone.

She swam down from a cloud like some kind of dragon. She had tiny silver fish darting around her, too. Yeah, very weird. She danced before my eyes, her body wiggling and spirally but her head unmoving, looking deeply at me. Her skin was black and her eyes undulated brown and tan like turbulent river water. I don't know what she told me. All I heard was the sound of bubbles when she moved her lips. But I know she was talking about why I'd thrown myself off Desire's Drop the day before. I just knew.

Okay, so three times during my teachings with Gambo I almost died. I mean, really died. Two of those times were when I fell down Desire's Drop. But once, well, I threw myself over it. Let me tell you about that incident. A little. It had been a rough day and I was sitting at the edge of the precipice, gazing out. My mind was clear, I felt at peace. I felt good for once. It was a cool evening. Gambo was preparing dinner. The camels were quiet.

But something swept into my mind. It was like ink polluting perfect blue waters without causing even the slightest ripple. Despair, gloom, hopelessness, doom. The air was suddenly warm and dry. I opened my eyes. Undulating and churning before me, filling Desire's Drop was a black vortex of nothing . . . and it was alive. The monster from the fields outside the cocoa farm!

My mind didn't register this at the time. It didn't register anything but suicide. *Now!* I thought. It was like I was already dying. Everything was going black, fading. It was smothering me. I got up. My legs felt like weights.

I ran carrying those "weights."

I jumped!

Hot air on my face. Darkness quenched all thought. Only the sound of wind rushing past my ears. The taste of un-right air in my mouth.

I remembered Gambo's hands wrapping around my chest and then an enormous burst of lightning. I remembered screaming and sobbing. By the time he set me back on the ground in front of our cave, we were soaked with the rain we'd both brought. I was so ashamed. I'm all about life. Always been. No matter what happens to me, that's the side I take. I would never do something like this! Yet, I had!

For that day and night, I refused to eat or drink, or bathe. I refused to speak to Gambo. I just sat there at the edge of the drop staring, thinking: *How could I do that? How!?* Maybe that's why the goddess decided to speak with me that next day.

She spoke to me about the pursuit of the "dark beast." She spoke of Gambo and me. I think. I'm not sure what she said. As I said, she communicated in bubbles. But I know this is what she spoke of. Does this make sense? Not to me either. But it does. Gambo and I never discussed what happened. *I am not weak,* I kept thinking. Then I'd think of the dark beast. That was when I first started suspecting that Gambo and I were . . . infected, maybe. By the dark beast. I think this was when I started to crack up a bit. Maybe it would have been better if Gambo and I had talked about this back then. Instead, we pretended it didn't happen.

The second time I saw a god, I cannot explain so well. It was more of a silent but overwhelming presence that descended on me one night. That's all I'll say of it.

Despite growing up in a Catholic household and then being around the hard-core Muslims of Niger, I consider myself an agnostic with a hint of atheism. I don't know what I saw those two days, really. Gambo said that two gods once died and lived up in these mountains. Maybe I believe that. Maybe I don't. Does what I believe matter?

Anyway, because of my lessons with Gambo, I knew what sparkling lizards tasted like—silver and copper with a hint of salt. After eating one, a skilled rainmaker can bring in a hurricane the size of what used to be the African continent. Or call down lightning so gigantic it can obliterate a whole town. All mysticism is old. Even the new kind.

Gambo was the perfect example of what mysticism can do. The man took on the stature of a short black man of maybe forty. You know, like his co-husband, Buji. Plus Jaa is short and I guess she must only like short men. But Gambo was an Aejej and he'd seen a thousand years. Really, he's more like a man with a dragon trapped inside him. Or maybe more like a dragon trapped in a man's body. He's wind, heat, force, mysticism, and myth. You'd be stupid to cross him.

I got to witness a man do exactly that. Actually, it was

closer to five armed angry men. We'd been living in that cave for four months and Gambo had finally deemed me ready for the last part of his lessons. For this, he said, we had to travel to the highest point of the mountains, L'Aïr Massif. On the way, we had to pass through an oddly sizable town for these parts. It was called Wàhalàà. I should have known there would be trouble. "Wàhalàà" means "crisis," "worry," or "trouble" in Hausa.

The people in Wàhalàà were rough. It was cold up here, too. All the women wore black heavy burkas, at least I thought they were women. Who could tell? The men wore black pants and long-sleeved caftans and bushy long beards. Even the children tended to wear black or dark clothes. And everyone looked at you with a suspicious scowl. The women kept making the evil eye at us. No one spoke to us. Granted, they probably weren't used to strangers, but come on. The place was a nest of hostility.

But you know what's funny? They didn't only treat us this way; they treated each other the same way. No one said hello to one another. We saw a fight in the street and no one helped as the smaller man got the camelshit kicked out of him by two bigger men. A little girl tried to pick my pocket, and when I slapped her hand away, she spat at me and kicked me in the shin before running off. I'll bet every man, woman, and child was strapped with some sort of machete and had been schooled in the art of robbery and violence.

"They say there's a stream that runs under these parts that makes them this way," Gambo said. "They weren't like this before the Great Change."

Needless to say, we only drank water from our capture

station and we only ate food from our supplies. It took us about two hours to get through most of Wàhalàà. We walked beside our camels, as opposed to riding them. We didn't want to look too flashy. The place was like a den of wolves, so it was best not to rush, either. We almost made it.

I was smiling to myself because about a half-mile away I could see the last of the sand-brick buildings. The town limits of Wàhalàà. *We're going to make it,* I thought to myself as we passed a house with a sulky-looking toddler sitting in the doorway. A supposed woman in a black burka quickly came, grabbed the child, and slammed the door. I sucked my teeth and turned to Gambo.

"These people are rotten as . . ."

He was looking at something behind me. I turned around just as one of the men grabbed my arm. Another quickly grabbed my other arm. They yanked Gambo and me into a nearby alley. There were six of them. Some other thugs were trying to pull our camels away. The camels roared and fought, refusing to budge; I was so proud of them. I hoped my camel would also spit and bite. He did. Imagine. Grown men, reduced to common thievery.

"Everything you have," one of the men demanded. He spoke in Hausa.

Three other men pointed sharp knives at Gambo's belly, the other two men did the same to me. Gambo and I were wearing our dirtiest clothes. He wore his long smelly thick caftan. I was wearing brown pants and a tattered T-shirt. The health of our camels must have given us away.

I laughed wildly at their stupidity. You had to forgive me; I was still somewhat delirious from the harshness of Gambo's lessons. "You people are such idiots," I said, still snickering. One of the men held his knife closer to my belly. But he looked worried. As he should have been. Then the fighting started. I defended myself well enough, but my continued laughter almost got me stabbed. I was pretty distracted. I knew some wild stuff was about to go down and I was looking forward to it. And it was all just so funny. Those men had no idea who they were dealing with.

A man was punching me in the gut, but I was watching Gambo. I wasn't about to miss what I knew he was going to do. Three men had him pinned to the ground. I saw him pucker his lips and suck in air. You could feel the air pressure drop, and there was this soft pulling sound. All the men froze, looking around. I shoved a man away from me. Gambo pushed two men aside as he got up.

He brought his hands together. It looked as if he was holding something gray-black. It was about the size of a basketball and round like one, too. Wind burst into the alley. He threw a piece of that ball at each man as they tried to run. They were knocked off their feet, landing motionless on the ground. Gambo didn't miss once.

Dead? I looked closely, feeling nothing at all but giggly hysterics. No, the man was unconscious. Gambo had tried to teach me to do this. "You learn to throw wind and you'll have no need of a weapon," he told me. But I could never focus the wind well enough to make it of any real lethal use.

"Come," Gambo said, stepping over the unconscious men, brushing dust off his blue caftan.

I chuckled some more when I saw more unconscious

men lying near our camels. I hadn't even seen Gambo handle them.

I was laughing because I was numb and just didn't care about anything. And for some reason this fact was hilarious to me. After all I'd been through, nothing scared me much. I'd been swept a mile into the sky by strong and weak winds. I'd been burned by lightning and shaken by something that looked oddly like an aurora borealis.

Gambo had gotten me to open myself to the sky. Trust me, you don't want to know what it's like to fall into the heavens. If there is a God, gravity is his/her/its greatest gift. I had spoken with the sky and goddamn it, it *had* a voice. It was loud, often angry, *always* changing.

If a cloud passed above, I could see its exact shape in my head. The weather, the clarity of the sky, dust storms, heavy winds, breezes, no breeze, passing clouds, dry air, especially rainstorms, all affected me. It affected me like an electrical pulse affects a nerve. I'd seen gods and a great consuming beast, thrown myself off a cliff, seen the ground flying toward me, and knew what certain death felt like. My dreams were turbulent when I slept at all. My body had grown muscular and I'd grown three inches during those months. To sum it up, I was more than a little crazy.

Gambo was taking me to the mountaintop. Here I would learn how to rope it all in, to keep it in control. Now that all the alterations had been made, he had to sew me up. Then I had to heal. "Your tattoos," Gambo said as he got on his camel. He climbed back down. "Come down for a second."

"What?" I asked getting down.

He stepped up close and looked at my face, frowning. "They've changed again," he said.

I rubbed the bridge of my nose. My face. Nothing felt itchy. "Does it . . . what's it . . ."

Gambo went to his camel bags and rummaged around a bit. He brought out a small mirror. Some bird chose that moment to burst out in a screechy song and one of the unconscious men groaned. A crowd was gathering nearby but no one had the nerve to approach us. Good for them. I needed to see my face, and if anyone had delayed this, I'd have smashed his chest in. My hands shook as I took the mirror. When I'd first gone into Ginen, my tattoos had changed from blue to red and white. What now?!

"I don't know what that's all about," Gambo said as I looked at myself. "Most rainmakers appear normal. They don't have markings traveling on their faces."

As if that's what I needed to hear. Was that supposed to make me feel better?

I looked closely at myself. The red and white tattoo that used to go from my forehead to the bridge of my nose had expanded across the flesh above both my eyebrows! It was like a big decorative red and white "t." I grimaced, tilting my head to catch the light. *Is this thing going to end up covering my entire body like some sort of cancer?* I wondered.

I giggled. The thought was absolutely hilarious.

━━━━

We didn't go all the way to the top. The camels couldn't have made it and it would have been too cold and snowy. I hate snow. And there were these groups of hairy hopping spiders the size of my hand that seemed to love it. I think that's even what they survived on. Wildly hop about and eat snow, that's all they seemed to do . . . until they found you in your tent and decided to bury you with snow. Apparently they didn't like any kind of warmth in their territory. They tried to bury the camels too. The creatures must have come from an opening to Ginen or one of the other worlds, because they made absolutely no sense.

We stopped at a fairly comfortable place. It was cool but not freezing; the air was crisp. No snow. No snow spiders. No baboons. Or any hints of the Great Change, for that matter. The plants and trees seemed native, as did the wildlife.

I felt good here. Even the camels seemed a bit happier. Aside from the lack of snow spiders, the plateau where we stopped was soft with short green grass. For about a week, Gambo taught me ways to meditate. He also encouraged me to go off and spend time thinking and taking in my surroundings. There was a place not far from where we camped where I could sit and see for miles and miles, past the mountains into the desert.

I would empty my mind as Gambo had taught me and just stare out into that openness. I'd do this for hours and not a cloud would gather in the sky. Not a cloud. It was during these times that I stopped laughing. And I thought about Ejii. What she must be up to if she were not in Kwàmfà. If she missed me as I did her.

I'd reached out to Kola and felt her. She was fine. Flying. Eating some sort of strange tasty rodent. But she was very far and my connection with her was fuzzy at best. I was healing.

But there were parts of me that needed more than meditation and a peaceful environment.

One night, when Gambo was snoring in deep sleep, I brought out my e-legba. I watched an interview with a man claiming he'd lost his private parts after shaking hands with an attractive woman. He looked harried and sweaty.

"And they are still gone!" he stressed. "*Biko!* Someone must help me find the culprit, *o!*" I frowned. I mean, what was there in place of his equipment? Just an empty space?

"Look at this man," I whispered. I sucked my teeth. "No self respect. He should just go find the cure instead of putting his face on the news."

I did a quick search for the latest *Felecia at Large* show. There it was. An icon with a close-up of my mother's face. Today's show featured my mother interviewing a woman who'd turned into a giant spider after running away from her husband. All but her head was arachnid and the only way she'd speak to you was if you fed her a ball of goat meat. My mother wouldn't need to try that hard to make this unexplainable situation look bad. The Great Change definitely caused some weird shit, no doubt about that. Especially when you were in the wrong place at the wrong time, like this woman probably had been.

I was about to click on it when something else caught my eye on the screen. A link titled, "Interview with the Obidimkpa Media Moguls!" My body went cold.

I stared at my last name. Obidimkpa. I didn't use it. For one thing, it inspired that stupid question: "Are you related to Chika and Felecia Obidimkpa, the people who own the internet?" I don't know why people think my parents own the entire camelshitting internet! Who can own that? No one even knows why it's still working! Who's paying the bills to keep it going? No one asks that. My parents are opportunists; that's all. Manipulative, money-grubbing opportunists capitalizing off of people's fears of the future! That's why one of their publication networks is called the *Old* Naija Times! Naija is slang for "Nigeria."

Anyway, I clicked on the link. "I don't know why I torture myself," I grumbled.

My mother looked perfect, as always. Her dreadlocks piled on her head in a sort of crown, not a bit of her natural-toned makeup smudged. Her intense gaze made the journalist interviewing them sit up straighter. My father looked like the arrogant bastard he was. Conceited, bloated with power and control, he was the ruler of the world in his eyes, and everyone should bow down to him because he was always right.

All they did was look smug and brag. And the journalist interviewing them happily encouraged them by asking questions about their money, their "media empire," and how they spent their free time with rich and famous people. They laughed heartily, chuckled softly, smirked, cocked their heads. They were the picture of prosperity and fame. Disgusting.

E-legbas ran from pricey to dirt cheap. And Nigerian Net was free. Even the poorest farmer, even a man living on the streets could tune into this interview. I'm sure my parents' bragging was making a lot of people feel like camelshit. I gnashed my teeth as I watched and listened.

The journalist sat back, crossed one short leg over his other short leg, and clasped his knobby hands together. He was a very dark-skinned Yoruba man who seemed to enjoy hearing his voice as much as my parents enjoyed hearing theirs. "Tell me about your son, Dikéogu," he said.

My mouth fell open. I held my breath.

The journalist leaned forward. Footage of an interview I did six years ago popped up on the side of the screen. I'd hated being interviewed. Thankfully, my parents put a stop to them once I started getting struck by lightning.

My mother's face betrayed nothing. But my father's face went through a series of events. First he started blinking a lot. Then he smiled. Then he frowned. Then he plucked at his beard, looking troubled and hurt. I could have vomited. Such theatrics! My mother took his hand.

"Oh, Dikéogu," she sighed. "It's been almost a year and half and my husband still has trouble talking about it." *Then why are you putting your face in everyone's face?* I wanted to shout. *Why have you been gallivanting all over the place like nothing happened?!*

She paused, all fake dramatic. Then she looked right at the camera with super sad eyes. Pouting her lips and furrowing her brow, she said, "It's such a tragedy that our only son, our only child, would die of such a normal, common disease. We Africans have been dying from malaria since the beginning of time." A single tear ran down her cheek.

I slammed my è-legba to the ground. The monitor cracked, making a sad beeping sound as it shut off. I dragged my fingers in the dirt, scratching, seething. Lightning flashed just above my head. Tears dribbled from my eyes. *Dead!* I thought. *"Normal" disease?!* All I could see in my mind were her fake sincere eyes. My father had looked down, a fake pained expression on his face. I shook with fury. *Lies! All LIES!*

I threw my things in a satchel. Gambo was still sleeping despite the lightning I'd let loose. Good. I sneaked off, hopping quietly down the rocks. I was totally unafraid of the tribe of baboons watching me or the wild screech of a very large bird hovering overhead or whatever the hell chittered in the dark not far to my left. Unafraid of the fact that I was high in the Aïr Mountains, on my own.

I was heading for Southern Nigeria, home. My teachings unfinished.

═══

When I reached the bottom of the mountain, needless to say, I was a changed person.

My head was so full.

I was strong.

I was weak.

I was shaky.

I was alone.

Rainmaker

There was something lurking in the dark that day in the savanna outside the cocoa farm. I told you about it but not really. Can I trust you? I don't think I can. I don't think I can trust anyone anymore. Except Kola. Kola knows what I saw. She was there. I didn't tell Ejii.

I close my eyes and it's there. Skulking. Deep like the ocean. Churning like Jupiter's red hurricane. Old like a Ginen tree. Dangerous like the death of a family. Gambo must have seen it too.

I have a notebook now. They gave me one. As if that will gain my trust. The paper is crude but the pen I use is one of those pens from Ginen. It's actually an ink-producing plant. Place it in a bowl of water then put it in the sun each day and its ink never runs out. It draws a dark red, like blood. The line is thick and smooth.

I draw the weather, filling the pages with loops, zigzags, swirls, spikes, circles, and blinking eyes. All the white space is occupied. My drawings are dense like the jungle I saw outside of Timia. It helps more than all this talking. This talking is like bloodletting if bloodletting worked. It leaves me weak. But drawing, or what I prefer to call scribbling, it's like an umbrella in a rainstorm. It's a bottle of water in the middle of the desert. It's something to do in prison.

But even in the pages that I fill with drawings, the clouds gather . . .

CHAPTER 5

Cockroaches

Except for Kola's absence, I was fine being alone.

Under the billions of stars, the land alternated. There were bizarrely shaped black rocks, high sand dunes, and hardpan populated with stunted dry trees. These parts were the Sahara Desert of the past, I think. Then there were the small spontaneous forests, which you never knew whether they were full of things like trees that would throttle you in the night or bushes heavy with sweet strange fruit. I avoided them completely—only if I were desperate would I break this general rule.

I was four days into my trip south when I woke up and saw the craziest thing. I'd slept just outside of the city of Timia. I planned to go there come morning to see if any caravans or trucks were heading south. I had money. Gambo had given a goodly amount for personal needs before we'd taken down the cocoa farms. I'd had little reason to spend it. So I had more than enough to buy either a camel or a ride. I was going to use my shabby look to keep the prices low.

My plans would have to change. Beyond Timia was the largest forest I'd ever seen. No, not forest, jungle. Even from where I was I could see that it was dense knots of trees, bushes, plants, and flowers. And it was noisy like a zoo. Squawking, cawing, cheep-cheeping, twittering, it was a symphony of displaced wildlife. Birds and swarms of insects were flying to it from all directions. I saw a group of sand foxes trotting toward it, too.

"It'll be gone by tomorrow," I mumbled. I decided to go into Timia, get a hotel room, and take my first real bath in months.

———

The roads were clear. Only a scooter every so often. Everyone else was on foot or camel or mule. Most of the people were obviously New Tuareg, but there were plenty of Hausa, Wodaabe, Fulani, and Old Tuareg. You could tell by accents, the way people dressed, the way people walked.

The buildings and homes were closely packed, some built with brown mud brick, and the more modern buildings were made of adobe and brick. Dry-looking trees and brown-green low grass grew between everything. Yellow weaver birds noisily occupied treetops with their complicated basket-like nests. There was always dust in the air. It was a dry dry city full of mazes.

After an hour, I finally found a hotel with a balcony. The cost was cheap. It was clean. And it was obviously owned by a couple of Ginenian immigrants. The number of plants growing in the lobby was ridiculous. It was practically a forest in there! Ferns, green creeping plants, spider plants, spiky plants, small palm trees. Plants that suctioned themselves to

the ceiling and hung down. And there were wall geckos lurking between the leaves and some kind of gray-furred monkey-
like thing peeking from behind the counter.

I pushed a thin vine out of my way to get to the lobby
counter where a tall woman and man sat on tall chairs. They
wore stiff garments lined with tiny colorful beads. Definitely
Southwestern Ginenians.

"I'd like a room, please," I said in Hausa.

The woman's eyes went right to my facial tattoo. People
really have problems. Everyone behaves as if their shit doesn't
stink. I mean, I know my facial tattoos look a little crazy, but
can't people make an attempt not to stare?

"Just you?" she asked. I paused, frowning. I couldn't for
the life of me tell what language this woman spoke. It was
the same when you crossed over into Ginen before the Great
Merge. I guess whatever strange mysticism had been at work
before still was, because though I didn't know the language,
I understood her.

"Yes," I said. "I just need one small room."

"You don't belong to anyone?"

Can you imagine? This woman wasn't even from Earth
and she had the nerve to look at *me* with suspicion. How long
could she have been here? The Great Merge happened, what,
barely a year ago?!

"No," I said, gritting my teeth. I looked her in the eye,
something I knew slaves didn't do. "Do I look like I belong to
someone?"

"You've got those markings, though," the man said, narrowing his eyes at me.

"Look," I said with a sigh. "I'm tired, I'm hungry, and I

really need a bath." I leaned forward. "I can pay. The prices posted are reasonable . . . just shut up and give me a room! Honestly!"

The man puffed up like some angry rodent, his brown face taking on a red tint. He wagged a finger at me. "Disrespectful plant-less ingrate! You should be . . ."

The woman pushed him back. "You speak to either my husband or me like that again, boy, and I'll set a plant on you that you will never be able to pull from you skin," the woman said calmly.

"Don't call me 'boy,'" I snapped.

"Fair enough," she said. She paused, inspecting me. Then she nodded. "I'll rent you a room, but only because I like the idea of taking your money." Then under her breath, as she brought out some paperwork, she said something that gave me pause: "Better a slave than a filthy Changed One."

I said nothing, taking my room key.

Imagine being able to do the things I could do, having been on the adventures I'd been on, yet having people only able to see the mark of the worst but shortest time of my life. Still, this mistake people made turned out to be a very big blessing.

=====

My night in Timia was . . . interesting. The damn hotel was . . . overly occupied. This was the reason for the cheap prices. Take my bathroom, for example. When I took my long-awaited bath, a small group of bright green bug-eyed tree frogs sat on the walls enjoying the mist. Wall geckos scrambled about the ceiling. A small squirrel-like creature with red fur skulked about my bedroom as if it owned the place. Surprisingly, it left no feces.

My balcony, where I slept, was occupied by large green grasshoppers who sang a bristly tune all night. I slept, but the noise gave me strange dreams about leaves, moist plant stems, and flying insects, and of course wind. My dreams are rarely without wind, even when inspired by strange grasshoppers. Thankfully, no nightmares of the consuming creature from the cocoa fields and Desire's Drop.

That hotel was exactly the type of place Ginen folk would create when on Earth . . . at least until they could procure some abode seeds to germinate into proper Ginen homes. Still, the hotel had plenty of guests, mostly Ginen immigrants and travelers who couldn't afford any better.

I woke up with the taste of seeds in my mouth. Three stories below, people bustled about, preparing for the morning. I had a perfect view of the south side of the city and the desert. The forest was still out there, extending from horizon to horizon. It would be another day before I'd reach Timia. Great.

I was restless, itching to get going. I had nothing to do here. Nothing to practice. Nothing to learn. Nothing to prove. Nothing to overcome. I still didn't miss Gambo. Not yet. Though I felt guilty about leaving him. *He'll probably fly right to Kwàmfà*, I told myself. This was probably true, as Gambo had told me he could change into wind (though he never chanced changing into a storm) and travel miles and miles without the need of food or water. But this strong possibility didn't make me feel better.

My nerves sang with remnants of my lessons and my head still ached. My bones were still sore and I was still exhausted. I went back to sleep.

The next day, the damn forest was *still* there. I ate from my supplies, went back to my balcony and slept again. The exhaustion that came over me was totally unexpected. It was like a tide that kept coming in. I slept for a whole week, only getting up to check if the forest was still there, eat from the food I had, relieve myself, bathe, or practice a few of Gambo's more benign lessons. I think Timia enjoyed the brief rain showers I accidentally brought in whenever I practiced. So did that damn spontaneous forest that refused to leave.

I was running low on food. Plus I needed to get out of the hotel. I decided to go to the market and find someone to fix my e-legba. When I got there, I received a rude awakening. The market was near the northern part of the city, right beside the city's main church and mosque. I should have taken that as a warning. There's always trouble when there is a church and mosque side by side. Between them, a breeze blew dust, straw, and plastic bags high into the sky. Ominous indeed.

The moment I stepped into the market, I wanted to leave. I hate crowds. Too many shoulders rubbing, too little room to breathe. Too much can happen. And with all the colorful flowing garments and various colognes and perfumes, it was like walking through a forest of over-scented curtains. But there were so many things for sale. And for once in my life, I had money.

I bought a bag of chin chin from the most annoying old woman ever. She wore a spotless white boubou. Regardless of her super-tall, perfect white head wrap, she was still short as an eight-year-old. She acted like one, too. She'd looked at my tattoos and made the usual snap judgment. I was used to this. But the way she barely spoke to me and refused to look me in the eye, that was something else. I wanted to punch her in the face, it was so rude. I snatched the bag from her, paid and moved on.

I moved to the middle of the market as I crunched on my chin chin. Whoever made the chin chin used too much sugar. They tasted like tiny sugar cookies instead of the slightly sweet fried pastries.

A man was selling small plants. He claimed they would keep a room smelling fresh. A woman sold dried ants that supposedly cured stupidity. Bush hoppers, mechanical men, pens that never ran out of ink. Though most of the buyers were New Tuareg, this part of the market was obviously dominated by Ginenians selling Ginenian items.

I walked for an hour and still couldn't find an electrician. I wasn't too worried; the market was large. I entered the area where foodstuffs were sold. I picked out a loaf of bread, some dried goat meat, and a bag of sticky dates. I had to snap at the seller a bit because he was treating me like I was made of camelshit. I couldn't care less whether he made eye contact with me or spoke to me, but I wasn't going to allow him to sell me stale bread, old dates, or the bony parts of the goat-meat chunks. I was looking at a very nice pineapple when I looked up and met the eyes of a shadow speaker boy just before a man selling peppers shoved him away. The boy couldn't have been older than eight or nine. He held several bills in his hand. Easily enough to buy what he wanted.

"Get out of here," the man said. He spit at the boy. "Filthy cockroach! Don't even *touch* my peppers!"

The boy stumbled back, looking at me for help. I took a step toward him. The boy looked to other people. No one but me met his eyes. He was a plump, light-skinned little boy. Possibly of Middle Eastern descent. Well-dressed, too. His large cat-like eyes must have seen everything. He was probably too young to understand any of what the shadows told him. The man raised a hand to slap him. The boy took off. I felt ashamed of myself for freezing. I was just so shocked at the man's behavior. The boy was trying to *buy* some peppers, not steal them.

"Should burn him alive," I heard a woman mutter.

"Don't worry," the man selling pineapples told me, giving me an apologetic smile. I was about to ask what he expected me to worry about, then I decided against it. "My products have never been touched by a Changed One," he said. I worked hard to hide my disgust. Now I, a slave in this man's eyes, was an acceptable customer. I bought the goods I'd picked out, but only to avoid suspicion. I looked around a little. I didn't see the boy.

I walked around the market all day. Listening and observing. I had the usual problems. Groups of aggravating little kids followed me around, snickering. Those kind of kids can practically smell when someone is alone and not from the area. They snickered about my shabby clothes and my "ugly" slave tattoos, commenting that I must have been a particularly difficult slave. Irritating. It took effort not to turn around and zap them or blow them away. Of course, that would have brought down the wrath of the entire market of Changed-haters on me.

Merchants eyed me suspiciously. A man tried to sell me cocaine. Another tried to sell me mystic moss, a hallucinogenic substance from Ginen that will turn your teeth and corneas green, and make you unhinged within weeks. I was followed by some shady-looking men for a while, too. *Probably gangsters*, I thought. I kept my cool.

But I almost lost it when I saw a metalworker woman harassed by a group of women when she tried to buy some cloth. What was wrong with these people? The metalworker's clothes were tattered, but the woman *did* have money. Someone slapped it out of her hand. No one picked it up.

"Cockroach bitch," a woman snapped. "Get out of here before you make us all barren."

"Go into the desert and die," another woman cried.

Again I heard that name, "cockroach." It seemed that any Changed One with obvious physical features was run off, hassled, spat at. The ones who came to the market must not have had people who could come for them. The metalworker woman stopped to catch her breath in front of a man selling specialized chocolates. He spat at her to get away from his stand.

That was enough for me. I quickly went back to my hotel. If I hadn't, I'd have electrocuted that chocolate seller. I'd have burned his nasty chocolate stand to a crisp. I'd have burned down the entire market, men, women, and children, and then brought in a storm to put out the fire and wash it all away. Because something was rotten about this place.

Better to leave.

I had been out of touch with society for too long. Things seemed to have changed. *Is this just a problem of Timia or are other places like this?* I wondered. *When did people like me be-come* cockroaches? I laughed. Cockroaches were the only creatures that could survive a nuclear explosion. Did Gambo, Buji, and Jaa know about this stupidity? Did Ejii?! I didn't want to think of what they'd do to her.

When I got back to the hotel and looked to the south, the spontaneous forest was gone. "I'm not safe here," I mumbled as I quickly walked back to my hotel. But I also wasn't quite ready to leave Timia yet.

CHAPTER 6

Tumaki

I found the electronics shop two blocks from the hotel. All I needed to do was go in the opposite direction of the market.

The small store was packed with all sorts of appliances and devices. A few were from Ginen, like the solar-powered e-legba that was part machine and part plant and a very small unhealthy-looking glow lily. Most everything else was very much from Earth. Thin laptops, standard e-legbas, all kinds of coin drives, batteries, and hardware like bundles of wiring, piles of microprocessors, digicards, and every kind of tool you could think of. It was a tinker's dream. It was my nightmare. Way too cramped. I planned to be quick.

To make things worse, the place was air-conditioned. My skin instantly started to protest as soon as I walked in. I wrapped my hands around my arms as I stepped up to the counter. A woman stood behind it. At least I thought it was a woman. I'll never get used to the burka. Maybe it's the southeastern Nigerian in me, but those things are creepy.

About fifty percent of the women in Niger wore them, though not so many in the town of Kwàmfà because of Jaa. The standard burkas are made out of stiff cotton, and a cotton screen covers the women's faces. You can barely see their eyes. These women, especially when you see them walking down the street at dusk or dawn, scare the hell out of me. They look like ghosts, all silent and mysterious. No, I've never liked burkas.

"Yes?" she asked. Okay, so I had been standing there staring. I never knew whether I was supposed to speak to these women or not. And since I couldn't see their faces, I was even less sure.

"I . . ."

She sighed loudly, rolled her eyes, and held out a hand. It was a careful hand. My mother would have described it as the hand of a surgeon. Her nails were cut very short, the palm of her hand slightly callused. Her fingers were long and they moved with a precise care that reminded me of the antennae of an elegant snail.

"Hand it here," she said.

I gave her my broken e-legba.

She turned it over, tapping the "on" button. The damn thing only whimpered. Never have I been so embarrassed. All e-legbas do that when they're broken. There are different whimpers, weeps, moans, or groans depending on the type of breakage. What kind of obnoxious engineer programmed them to do that? It's bad enough that the thing is broken. Why should a machine act like a whiny child?

"What'd you do to it?" she asked. As if my e-legba was some living creature.

"It's a long story," I said.

She turned it over some more between her antenna-like fingers. She laughed. "This is practically a toy," she said. "This is your only personal device?"

"It's a prime e-legba," I insisted, indignant. "An electrical god of the best kind."

She laughed her condescending laugh again. "A lesser god, if a god at all. With a weak solar sucker, sand grains in the fingerboard, a faulty *and* cracked screen, and probably a smashed-up microprocessor."

It gave a sad pained groan as if to stress her points. I wanted to grab and hurl it across the room. *What do I need it for anyway?* I thought. But in the back of my head, I knew I wanted to watch my mother's news program. And I had a copy of *My Cyborg Manifesto* on it and a much-needed Hausa/Arabic dictionary, and it picked up a fairly decent rap music and Afrobeat station whose signal seemed to remain strong wherever I went.

"I can fix it, though," she said after a while.

"You?" I asked.

She looked up, her dark brown eyes full of pure irritation. I stepped back, holding my hands up. "I'm sorry," I said. "I . . . my mouth is what it is."

"It's not your mouth that bothers me," she said. "It's your brain. My *mother* owns this shop. Not my father. Does that surprise you, too?"

I didn't respond. It did surprise me.

She nodded. "At least you're honest." She paused, cocking her head as she looked at me. Then she brought my e-legba to her face for a closer look. As she inspected it, she talked to me. "My mother's an electrician. She taught me everything I know. My father's an imam. He tries to teach me all he knows, but there are some things that I cannot digest." She laughed to herself and looked up at me. "You aren't Muslim, are you?"

"No."

She grunted something that sounded like, "Good."

"But you are, right?" I asked.

"Sort of," she said. "But not really."

"Then why do you wear that damn sheet?" I asked.

"Why shouldn't I?"

"Because you don't want to," I said.

"You don't even know me."

"Do I need to? A sheet is a sheet." I saw her eyes flash with anger. I kept talking anyway. "Doesn't matter if you look like a giant toad with sores oozing pus. You shouldn't . . ."

She pointed a long finger in my face like a knife. "You have got to be . . ." She stopped. I saw where her eyes flicked to. My tattoos. And I could tell she got it. She understood.

"My mother and I are electricians and this town is domi-nated by patriarchal New Tuareg ways and even stronger patri-archal Hausa, Tuareg, and Fulani ways. People here still . . . expect things. My mother and I play along. My father, well, he prefers us to play along, too. Everyone's happy."

"Except you have to live under a sheet."

"Business is business," she said with a shrug. "It's not so bad. I get to be an electrician who is female." She looked me in the eye. "Plus, sometimes I don't want people looking at me."

That was the excuse Ejii often gave whenever she wore her burka. I didn't buy it from Ejii and I didn't buy it from this girl.

"Well, other people's problems should be their business, not yours."

"In an ideal world, certainly," she said. "So can you pay?"

"Yes."

"In full?"

"Yes."

She looked me in the eye, obviously deciding whether she could trust me. She brought out a black case and opened it. Her tools were shiny like they were made for performing surgery on humans, not machines. She started to repair my e-legba right there. It was a simple gesture, but it meant a lot to me. She'd looked at my tattoos, seen them, yet she trusted me.

Minutes later, a woman came in also draped in a black burka. Her mother. I was about two feet away from her daughter. It was too late to step back from the counter.

"*As-salaamu Alaikum,*" the woman said to me, after a moment's pause.

"*Wa `Alaykum As-Salām,*" I responded, surprised. She glanced at my tattoos, but that was all.

People came in and out of the store. Her mother helped customers, sold items, chatted with them. But I was focused on the electrician fixing my e-legba. I ignored my claustrophobia and the freeze of the air-conditioning. I didn't want to leave. I didn't want to move.

She had my e-legba in pieces within three minutes. She tinkered, fiddled, replaced, and tinkered some more. After about an hour, she looked up at me and said, "Give me a day with this. I need to buy two new parts."

"Okay," I said. "I'll see you tomorrow, then."

From that day on, that store became my second home. Her name was Tumaki.

CHAPTER 7

Poetry

My e-legba was nothing to Tumaki. She could take apart and rebuild the engine of a truck, a capture station, an entire computer! She could even fix some of the Ginen technology. You should have seen what she did to that pathetic glow lily that I saw the first day I was in the shop. She got that plant to do the opposite of die. Once, she tried to explain to me her theory of why nuclear weapons and bullets no longer worked on Earth. She started talking all this physics and chemistry. I remember none of her words, but I fully remember the intense look on her face.

She was a year older than me and planned to eventually attend university. I wasn't sure if she liked or just tolerated me. When I was around her, I couldn't stop talking.

"We just use pumpkin seeds," she told me one day while she worked on an e-legba. We were talking about how to make egusi soup.

"See. That's where you people go wrong when you make the soup," I said.

"Us people?" she said, as she unscrewed some tiny screw.

"You people. Yeah. You know, those of you who live here in Timia," I said. I shrugged. "Anyway, we Nigerians call it egusi soup for a *reason*. Because we use *egusi* seeds. Goat meat, chicken, stockfish, fresh greens, peppers, spices, and ground egusi seeds. What they serve in the restaurants here is a disgrace."

"Fine, we'll call it pumpkin soup, then," she mumbled, as she worked in another screw. "Makes no difference to me."

"Ah ah, I miss the real thing, *o*," I said, thinking of home. "With pounded yam and a nice glass of Sprite. Goddamn. You people don't know what you're missing." I wished I could shut up. I didn't want her asking me any new questions about home. All I'd told her was that I was from Nigeria.

She only glared at me and loudly sucked her teeth. I grinned sheepishly. I was just talking, totally drunk on her presence. No matter how much rubbish I talked, though, she never got distracted. She could listen to me and work on a computer like she had two brains. Tumaki was genius smart. But she was also very lonely, I think. I figured this might have been why she didn't tell me to get lost. Maybe it was also why only two weeks after I met her, she did something very unlike her.

———

I was half asleep when I heard the banging at my hotel-room door. It was around two a.m. I don't know how I heard it, as I was outside on the balcony in deep REM sleep. It was rare for me to sleep this well.

My teachings with Gambo left me so awake and jittery. There were days where I felt like I'd eaten ten kola nuts. I felt like I was in fast motion, electrified, my heart beating fast like a rabbit's, cold sweats. Once, while I was showering, this electrical feeling started at my belly. I managed to jump out of the shower just as a huge blast of wind burst from my navel, nearly knocking the bathroom door off its hinges. Thankfully, the balcony door was open. I spent that entire day in meditation. I was such a mess.

When the banging on the door didn't stop, I got up, stumbled across the room, no shirt on, mouth gummy, crust in my eyes, smelling of outside and my own night sweat, barely coherent. I opened the door and came face to face with a black ghost. Death had come to finally take me. That thing from the fields outside the cocoa farms was back.

My eyes widened, my heart slammed in my chest. If my mind hadn't finally kicked in and my eyes hadn't adjusted, I'd have brought an entire storm into the hotel room to fight for my life. Tumaki would have learned the secret I continued to keep from her and then I might have accidentally killed her.

My control of my ability really was camelshit. And that thing from the cocoa fields . . . I still refused to think about it. Not a good idea, since when I was suddenly forced to face the memory, I almost went crazy with fear.

"Tumaki?" I whispered, stepping back. I ran my hand over my dreadlocks. They were probably smashed to the side. I must have looked like a madman.

She laughed. "How'd you guess?"

A thousand emotions went through me. Delight, pleasure, embarrassment, excitement, horror, fear, confusion, worry, irritation, fatigue. I slammed the door in her face. "Shit!" I hissed, staring at the closed door, instantly knowing it was the wrong reaction.

She banged on the door. She was going to wake my

neighbors. I quickly opened it. "What the hell are you do-ing?" she snapped.

"Trying to save my neck," I said.

She sucked her teeth loudly. "Let me in," she demanded.

Oh my God, I have no shirt on, I realized. My heart pounded faster. I looked down both ends of the hallway. I saw no one. But who knew who might have been listening or peeking out. I grabbed her arm and pulled her in. "You could get me killed by coming here," I whispered. I didn't know what to do with myself. Tumaki's family was highly respected. She was the imam's daughter! No girl went to a boy's hotel room in the middle of the night! Period. Especially not to meet a guy like me. Especially if anyone got a sniff that I was a Changed One.

"Nah," she said. "They'll just chop off one of your hands."

I pointed at her as I looked for a shirt. "Not funny," I said. My room was tidy, as I barely had use for it. I don't like messes. My clothes were neatly folded on one of the beds. Four shirts, one caftan, three pants. I grabbed a semi-clean cotton shirt. "What are you doing here?"

She shrugged and walked past me to my balcony. The scent of the incense she liked to burn in the shop touched my nose. Nag champa. I loved that scent, though when I bought some and burned it in my room, it didn't smell as good. She stepped over the mat I'd been sleeping on and took in the view. She inhaled and exhaled. "Nice," she said.

"Tumaki . . ."

"You sleep out here?"

I sighed loudly. "Yes."

"Why?"

"I like to," I said.

"You don't like the indoors."

"No."

She looked back out. "Makes sense."

There was a cool breeze. This was probably what had allowed me to sleep so well. Despite her presence, my head still felt a little fuzzy. It had been a while since I'd slept that deeply, and to be ripped from that kind of sleep was no fun. "Tumaki, your parents are going to . . ."

She laughed and whirled around, her eyes grabbing mine. "Let's go to the desert!"

"What?"

"Just outside of town," she said. "For a little while. I never get to do anything."

I opened my mouth to protest.

"I'm often in my library late into the night. Sometimes I sleep there," she said. "They assume that's where I am if I'm not in my bed. They can't imagine me being *anywhere* else but alone in my library. Trust me."

We could have taken her scooter, but we walked. I didn't know how to drive one, and even at this time of night, too many people would remember a woman driving a man on a scooter. It was *always* the other way around.

For once, I was glad she was wearing her black burka. In the night, you could barely see her. But I didn't have to see her to be aware of her proximity. It was the first time we were completely alone together—no mother in the back room or customers looming. But it wasn't the first time I felt this strong attraction to her. It didn't make sense. I didn't even know what she looked like! But the sound of her sweet voice, the smell of her nag champa, the dance of her graceful hands, just being close to her, I've never felt anything so real.

Each time I stepped into that shop, my heart started hammering. I'd get all sweaty. My mouth dried up. When I was talking to her and she had to leave for one second, I felt impatient. She was my last thought before I went to sleep and my first thought when I woke up. Tumaki, Tumaki, Tumaki. I hated feeling like this. No, I didn't trust it.

I was fifteen going on sixteen with no real experience with women. Well, there was Ejii. I definitely liked Ejii. But that had really never taken off. Two Changed Ones? It was a lot. But this thing with Tumaki came out of nowhere. Didn't I come to Timia thinking I'd be there only a day? Then wasn't my stay about finding a way to stop the discrimination against Changed Ones? I didn't like things that just came out of nowhere. I didn't like surprises.

"I wanted to go see that spontaneous forest so badly," she said as we walked in the moonlight.

I laughed and shook my head.

"I did," she insisted. "But I didn't have anyone to go with."

Tumaki had told me that all of her friends had been married off. Now she barely ever heard from them except for baby announcements. It was as if they had entered a different world. They had, in a way. The Married Woman World. In Timia that world had no place for friends.

"Spontaneous forests can be dangerous as hell," I said. "Especially when you don't know what you're doing."

"Not all the time."

"You want to take that risk?"

"Yep."

I almost laughed. She sounded kind of like me. I was glad that damn forest was long gone. I think she'd have gone in there and I'd have had to go after her. As we passed the last building, a man on a camel slowly passed us on his way into town.

"*As-salaamu Alaikum,*" he said to me.

"*Wa `Alaykum As-Salām,*" I responded, trying not to meet his eyes. Tumaki stayed quiet. Every part of my body was a sharp edge. How must we have looked heading into the desert with nothing but ourselves? *Oh Allah, they are going to lynch me, o,* I thought.

"Relax," Tumaki said when the man was gone. "He didn't know it was me."

"You knew that guy?"

"He's my uncle."

Before I could start cursing and going ballistic, she grabbed my hand. Her hand was warm but not soft. I stared down at her hand in mine. I didn't know what to say or do. I considered snatching my hand away. She was the kind of girl who would slap the hell out of you if you did something to her that she didn't like. Don't let the burka fool you. I'd heard her tell off a man who'd tried to cheat her on the cost of an e-legba repair. She'd handed the man his masculinity on a silver platter.

"Dikéogu," she said. The sound of my name on her lips . . . *let them cut off both my hands,* I thought. I wasn't letting go of her hand for anything. "Come on," she said pulling me along. "No time for you to start losing it."

━━━━━━

We didn't go out far. About a mile. Timia was still within shouting distance. Between the light of the half moon and the dim light from Timia, it wasn't very dark here. By this time, the thought of having a foot or hand chopped off or being publicly whipped for fornication, attempted rape, or some other fabricated camelshit had faded completely. Tumaki filled my mind like a rainstorm. And I knew she liked me, too. The cool breeze was still blowing and she opened her arms as if to hug it. Her burka fluttered. She looked like a giant bat. I laughed at the thought.

"I *love* the wind," she said, her eyes closed—at least I thought they were.

I suddenly had an idea. I focused on the breeze and the rhythm of my breathing. The breeze picked up. Tumaki laughed with glee, her burka flapping hard now.

"When I was a little girl, before I had to start wearing this thing, I used to run outside on windy days," she said. "There was this one day in the schoolyard where suddenly this giant dust devil whipped up! Everyone went running away from it. I ran *to* it."

She laughed and whooped, whirling around. I increased the breeze to a wind.

"I managed to get in the middle of it," she said, raising her voice over the wind. "It twirled me around and around and around. I thought it would suck me into the sky! My skirt lifted way up and everything." She turned to me, her burka billowing around her. "My father beat the hell out of me that day. For shaming Allah. I have a scar on my face from it."

A ripple of anger swept through me at the thought of this. I lost control of the wind. *Whooosh!* It swept from the desert floor to her ankles and blasted upward, taking her burka with it. We both stood there watching it flutter back down many yards away. Then slowly our eyes fell on each other.

Almond-shaped eyes. Skin dark like the night. Soft thick lips. The African nose of a warrior queen. She was taller than me and lanky in her red T-shirt with a yellow flower in the center and an orange patterned skirt that went past her knees. She wore her thick hair in two long cornrowed braids; the moon made it black but I suspected it was closer to brownish red. She had a long scar on her left cheek. Her hand went right to it.

A crucial layer of ourselves revealed. She knew what I was. I knew what she looked like. There was a flash of lightning from above. I could feel it in every part of my body and soul. It started to rain. We got soaked. But we didn't care. We ran around in the sandy mud and lightning and rain. We threw mud at the sky. We laughed and screamed and it rained and rained. Was it because of me or the will of the skies? Both, I'd say.

I grabbed her wet hand and pulled her to me. The first time I ever kissed a girl was accompanied by a chorus of simultaneous lightning, thunder, and a torrential rain, and it tasted like the wind and aquatic roses.

CHAPTER 8

Glow Lily

Tumaki wore her brown-red hair cornrowed at the shop or at school. Basically whenever it was under a burka. When she was at home or with me, she let it out into the big bushy tangled Afro that it wanted to be. I liked it best when it was out. So did she.

Her parents knew little about us. They only saw me in their shop, when I'd come around. I wasn't stupid. Her parents were progressive, but they were still Muslim. I was lucky they allowed me in the store to speak with her for ten minutes.

Her parents had named her well. "Tumaki" meant "books" in Hausa. During those wonderful six months, I spent most of my time in two places, Tumaki's arms and her library, which I learned was an underground room behind their house. She'd made the place hers. Her space. That was the only reason I could stand being in a small underground room. The room was like Tumaki's soul.

She'd even reinforced the walls with concrete all by herself three years ago. She'd also installed a winding metal staircase. She said she hired some guys to help with it, so I guess the library wasn't *completely* secret.

"This room just appeared about four years ago," she told me. "My mother believes it was made by one of those giant underground worms. It might have dug the hole for eggs and then decided that it didn't like the land or being too close to people."

"I believe it," I said. Ejii had once told me about "reading" the mind of one of those weird worms. She said it was obsessed with the number eight or something. The creatures definitely had strong opinions about stuff.

Tumaki had tons of books stacked down there. Books on physics, geometry, geology, African history, nuclear weapons, novels, biographies, how-to books, old magazines. She didn't discriminate. She loved information. She had a couch and two tables and gold satiny pillows with tassels. Glow lilies lit the room. The place was always cool even during the day. It smelled like the nag champa she loved to burn and the curry she liked to eat. And she liked to play soft Arabic music.

We didn't go back out to the desert, but we did explore the more progressive parts of Timia. We went to late-night tea shops where people spoke freely, teacups in hand, about whatever was on their minds. Once in a while people talked about Changed Ones, mostly as if they were the scourge of the Earth.

Usually when there was Changed One bashing, we'd stay for a long while. I really wanted to understand the root of their hatred. Fear, arrogance, ignorance, you take your pick, those people seemed to suffer from all those. But eventually, I'd start getting really steamed. The way those guys would talk (always guys, women never spoke in the tea-shop discussions), it was like they hadn't been on Earth during the Great Change. Like they were untouched by it. They thought they were so "pure." It was ridiculous. More than once, Tumaki had to drag me out before I threw hot tea in someone's face. The last thing I needed was for people to know I was a Changed One.

Tumaki and I were always quiet as I walked her home on these nights. After that night in the desert, Tumaki and I didn't speak of my abilities. She didn't ask about them and I didn't really want to talk about them. She knew I was a rain-maker, what more did we need to discuss?

We went to secret poetry slams held by students, usually in empty or abandoned buildings. Here I heard some of the worst poetry ever, but Tumaki seemed to enjoy it and none of these people bashed Changed Ones. So, though I made it a point to tell her the poets stank, we kept going to them. She knew most of the students here and again her burka pro-tected her, as it did the identity of most of the women there. If word ever got back to her father about her being out at night *and* with me, she'd have more than just a scar to show for it.

"But my father isn't the monster you're imagining," she insisted during one of our conversations about her scar.

"Any father who puts a mark on his child is a monster," I said. "I don't care if he's an imam."

I'd never spoken to Tumaki's father. Tumaki had tried to introduce me once but I wasn't up for it. He was one of those "big chief" men in Timia. The kind who struts around fol-lowed by guys who will admire even the toilet paper he wipes his ass with. His expensive embroidered thick cotton robes were always a heavenly white; how do you keep your clothes that white in a place where there is so much dust, eh? His long beard was bushy and dyed red, his hair cut short, not one gray hair on his head. You could tell he was a proud proud man. I didn't like him.

"You don't know him," Tumaki said.

"I beg to differ," I muttered. I'd known many like him, including Chief Ette, including *my* father.

That afternoon, she asked her mother if she could take the day off from the shop. Then she took me to the market square to see her father speak. We stood out of his sight, beside the booth of a man selling dried grasshoppers. The seller absentmindedly munched at a grasshopper leg as he listened to Tumaki's father speak.

Her father sat on a table before about a hundred young men who sat on the ground. He had their full attention. Every single one. I wished I could command that kind of attention . . . in a positive way.

Around them, the market went about its business, but people were obviously preoccupied, listening to Tumaki's father. I spotted her mother on the other side of the square. She was trying to be inconspicuous as she stood in the shade of a cloth shop. Even the shadows couldn't hide the pride on her face.

"And then whoooosh! The sweetest-smelling wind ever imaginable," her father said. "Everyone agrees the smell of the Great Change was like billions of blooming roses. It made your skin feel new, soft like a baby's backside. Allah is great, *quo*. If you were not there to witness the Great Change, you will never be able to fully imagine it. The Great Change was Allah's return. All its results are Allah's will."

He paused dramatically, then his eyes widened and he pointed his index finger up beside his head. "Now you have

these *foreigners* who know nothing about us. Who do not respect local traditions. They slaughter cows indiscriminately.
They consume goat milk." He spat to the side; several men in
the audience did the same. "And have you ever shared tea
with these people? They take one cup and then get up and
leave. When there is a whole pot left! What kind of nonsense
is that?" Several people in the audience sucked their teeth
and grumbled. I noticed more, however, were starting to look
around, uncomfortable.

"They openly disrespect Islamic tradition. Look at all the
addicts addicted to that . . . that drug, mystic moss. How
many die from eating other people's personal peppers? A
whole family died from them a month ago when a woman
mistook one for a normal pepper and used it to make stew."

"And the worst thing," he stressed, his voice rising. "The
worst thing is that they come here and think they can tell us
that we have gone wrong. They say the Great Change has
made the Earth and its people unnatural. They doubt the will
of Allah. They take their own lives for granted." He narrowed
his eyes and looked at his audience and then around the
market. "You know who you are. You know who you are."

My mouth practically hung open. Beside me, Tumaki gave
me a small smile and nodded. Tumaki had insisted that her
scar had been an accident. A stupid mistake of an overprotect-
ive father. I'd scoffed. "Why do you protect him?" I'd asked. I
was sure he'd done it on purpose, because he was afraid of
the power of her beauty. I assumed he was the usual non-
progressive ego-driven type of man that I was used to seeing.
Okay, so I had to revise how I felt about Tumaki's father.

He was a traditional imam, certainly, but this man was open-minded. And the man had balls. The "foreigners" he was griping about were Ginenians. No one did that! The people of Timia practically worshipped Ginenians. And though he didn't openly say it, the meaning was clear: he was *defending* Changed Ones. Can you imagine? In a town where they were treated like, well, cockroaches, here he was saying that they were the "will of Allah." Maybe Tumaki's scar *was* an accident caused by the hand of a scared father. Maybe. Even people who do good things can still do terrible things once in a while. He should have never scarred his daughter's face. I don't care what was going through his damn head.

More people gathered. Women, veiled, unveiled, burka-ed, gathered at the periphery of the all-male audience. There was a young girl standing not far from me who I think was a metalworker, as Tumaki's necklace was softly pulled in the girl's direction.

"We all keep up with the news," her father continued, now smiling broadly. Several in the audience grunted. I almost laughed aloud. I knew where he was going with this. "Yes," he said. "Yes, the *Old Naija Times*. Bringer of news from all over West Africa. For the old *true* African. These people are almost as bad as the foreigners. These are not 'old' times, these are new *changed* times."

I laughed, quietly cursing my parents. There were some boos. A few Ginenians had come to listen, too, and some local people simply didn't like what they were hearing. But mostly there was silence, attention, and a deep sense of fear. His words were obviously inflammatory, but many agreed with him. He was tapping into Timia's quietly festering disease. That thing that was on everyone's mind that no one dared to speak of.

He spoke with a casual eloquence that made you listen, consider, and fear for his life and your own for being there. You could see where Tumaki got her humanity. I felt my heart in my throat when I glanced at her as she looked at her father. I knew I had to deal with my parents eventually. *Not yet*, I thought. I couldn't imagine leaving Tumaki. *Will she come with me?* I couldn't imagine that, either.

When her father finished speaking, I still refused to meet him. No one wants to meet that kind of man while knowing you've more than kissed his daughter. No way.

====

Not long after that, invigorated by his speech, Tumaki and I went into the part of Timia where drug deals, prostitution, and other illegal transactions happened. It was her idea. I'd seen such places plenty of times since escaping the cocoa farms. I knew damn well that they existed and thrived. But I guess Tumaki was pretty sheltered.

"I need to see it," she told me.

One thing I noticed about Timia's ghettos is that you didn't see one Ginenian. You saw them at the poetry slams and always in the tea shops but never ever in ghettos. I guess that was sinking too low for them. At other times, Tumaki and I just walked the streets at night. Because we could. And I knew Tumaki liked the risk of it, though deep down she knew that I'd never let anything happen to her.

Nonetheless, we spent the most time down in her library. We didn't have to wait until night to go there. I'd meet her there after she finished school, when she didn't have to work or on her days off on the weekends. We'd simply read and enjoy each other's company. It was the first time I'd really had a chance to sit down and educate myself since my abilities had begun to manifest. Back home, school was not a good place for me. I was "The Boy That God Was Angry With," "The Kid Who Kept Getting Struck By Lightning," the butt of everyone's jokes.

"This book was amazing," Tumaki would say, shoving a thick book in my hand. Or she'd say, "You've got to read this! It'll change your life!" I couldn't not listen to her. I was in love with her, I guess . . . if I want to use that cliché, overused, damn-near-meaningless term.

Anyway, I must have read hundreds of books in those months. Reading kept thoughts of my parents at bay. And it helped me make sense of the intense discrimination I saw in Timia. I was slowly running out of money, but I'd cross that bridge when I got to it. *I could get a menial job or something,* I figured. I wasn't thinking about my future at all. Thankfully, my hotel room was dirt cheap (they even knocked down the cost if I helped them pull weeds from the lobby plants).

The reading Tumaki urged me to do helped to soothe the storm in my head whipped up by Gambo's teachings and my parents' idiotic interview. There is something about reading, and not just novels—learning and seeing and understanding things, too. It really is food for the soul. But it also *stirred* my soul. She had me read about all the worst things human beings have ever done.

"Best to know where you've been to know where you
need to go," she said.

I read about witch hunts, persecution, racism, tribalism,
infanticide. I read about the genocides that had taken place
all over the world. Germany, Rwanda, Bosnia, Sudan, Kosovo.
I memorized the eight stages of genocide—classification,
symbolization, dehumanization, organization, polarization,
preparation, extermination, and denial. I, of course, read ex-
tensively about slavery and those who fought for freedom. I
read about the pollution and eventual nuclear destruction of
the environment. I had terrible nightmares during this time,
but like my teachings, it was worth it.

I found a book on those medicinal butterflies that Asibi
had wanted to cultivate and sell. It was a recent book and it
was very slim. I read it cover to cover. I read about camels, I
read *The Autobiography of Malcolm X* (I usually don't care for
super old books like that when it's not history, but I liked this
book very very much). Tumaki made me read some of those
novels about Muslim women . . . not bad, except for the ones
that were mostly about perfumed and oiled girls dodging eager men and landing a rich princely husband.

I swear, between my teachings with Gambo and my time
with Tumaki, my brain probably doubled in size.

Rainmaker

Tumaki didn't wear make-up. Even without the burka she had no need for it. She only lied when she had to. Like when her mother asked about me. She told her that I was just a friend and that I was harmless. Her mother would have had me beheaded if she knew that I knew every part of Tumaki. Every part.

Tumaki wasn't deceptive, and because she grew up around trust, it was easy for her to learn to trust me. And she quietly worked hard to earn my trust. At first, I couldn't see past her beauty. Then, as time passed, yes, I began to trust her. Bit by bit.

You think of the times in your life where you actually accomplish something useful and good. Where you create love and beauty. Then when you reach the bad ugly place, where everything is a rainy prison, you understand that life is meant to be lived. It's meant to be lived. We are meant to go on.

That's what I tell myself here as I scribble my shapes and designs on these pieces of paper. Each day we get closer and each day those good days with Tumaki get farther and farther away. Soon it will be as if they never happened. It will be as if none of this happened. It will only be the wind, the rain, the lightning, this great storm.

CHAPTER 9

Paradise Lost

Now, listen.

I'm not telling the story of my relationship with Tumaki. That was gloriously normal. Textbook stuff. She and I were good together, when you didn't count all the outside stuff—like her being from a Muslim, fairly well-off family, and me being Changed and an ex-slave who'd been rejected from his basically Catholic, stinking-rich family. I told Tumaki a bit about my past. And she didn't ask about it much. She knew the basics. My secrets were not her preoccupation.

The story I'm trying to tell started when Tumaki's father disappeared.

Recall the incident I saw with the little boy shadow speaker. I saw so much of that in Timia. Changed Ones treated like radioactive, cancer-causing, evil infidel waste. Threats to small children and wholesome family values. We caused women to become sterile. We were the cause of all that had gone wrong. It was the Ginen folk spreading these stupid rumors.

But local people took to it like fish to water. They loved the Ginen folk like people love superstars and the wealthy. You could see it in their eyes. Women would swoon over the young Ginen men. Men would chase after Ginen women like they'd lost their damn minds. I have to hand it to the Ginenians, they had style. Their clothes were always the most fashionable. They had a way of speaking that sounded like music to your ears—I think some of this had to do with the mysticism involved in their language. They had money from selling their rare items.

It was the people, the natives of Niger, who took to calling Changed Ones (and anyone who sympathized with or gave birth to them) "cockroaches."

It was a slow disease in Timia. I might have left that city if it weren't for Tumaki. Hiding away in her library, I didn't realize how bad it was getting. Not until the day she came running down the winding staircase, shaking, eyes wide and wet. I'd been waiting down there for an hour.

I jumped up and ran to her. "Tumaki! What . . ."

She snatched her hand from mine as she threw off her dark blue burka and let loose a string of obscenities that impressed even me.

"What?!" I asked again. "What happened?!"

"My papa!" she shouted. Her left eye was twitching as she sat down on the couch. She stood up and started pacing. Then she made to go up the staircase. "I have to make sure!"

I grabbed her hand. "Will you tell me . . ."

She whirled around. The look on her face made me back away. I thought she was about to punch me. "They took him!"

"Who?"

"Some men." She shook her head. "And one woman. All of them strong like oxen. People were cheering! How can that be? People of his own home!"

"But why?"

"People are suddenly disappearing all over Timia," she snapped. "Haven't you noticed?"

I shook my head.

"Oh Allah! They took my papa, *o!*" she wailed. She screamed and moaned. I didn't dare touch her. Eventually, minutes later, she knelt down and was silent. She shut her eyes. When she opened them, she was calm. She stood and grabbed my hand. "Come, Dikéogu," she said, her voice steady, her eyes blank. "I don't care what my mother says."

We went up the stairs, across the yard, into her house.

Her mother didn't care, either. She didn't ask why I was with her daughter alone or why she was without her burka or why I was in her house. It was the house of wealthy folks. It reminded me of my home in Arondizuogu, but not as obnoxious. The floors were wooden, not marble. The furniture was plush, sturdy and well-made but probably not black leather imported from Italy.

There was a large picture with a white silk veil over it. I assumed this was a portrait of Tumaki's father. The house reeked of burned rice, and Tumaki had to run to the kitchen to turn the heat off the pot. Her mother just sat there on the couch. She wore no burka and she stared blankly ahead. This was my first time seeing her face. Tumaki was the spitting image of her mother.

"It was only a matter of time," her mother whispered. "Of course they'll take the imams first. Right there in the mosque. They have no respect."

Tumaki brought her a glass of water. Her mother took it absentmindedly. Tumaki looked at me and then back at her mother.

"He should have kept quiet." She whimpered. "He used to watch windseekers fly about at night when the bats were out, when they thought no one would see them." She set the water on the rug beneath her feet.

That day, I moved my things from the hotel into Tumaki's home.

===

I walked the streets, letting people assume I was a slave. The slave of Tumaki and her mother. I went shopping for them. I helped Tumaki in their electronics shop. I went to tea shops to listen to gossip. Some people, government officials of some sort, or so people thought, were finally doing what "needed to be done," some drunken blockhead said. Everyone, including me, mumbled assent. He sipped his tea and nodded. "Soon this city will be free of Changed Ones and troublemakers," he said. More mumbled agreement, this time a bit livelier.

It was all happening so fast.

===

Within one week, I stopped seeing Changed Ones with obvious characteristics in Timia. No windseekers; they brought wind wherever they went. No metalworkers; they attracted things like earrings, necklaces, and keys just by standing near people. No shadow speakers with their weird eyes. Professors started disappearing, too. And certain students, many of whom we'd seen at the poetry slams.

Two weeks later, Tumaki's parents' shop was ransacked, then burned down. Two days after that, her mother disappeared from her own bedroom.

The streets were busy and dare I say jubilant. Something was very wrong with these people. It was as if they'd been programmed and then the program had been turned on.

Tumaki and I dragged as much food and water as we could and hid in the library. We read books and enjoyed each other, but avoided talking about anything serious. Especially about the fact that I was a rainmaker and she was a female electrician and student. We were down there for three days. By the third, we were smelly, hungry, and angry. And then we heard people rushing down the stairs.

Now, when you've been cooped up for that long in a small room, you become concentrated. You know every sound. You know every angle. And you're a bundle of nerves. We'd been waiting for three days for something to happen. Tumaki had her mother's best hammer. I had myself. But nothing could have prepared us for what came down those stairs. There were four of them. Tall, dark-skinned, bald, even the woman. They wore white long caftans, the woman in a white flowing dress made of the same flawless material. They moved swiftly down the winding stairs and they made not a sound. I mean, not . . . a . . . sound. Silent as ghosts. Once in the room, they flew right at Tumaki and me.

I shoved Tumaki behind me. She tried to shove me behind her. It didn't matter. With my peripheral vision I saw one of them zip right at Tumaki, grabbing her in his clutches. It all seemed to happen in slow motion. I turned, my mouth open. He slammed Tumaki against a bookcase. She winced, mournfully glancing at me. He had teeth like a snake, fangs. *Vampire?*

"Let her g—" I was grabbed from behind.

But I saw it sink its teeth into Tumaki's neck as she raked her nails across its face. Its skin tore away, but there was no blood. It didn't let go. Tumaki's eyes went blank.

I was grappling with the woman, trying to get back to Tumaki. She said into my ear, "Where do you think you're going, cockroach?" Two more of them grabbed me.

I didn't hear a sound from Tumaki. But I heard the sound of her hammer dropping to the ground. In all that scuffling, I heard that.

I'd had enough. I stopped fighting. I focused. I let burst the most powerful surge of electricity I could produce. It made a low deep deep *thud!*

Screeches like you would not believe. Like rabid rats trapped in a tiny tiny cage. Spitting and hissing and high-pitched screeching. They fled up the stairs. I don't know if they flew or ran or oozed or what. All I knew was that they took Tumaki. She was gone. They must have picked her up like a sack of dried dates. They'd sucked the life from her and then they took her.

"Oh Allah, what is this, o?!" I screamed. Then I just screamed and screamed until a darkness fell over my mind.

The only gift my father really ever gave me was a thick book about an Igbo poet named Christopher Okigbo.

A line from his poetry: "For the far removed, there is wailing."

———

It was several things about Tumaki.

It was her books. It was the fact that she *hid* her books. Maybe one of the men who'd helped her install the staircase that led down to her library had told on her. It was her tinkering. It was how she knew to wear her burka despite all this. It was her pride. It was her wanting to attend university. And it was probably her parents.

I have no doubts about why they killed her.

———

I went mad. Plain and simple. I couldn't handle it. Darkness crowded in on me. Down there in her library, all alone. I barely noticed. Tumaki was gone. Her eyes had gone out. Like a light. I loved her. I was consumed by terror, shock, rage, shame. I tore at the neck of my caftan. I had no one left. A breeze lifted up around me.

Something oozed up through the library floor like some ancient crude oil, pooling around me, whispering and sighing. It was opportunistic, searching for a way into me. Oozing around my feet: the Destruction. I wanted to destroy all things. Murder, mayhem, havoc. Crush, kill, destroy. "Yesssss," the darkness whispered to me, like the sound of whirling sand. "Sssssssssss."

My grief made me retreat into myself instead of taking it

out on what was around me. I was lucky . . . in a way. In another way, I wonder if I'd have been better off succumbing to the thing from outside the cocoa farm that seemed to have followed me into Tumaki's library, like some lethal black smoky snake that had waited for the right moment to strike.

A large chunk of my life just after this remains mostly a blank, and the few short moments that I remember were just more badness. I do not recall leaving the library, or Agadez. I briefly recall, some idiot of a man grabbed me and told me I was going with his family to Agadez. He needed someone to help him with his camels. He read my tattoos as the mark of a slave. I let him. In Agadez, I slipped away in the dead of night. My memory is mostly blank for those weeks. In the following months, I'd mentally surface for an hour or two, finding myself in this town or that town. I'll not talk about the worst of it.

My mind was unhinged. I forgot about Gambo. I forgot about Ejii. I forgot about the magical nsibidi pact that had forced peace and was set to expire in a year. I forgot about my goddamn parents. I forgot about setting people free. I forgot about my owl Kola. I forgot about the dark beast that seemed to be following me. I forgot Tumaki. I forgot myself.

Somehow I ended up nearly dead in the desert, squinting up at that tall man whose face was covered by an indigo veil. I think it was being nearly dead that finally woke me up.

The closeness of death has a way of clearing even the most damaged senses.

Rainmaker

It looked like I was wandering, but, as always, fate was leading me toward something.
I have no trust in fate.

Those times of blankness were so bad. I don't know the name of the village where it happened, so don't ask me. I just know it was during my blank time. It was something in the Tuareg language of Tamarshak. It meant something about cows and straw and happiness. Too peaceful a name for a village full of crazy people. I don't know the location either. It was not far from Agadez but far enough.

That's all I'll say about it.

CHAPTER 10

Kel Ataram

From where I lay, the man looked eleven feet tall. His flowing indigo robes made him even more intimidating. He also wore a long piece of indigo cloth wrapped around his head. The only parts of his body that were visible were his hands, his eyes, and the bridge of his nose. His eyes were blue, his skin almost as brown as mine. In his big, rough-looking hands, he carried a shiny sword with three grooves down the center. My throat was too dry to make any sound. I had nothing to say anyway.

He saw that I was alive and laughed this big wheezy laugh. He sheathed his sword, clapped his hands, and said something in a language that I didn't understand. I heard many other men laugh too, commenting in their weird language. It sort of sounded Arabic, a little, and slightly West African, too, but mostly something else. I heard no female voices.

There were about thirty of them and about fifty camels. Gradually, my brain began to grind again. This was a caravan coming most likely from the town of Bilma, as the camels were weighed down with pillars of salt. The camels were a variety of shades from white to a deep tan. This meant these men were wealthy.

All of them wore garments and veils of a deeper blue than my own. Indigo. They were Tuareg. The infamous Blue People known for their indigo garments and irrational dislike of strangers; as if in the Sahara strangers weren't the norm. But the Tuareg also loved freedom and were a rebellious people. This was the main reason why many of them preferred to keep being nomads. Ironically, the Tuareg used to enslave the people who would later become a nomadic people known as the New Tuareg. Ejii's father was New Tuareg.

"Tumaki," I softly said, my voice cracking.

The man looked down at me, a curl of granite-black hair falling over his left eye. He pushed it back under his veil. "We have little use for books," he said in Hausa, stepping forward. "But we enjoy a good story. What is yours?"

He helped me up. He had to pull hard, I was so weak. The first thing I noticed was that, though he was tall, he didn't seem as tall as I had thought he was. *No,* I thought. *He is tall . . . I'm just . . . I'm just not as short as I used to be. Shit, how long has it been?* I immediately doubled over, dry heaving, every bone in my body screaming in pain, my mind shrieking with awareness, all my muscles clenching.

"How long have you been out here?" he asked.

"Don't know," I mumbled, my hands on my knees. My mouth tasted like sand, was grainy with sand, was dry as sand. I took a deep breath and then slowly raised my head to look up. The sky always made me feel better. The sun hadn't made it very far up yet. It was early morning. There was wind way way up there. I could feel it—shifting, running, coiling, swirling, cool and light. I realized another thing. I could feel the wind thousands of feet in the air as if it were blowing past my cheek. I wasn't out of practice. Again, I wondered how long it had been. And for the first time, I wondered what I'd been doing.

Despite the rising temperature, I was freezing. All I wore was a thick, dark blue caftan and pants. Rough clothing from a rough year. The Tuareg men all stood looking at me. The color of my clothes was probably what saved my life.

═══

"I am Byah Byah," the tall man said. He held out his hand. If I weren't so out of it, I'd have shuddered. I'd met Tuaregs before, obviously. Shaking hands with Tuareg men is like participating in a duel. You step to each other with polite smiles and lock eyes. Then you shake hands over and over, typically by the fingertips. The tricky part is knowing the right time to *end* the handshake. Too soon is rude and too long is also rude.

As I stumbled through the ritual, he sized me up, looking hard at my tattoos.

"My name is Rasaq," I said. I coughed again. My throat felt like I'd guzzled a gallon of whiskey. I'd once read about a rainmaker long ago whose name was Rasaq. The man lived in the times before the Great Change. He was hired by a family to avert a storm threatening the burial party of one of his relatives. Rasaq had dedicated his entire life to Shango, the deity of lightning. When he went up a hill to beseech Shango, he was struck dead by a bolt of lightning. Seemed like a fitting name for me at the time.

Byah Byah eyed me suspiciously. Because of his veil, I couldn't tell if he was smiling or irritated. Then the sides of his eyes crinkled with amusement. "Fair enough," he said.

"Why do they call you Byah Byah?" I asked. "You must have the beard of a wizard to have a name like that." Byah Byah was slang for "beard," at least back where I came from.

"Or the beard of a holy man," he said with a wink. Then his eyes fixed on me with great intensity. "We Tuareg value our true names," he said. "Byah Byah is what you will know me as, as I will know you as Rasaq." Only three others introduced themselves to me, all with equally non-Tuareg names. It was difficult to tell them apart without seeing their faces. A short man with brown eyes and yellow-brown skin said, "I'm Mekka."

"I'm Dem," a man of average height with blue eyes and wrinkle-free dark brown skin said. He seemed about my age and he looked me up and down as he spoke. I didn't like that. And my handshake with him was too long.

"I'm Ali," a tall stick-figure of a man said. Even his garments couldn't hide how lanky he was. He bent to shake my hand and look closely at me. Now this man I could tell was old as time. I wondered why he was traveling the salt roads. From what I knew, only the strongest men in the community did this. His eyes were dark brown and knowing and his wrinkly skin was near black.

Everyone else seemed uninterested in me or my plight as they kept slowly trudging along on or beside their camels.

"You want to finish dying out here or will you come with us to Kwàmfà?" Byah Byah asked.

The name rang a loud bell in my head. It rang and rang,

flooding my mind with images. Ejii in a long yellow dress. An adobe house with a garden in the back. A market where Changed Ones bought food freely. A graveyard. There was a graveyard. I blinked. Remembering. *There was a pact,* I thought. *How long has it been?!*

My mouth hung open; my eyes were blank. When I said nothing, Byah Byah patted his tall, blue-eyed camel. He mounted it the Tuareg way: grab its chin, climb right up, and jump into the saddle before the thing can bite the hell out of you. A primitive method, in my opinion. It always seems to anger the camel. His camel was no exception as it roared and grunted irritation.

Once the man was settled on his camel's back, he looked at me. "Get on."

I blinked, snapping out of it. Then I smiled weakly, thinking of so many things, the main one being, I wasn't ready to die.

━━━

For hours, the Tuareg caravan traveled swiftly. Most of the time I slept on the camel as it walked. I've always been good at sleeping on camels. Byah Byah gave me some flatbread and some water and I managed to get it all into my stomach. When evening was approaching, we stopped.

Byah Byah climbed off his groaning camel. I nearly fell off when I climbed down (I was still a little weak). I stood beside his camel as everyone stretched their legs and went about setting up bedding. Someone switched on a capture station. Men made fires. The camels were given buckets of water and hay. My stomach growled and my muscles ached. I felt like camelshit.

About a half hour later, dinner was served.

"You sit here," Byah Byah said, leading me to the warm fire and pointing to a wooden mat. I sat and crossed my legs, the smell of food making me dizzy with hunger. *How long has it been since I've eaten a meal?* I wondered. I didn't know.

For the first time, I tentatively glanced down at myself. My hands looked rough and veined. My forearms, they looked like a man's, more muscular than they'd ever been. How far had I walked or run, how hard had I worked? I shook my head, not wanting to think or see more. I gazed out at the evening. Out in the Sahara, sunset is the most pleasant time.

An enormous bowl of rice and lamb stew was served. Everyone gathered around the bowl and ate using wooden spoons. I remained where I was by the fire. I was hungry, but I found it hard to get up to go eat. Eventually, Byah Byah came over and handed me a spoon. I slowly got up. To not eat their food was rude, I knew. The rice was moist, the stew a burst of pepper, tomatoes, spice, the meat was chewy and burned, just the way I liked it. Delicious. I ate more. The men around me nodded, smiled, and grunted approval.

When we finished eating, of course, tea was served. The people of Niger were crazy about tea, especially the Tuareg. Tea in the morning. Tea in the afternoon. Tea when you meet with friends. Tea when you're alone and irritated. Tea when you're happy.

I mean, in Nigeria, I had grown up drinking it too; my mother said it was one of the remnants of British colonialism. But with the British, wasn't it an adopted tradition from

Asia? Anyway, in the Sahara, tea had a more intricate meaning. Like shaking hands, the ritual is crazy elaborate.

To turn down someone's offer of tea is like a slap in the
face. To refuse the second and third cup is equally as rude.
When someone makes tea for you, you stay and finish the
entire pot with him. If he makes bad tea, this can be pretty
annoying. Usually they drink green tea, mint-garnished being the most popular. The first cup tastes bitter: it represents
death. Sugar is added to the second cup to make it sweet like
life itself. The third cup is also sweet and represents love.

I sipped my last cup. It was as strong, cloying, sweet, and
minty as the second cup. Good tea. And it did make me feel
better. Or maybe it was more the food in my belly.

"So why were you out in the *Tinariwen* trying to kill yourself?" Byah Byah asked. As I ate, conversation had swirled
around me. However, up until now, no one had aimed it
at me.

"*Tinar* . . . what?" I asked.

"The Deserts."

Everyone, man and camel, was turning in to sleep now,
except Byah Byah, Ali, and the boy named Dem. Really, I just
wanted to be left alone. Things were starting to come back to
me. Not only memories about what had happened in Timia,
but . . . other places too. And much of that was not pleasant.

"It's a long story," I said.

The old man named Ali said something to Byah Byah,
and Byah Byah grunted and nodded.

"What could *you* possibly have seen that's so bad?" the
boy named Dem asked.

I frowned at him. I wasn't sure if the twitching of his left eye was a trick of the light from the fire or caused by sudden, pent-up anger. I laughed bitterly. "Oh, you have no idea."

He just looked at me. I wished the members of the group would take off those damn veils. There weren't even any women around. Who were they covering up for? How could people live like this?

Ali gave Dem a hard look. But Dem shook his head. "If he were one of them, he'd be bald."

My ears pricked and my heart flipped. "Bald?!" I nearly shouted, sitting up. "Have you . . . have you seen them, too?"

The three of them were quiet, all eyes on me. It was in this moment that I realized that I preferred them to remain veiled. There is nothing like having the eyes of Tuareg men on you. All the energy we normally pack into our full facial expressions, these people can funnel into their eyes. To see their faces at this moment would have been overwhelming.

"One of whom?" I insisted. My hands began to shake. Then the feeling traveled to the rest of my body. I started sweating, images flashing into my mind. Images upon images. Tumaki alive. Tumaki being bitten. Tumaki whisked away. Kola, my owl, my soulmate. An angry mob. That little boy. Celebrations in the street. Empty burning homes. The hot hot sun. A mosque burned down. A shadow speaker beaten in a market. A hotel inhabited by plants and wildlife. An underground secret library. Tumaki.

I shut my eyes tightly, clapping my hands over them, vaguely aware of Byah Byah, Ali, and Dem looking at me. There was a deep deep rumble of thunder from nearby and a cool wind picked up.

Two minutes passed. I remembered mental techniques to relax myself. I used them. Slowly, I opened my eyes. They were still staring at me.

"Please tell me," I whispered. "The people I saw . . . no, the *beasts* I saw, they too were bald. Even the woman."

Ali leaned forward, and before I knew what was happening, he pulled out a hair from my bushy head.

"Ow! What the hell . . ."

"Just making sure," he said, looking at the hair between his fingers.

Byah Byah was looking at the sky, whose stars were now hidden by clouds.

"Skin like chocolate," Dem said, after another moment. A good description, I felt. "Young but old. Tall. They were like vampires. But they moved like spirits and instead of changing into bats, they become fireflies."

We were quiet again. Staring at the fire. *I don't remember them changing into fireflies,* I thought. But then again, my memory was not what it used to be.

"I . . . I know she's dead," I suddenly said. "In the middle of all those books, they killed her, then they took her. They killed all the people with any kind of free thought. I should be dead, too." I looked at them, meeting especially Dem's eyes. Then I just didn't care. "I'm a rainmaker," I said, sitting up tall. "I'm no slave. Not anymore. And if the information is of any use, those vampire things hate lightning. They fled from it like terrified chickens."

"But it didn't kill them?" Ali asked.

"No."

"Who did you watch die?" Dem asked.

"My girlfriend," I said. "She was smart, an electrician, the daughter of an imam . . . and an electrician . . ."

"A woman electrician?" Ali asked. His tone annoyed me. It was almost as if he was condoning her death because she had the nerve to be smart, working, and female.

"She was damn good at what she did," I snapped.

"This was Timia?" Byah Byah asked.

I nodded. "They were killing anyone they could determine was Changed and anyone smart enough to understand that we are not a health threat." I frowned, remembering why I'd run away in Agadez. "They were doing it in Agadez," I said. "And . . . almost every town and village in a twenty-mile radius."

"Allah help us," Byah Byah whispered. "The same is happening in Bilma."

"Word is that these people, the Adze they are called, are working for someone," Dem said.

And that was when it all came together for me. The Ginenian migration. The Ginenians passing on their hatred of Changed Ones to the Earth natives. How this hatred softened natives up for the sweep of killing by the Adze. I gnashed my teeth. It all made sense. Chief Ette was behind all of this.

From the very moment I met him I knew the man was . . . a bad seed. That cruel bastard had no heart, or if he had one, his ruthlessness had smothered it long ago. The day of the Golden Dawn meeting in Ginen, as we stood in the Ooni Palace hallways, he'd looked at Ejii and deemed her useless because she was a girl. He'd deemed me useless because I'd been a slave. He'd called me "nameless," and "a nameless man is worse than a woman," he'd told me.

His wives had stood behind him, looking miserable, stepped on, and soulless. Chief Ette had been ready to wage war against Earth to protect his sacred land. To him, Earth was poison. A man like him would happily wipe out "diseased" Changed Ones in the name of "cleansing" the lands. It was because of him that Tumaki and so many others were dead.

———

The Tuareg were very polite in their way of pointing out that I was filthy and smelly. Dem brought me a bucket of water, some strong-smelling soap, a weak glow lily, and a small towel. "We're using a spot behind that sand dune," he said, pointing to my left a few yards away. I'd noticed men, one after the other, going behind there and returning. We were less than a day away from Kwàmfà. I guess everyone was cleaning up.

"Thanks," I said, standing up. My muscles ached with soreness.

"The water's warm," he said. "I put my thermal frog in there." He paused and added, "Make sure you bring it back to me."

I glanced in the water. Sure enough, there was a dark green frog happily swimming in the water. It swam to the bottom when it met my eyes. I'd never heard of such a thing, but then again, I'd been crazy for a long span of time. Who knew what else I didn't know? I didn't want to look stupid, so I nodded and just said, "Thanks."

I was glad for the privacy. I needed some time to think. It was absolutely freezing and the glow lily I had did nothing more than light my immediate vicinity. Anything could have been lurking out there in the darkness. I stared into it for a moment, remembering perfectly, vividly, like it happened yesterday, what Gambo and I had battled in the fields outside of Assamakka.

My freshly wakened mind twitched and I quickly pushed the image of the rolling blackness away. My stomach rumbled. I'd have to eat again before I slept. I smiled. I was actually hungry. A normal kind of hungry. I slowly undressed. Okay, so I was afraid of what I'd see. Who was I now? Would I have some weird scars? How much had I grown? As I took my pants off, I noticed that I had things in my pockets. I reached in. My e-legba. I smiled. At least I still had that. I clicked it on. The usual black screen with the rotating cowry shell came on. I felt a rush of emotion. Tumaki had installed this intro-screen just before her father disappeared. I'd been so happy in those days. And blind.

I touched the screen. My files and links came up. There was the link that showed my mother's latest program. Apparently she was interviewing a family that had recently immigrated from Ginen. In the brief description, it said, "Ginen family believes in old ways."

"Wow," I mumbled. "Twisted and hypocritical on so many levels."

There were several files on the screen I'd never seen before. Their icons showed that they were audio files. I clicked on one. Inaudible murmuring. I couldn't hear what the voice whispered, then whoever it was burst out sobbing. Suddenly I had to sit down. This was my voice. This was me. I clicked the file shut. I shut off the e-legba. I placed it on the sand beside me and stared at it. It was like hearing the voice of a ghost. A ghost of myself. Yet here I was, alive.

I noticed a bump sticking out of the side of my e-legba. I laughed to myself. *What'd I do to it this time?* I thought, not really caring. I picked it up and touched the bump. It was soft but firm, and it was only part of what was growing out of the back. It looked like a flat root of some sort. Possibly green in color, but I couldn't tell in the glow lily's strange lavender light.

"Whatever," I mumbled, setting it on my towel.

There was also a large wad of money in my pocket. I put it aside. From my other pocket, I brought out three pieces of folded paper filled with scribbles, loops, swirls. Not a section of the paper was untouched by ink. I knelt down close to the glow lily for a better look. "Wow," I said. The lines of the undulating designs swooped, zigged, zagged, and curved close to each other on the paper, within millimeters, but they never touched. I could stare at the paper for hours and still see something new. Flowers, ripples, stars, even the vague shapes of people. *Did I do this?* I looked at my fingertips. Indeed, they were stained blue and black.

I examined every part of my body. Not only was I taller and more muscular, I had a small scar on my left bicep that didn't look new, the bottoms of my feet were tough as actual shoes, a small leather amulet hung from my neck (had I been around a Wodaabe clan?). I touched my face, wishing I had a mirror. I didn't feel any scars, but who knew what my tattoo looked like, especially since I seemed to not be out of practice.

I dipped my hand in the water. It was warm, almost hot. The frog, which had been wading near the top of the water, swam back down again. "Whatever," I said again. It was Tumaki's thing to figure out the how and why of Ginenian items and creatures. Me? As long they did me no harm, I was fine. I soaped and scrubbed, mixing sand in with the soap. I had a lot of dead skin that needed to come off.

When I finished, I felt raw, clean and alive. I rinsed and sighed. As I reached for my towel, I accidentally knocked over the near-empty bucket. The frog leapt out into the darkness. "Shit!" I hissed, slapping my towel over my shoulder, grabbing the bucket and going after it. I wasn't in the mood to have Dem angry with me. He seemed like the type to hold a grudge. I chased the frog past the light of the glow lily and had to run back to grab the lily. Luckily, the frog had nowhere to go, so I was able to easily find it.

But it was a strong jumper, and each time I got near the stupid thing, it leapt again, feet away.

"Breeeee!" the frog sang as it jumped.

"Dammit, get back here!" I shouted. "A frog in the desert only has two options, dry up or get eaten!"

Finally, I managed to catch it. The minute my hands wrapped around the damn thing, it heated itself hot as an ember. I screamed and cursed, but I wasn't about to give up so easily. I managed to trap it under the bucket. "Gotcha!" I shouted triumphantly.

"Is this what you've been up to all this time?"

I froze. My eyes landed on his feet. His two petite, perfectly manicured, unused-looking brown feet. "Oh, come on," I mumbled. "You've got to be kidding." I slowly looked up to meet a mass of dreadlocks. They grew three hundred and sixty degrees around his head. The Desert Magician.

"You've been off my radar for about a year," he said. "I didn't expect to find you buck naked in the desert chasing a frog."

I slowly got up, wrapping the towel around my waist. I stood two feet taller than his four feet now. "I've fallen on hard times," I said. I didn't want to look at him. I'd seen behind those dreadlocks once before, when we'd entered Ginen that first time. Looking behind them was like having the shock of my lessons with Gambo all rolled up into a moment and amplified a thousand times. Doors opening, my life tearing, nerves searing. Ah ah, I didn't want to see behind the eyes of the Desert Magician *ever* again.

He put his annoying foot on top of the bucket. "Yes. Hard times, indeed. You were dying."

"I guess," I said.

"Should have stayed with your teacher," he said. Then he snickered, as if he had a great big secret.

I wasn't interested. "And my parents shouldn't have been assholes, but what can you do?"

"It's all one big witch's brew," he sang. "One rancid pot of stew. And none of you have a clue. In my point of view. Ha!" He looked at his foot, which still rested on the edge of the bucket. "Ah, that frog seems to be trying to burn its way out of that bucket." He brought his foot down, knelt beside the bucket and tilted it up. Then he snatched up the defiant frog. There was a sizzling sound as he held it, but the magician only chuckled. "Brave and stupid creature," he said. He kicked the bucket and it immediately filled halfway with water. He threw the frog inside.

"Thanks," I said, looking in the bucket. The frog happily swam in circles, softly bumping against the bucket's wall.

"No frog deserves a death like that," he said. "Walk with me."

I looked down at my towel. "Can I get dressed first?"

Would you walk into the desert with a riddle-speaking, trick-playing, four-foot-tall midget who's really some sort of spirit or god with dreadlocks growing around his head? I planned to make a run for it as soon as I got my clothes on. I wondered if he would pursue me into the camp. I'd just have to find out.

"No," he said, with a laugh. "You're used to running about like a madman. The towel will be fine. Come."

I cursed under my breath, clutching the glow lily. I was freezing. I grabbed the bucket, glad for the bit of warmth that came from it.

He hummed and danced a little jig as we walked. "These are the days of old and new," he said as he strolled. "Ancient and futuristic."

"Mr. Magician, I'm freezing."

"I beg to differ," he said. Then he laughed. "You've only just begun. No time to die yet." When he turned to me, he was carrying folded garments in his arms. They steamed hot in the cool air. "Leave your rags. Wear these riches," he said.

The cloth was very expensive. I could feel it in the stitching and weaving. *I'll bet these will fit perfectly, too,* I thought. I couldn't tell if they were black or just deep indigo.

I eyed him suspiciously, clasping my towel. "What's the catch?" I asked, my voice shaking from shivering.

He laughed, deep and husky. "Smart boy to ask, stupid boy to think you'll see your path as you walk it. Put these clothes on and listen to me. Then take the story where you will."

I hesitated. *Dammit*, I thought. *I wish I could see his actual face.* It seemed to be the theme of my encounters: Veiled faces, be they veiled by cloth or thick, long, sand-tipped dreadlocks. I took the clothes. What else could I do? Do you really think he would have let me go if I didn't? Okay, maybe he would have, but I was *freezing*. Parts of me that should never have been that cold were like blocks of ice as they tried to retreat into my body. The garments were traditional but really well-made. The pants came right to my ankles and the robes came to my knees. The clothes were still warm.

"Ah, there you go," the magician said when I was dressed. "Rags to riches." He motioned to my feet. "Well, not completely. But I don't think you need sandals."

I didn't. I could walk over hot coals and not feel a thing. We walked farther away from the camp.

"You are going back to Kwàmfà?" he asked.

I nodded.

"I am the Desert Magician," he said, as if answering a question I'd asked. "I find water where there is none. Deeper down the rabbit hole you creep, Dikéogu. But colorless green ideas continue to sleep furiously. Ask Chief Ette. Heh!"

I sighed loudly. The man was putting my head in knots and it was irritating as hell. My dealings with the Desert Magician were always like this. Rambling, nonsensical, with some kind of meaning so deeply buried that it gave you a headache searching for it.

"You people make such a mess of things," the magician said. "The mess gets messier, the deaths deadlier." He laughed hard. "Excellent entertainment. Better than television and even good theater. Dikéogu, how are your parents?"

"Fine," I snapped, before I could stop myself. The question surprised me. They were the last thing I wanted to talk about.

"Glad to hear it," the magician said. He paused, his locks swinging in the breeze. Definitely not *my* breeze. "I've stopped you to offer some information. You do understand that the pact has disintegrated."

I blinked. My heart sank. *So it **has** been a year,* I thought. *At least. I have been running mad for that long? Three years since the Golden Dawn meeting? Since seeing Ejii? My God!*

"Yes, in the three years, Jaa the Red One and Chief Ette have failed in becoming best friends. Big surprise there. Just like I am surprised when the sun rises." He laughed loudly. "So the story continues, this time down a darker path. But there is hope still." He lowered his voice. "The man Dieuri lives."

I threw my hands in the air. I'd had enough. "What?! Ah ah, this is . . . this is alllll total *camelshit*," I shouted. Tears flew from my eyes. I was all messed up. A year out of my life. Doing goodness-knew-what. I knew some of it, and those bits that I remembered were pretty bad. The nsibidi pact was disintegrated, which meant war was coming. Ejii, where was she? Tumaki was dead. My parents were assholes. Now this news of Dieuri, the Haitian scientist who created the Peace

Bombs that helped the entire Earth go haywire?! He was believed to have either thrown himself into the Caribbean Sea or sprouted wings and flown into outer space where he came from.

"Bring the rain," the magician said. "I am waterproof. Listen to me, rain boy who is no longer a slave, get it together. The last thing I need is for you to go bananas again. Although that would be quite exciting to watch. You're needed. The man Dieuri, the man who caused you all, he lives. If you want the real story, go and see him."

I sighed. *"Real story" of what?* I wondered. I needed to think.

"Go to Kwàmfà," he said. "But when the time comes, consider my words. Find him in Lagos. Ask around and you will learn where."

"How do I know you're on our side?" I asked.

"Did I say I was?" The magician laughed. "I just like a good story. Stories about war and full of battles? Boring as hell. Predictable. Not so spicy."

I was relieved when he finally let me go without any more nonsense. As I walked back to my old clothes, I thought about what he'd said. Lagos was far as hell, by vehicle, camel, or foot. And it was probably getting farther and farther away every day. As you moved further south, toward the equator, as the Sahara Desert and arid lands ended there would be more jungle. There would be bandits, people who have become strange. There would be creatures. And could I trust the magician anyway? Dieuri the mad scientist, alive?

And could I trust the magician? The frog in the bucket poked its head out of the water and said, "Breeeee!"

CHAPTER 11

Kona Bird

One thing I like about the Tuareg is that they sleep on straw mats outside, not in tents. They like to see the stars at night. So for once, I wasn't alone. I lay awake on my mat in my old clothes. I'd changed out of the ones the magician had given me. I wanted to avoid questions until morning.

Sleep wasn't going to come to me. I'd been mentally "asleep" for over a year. I wasn't in the mood for any kind of rest yet. I brought out my e-legba and clicked it on. Avoiding the audio files, I clicked on a video icon shaped like a tiny green circle. The circle cracked open, making a loud wet sound, like when you break open a watermelon. I looked around. The noise didn't seem to wake anyone around me.

Tumaki's face and shoulders appeared in a large box on the screen. I almost dropped the e-legba. *She's alive!* I nearly screamed. I had to fight not to jump up. Tears welled in my eyes and I had to breathe through my mouth. I felt so guilty about her death, like it was my fault. I should have done something. Now here she was. "Thank God," I whispered. "Oh, thank God!"

She wore no burka. Only a white T-shirt and a great big smile. She laughed and laughed, then she grinned and said, "I wonder how long it took you to find this. I put the icon right on your screen. Goodness. Anyway, I've put this file here in case you got confused when things started . . . changing on your e-legba. The process will take about eight months, I think." She smiled. "Seeds need time to grow. I like making things what they should be. Your e-legba was like a parame-cium. I've evolved it up to, let's say, a dolphin. Like dolphins, it looks cute and harmless but it is really a smart amazing organism. I say organism because I've implanted some . . . Ginenian software."

I paused the video. My stomach sank and I closed my eyes. This footage was old. Made maybe a day or so after I met her. When she'd fixed my e-legba. No. She wasn't alive. She was dead. I'd seen her killed. I un-paused it and watched the rest of the only thing I had left of Tumaki.

She'd made my e-legba a cyborg, part machine and part plant. That's what the thing growing out the back was. A root. Didn't I say Tumaki was a genius? No longer did it need a battery, because it was both solar *and* lunar. And thus, more durable. I could drop it on the ground, in water, in the sand, and it would be fine. And it could now pick up network sig-nals from as far as Saudi Arabia and even some of the other worlds with technology like Ginen and Agonia. And all the software on the e-legba had been upgraded.

"I did it because I could, and because, well . . ." She chuck-led and grinned. "I kind of like you." She'd made this mes-sage before she even really knew me. She'd secretly shown me her face when she had no clue that she would love me. Or maybe she did. Women and girls have a way of knowing and controlling the future, I think. Sometimes. The connected ones.

Eventually, I fell asleep with the e-legba clutched to my chest.

━━━━━

Whoop!

Even in my dreamless sleep I heard it. Something soft. Something large. I slowly opened my eyes. I stared at the sky for a moment. Its deep darkness and the position of the stars told me that about two hours had passed. The sun was still hours from rising.

I felt more than saw or heard her. I sat up. "Kola?" I grinned. She was close. She was speaking to me. Pleased to feel me, too. I scanned the camp. Everyone was fast asleep. Except Dem. I could see him some feet away, sitting up.

"What was that?" he whispered.

"Dunno," I said. But I was laughing and grinning. He probably thought I was nuts. I got up, as did Dem. We both turned to the left at the same time. In the firelight, it was a sizable shadow. About the size of a small car. Dem ran over to me.

"What's going on?" he asked suspiciously.

"Quiet!" I said. In my head I heard Kola hooting softly. She didn't want me to be afraid. I frowned, listening to her. She wanted me to . . . go toward the shadow. As my eyes adjusted, I could see it a little better. The firelight bounced off soft tan feathers, a narrow but powerful black beak, and fire-red eyes. A giant bird. In my mind, Kola told me he was a Kona bird of the Kona tribe. From Agonia.

Dem made a circle around his head with his hand and snapped his fingers as he stared.

"He's not a demon," I said, gazing at the bird. Kola wanted me to go with him.

I split my bundle of bills in half and gave Dem one of the halves. "Give that to Byah Byah," I said. "Take some for yourself first."

Without a word he took it. We shook hands elaborately. "Where will you go?" he asked, as we grasped and slapped. I winced a little because of my slightly burned hands.

"Kwàmfà," I said after a moment. Yes, it seemed right. "I'm sure I will see you there."

"I realize who you are now."

"I'm nobody."

"You're Dikéogu and you helped save the world."

I paused, surprised. When I spoke, my throat was tight with emotion. He knew who I was. "The-the pact is disintegrated."

"Yes, and there are monsters killing Changed Ones like you and free people like me," he said. He nodded. "That's why we go to Kwàmfà."

"I will see you there, then," I said. A tear rolled down my cheek and I winced. I needed to get myself together.

"Be safe."

I looked away. "You, too. Thanks for lending me the thermal frog."

He grinned. "You know, it doesn't need to stay in the water after it's heated it. I usually let it go out and forage for food. It comes back when it's done." He laughed knowingly, shaking and slapping my hands again.

"You're an ass," I said, laughing.

I changed into the Tuareg garments the magician had

given me. I even put the turban veil on. It would be good protection against the wind as we flew. My e-legba, a bag of dates from Dem, and my money were safely in my sturdy deep pockets.

The Kona bird's name was Kee. So Kola told me. His body was firm, his feathers tough but light. He smelled like orange peels and was partial to making a deep clucking sound followed by a shrill *keeeeee!* He did this just as we took off, waking everyone in the camp. As if I was paying attention. I was on a giant muscular bird climbing high into the sky. It was exhilarating. But even then, I missed Tumaki. I missed her so much.

I never saw Dem, Byah Byah, Ali, or the others again.

Rainmaker

Today was not a good day. It haunts me in my sleep but now it haunts me during the day, too. First there was the sound of a million cowry shells falling from the sky. My camel nearly threw me off, it was so afraid. The air here is dry like dead trees. You can barely breathe. But we keep going. It's all a bad omen. It will all come to a bad end. It's all bad.

I think about escape constantly. That's the only way I think I will be able to find him. On my own. These people will surely just kill him. Put him out of his misery. I know he's miserable. Like me. I am Dikéogu the Miserable. Always under its darkness. Like some giant umbrella. No rainmaker should be cursed with a giant umbrella.

We keep on. But trust me, I won't let them get away with this. When the time comes, I'll show them what makes rainmakers so dangerous.

CHAPTER 12

The Arrival

I wanted to kill the chief. I knew that now. I wanted to confront my stupid parents and then go out and kill that rotund evil symbol and head of all that is bad. I'd make the world a better, safer, more logical place. As I flew over the odd changing lands, these ideas hung in the back of my mind like an inevitable storm cloud. Rumbling, flashes of lightning in its bowels, an approaching sense of urgency.

Still, I remembered joy, too. As we flew to Kwàmfà, I thought about the delicious meal I would have as soon as we landed. Lentil soup, moi moi, and fried plantain. It was odd. Somewhere in that lost year, I'd lost my taste for meat. I was looking forward to hopefully seeing Ejii, Gambo, Buji, and Jaa, too. I wondered what they thought had happened to me. Maybe they thought I was dead. I kind of had been. I'd have a lot of explaining to do.

But deep deep in me, I rumbled and seethed. I thought of Chief Ette and his miserable women all lined up in a row. How easy it must have been to send the Adze to the Sahara region to kidnap and kill. How logical it must have been to him to send Ginenians to plant seeds of hate amongst the locals to soften them up for what would happen next. The man was easy to hate.

I leaned close to Kee's back. How he knew exactly which way to go was beyond me, but I suspected it had to do with Kola. *Where are you, Kola?* I wondered. I sensed her now, but only that she was alive and far away. Kee and I got on well. He flew like an eagle, harnessing all the power of the wind, barely having to flap his wings at all. And his wings were as silent as an owl's. But he didn't fly too high. For my sake, I suspected. Like me, he had a brotherly relationship with the weather. His wings vibrated whenever the air pressure shifted the slightest bit, just like a barometer.

"Do you like music?" I asked, after we'd been soaring for about an hour.

"Keee!" he said. I laughed. That sounded like a very enthusiastic "yes." I tested out several channels that came in nicely up here. When he started humming deep in his chest, I stopped. Classic Nigerian highlife. I felt like laughing and crying. My father loved this kind of music, too.

———

Kwàmfà spread below, all sturdy sand-brick buildings and dirt roads. Even from up here I could see that the town had changed. It was bigger, stronger. I laughed. Who knew what people would think of me swooping in on a giant bird? By now people had to have seen stranger things. I'd heard there was an opening to Agonia not far away, so people were probably used to sentient flocks of parrots and maybe large birds like Kee.

The flight to Kwàmfà had taken three days. The first night we rested in a small spontaneous forest that Kee chose. The giant bird was my only mode of transportation out in the middle of nowhere, so I was forced to trust him on the safety of the forest. Thankfully Kee was right. The forest was harmless. The trees produced normal coconuts and the only animals inhabiting it were some small snails on the trees and three ring-necked doves.

I should have slept well that night, but I spent most of it watching my mother's show and a series of insensitively reported news files about the disappearance of Changed Ones in Agadez, Timia, and Bilma. The reporters all had amused smiles on their faces, as if they thought Changed Ones were just sulky little kids trying to get attention by hiding. "Well, at least they are acknowledging that something is happening," I mumbled. I got about an hour's worth of sleep. The forest was gone when I woke up.

My second and third days of the flight were less pleasant. I spent them quietly being inundated with memories of the past year. Bits and pieces. I remembered arguing with a Hausa man and telling him off so thoroughly that he'd tried to swing at me. My memory continued to hide what I did to him. I remembered sleeping in a garbage dump because the garbage stayed warm at night. I remembered reveling in a thunderstorm while those around me cowered in buildings. Eating dry grass. Being led into a mosque and participating in prayer. Sleeping in a church. Winning a big pile of money in a dark dank room, dominoes on the table. It was like I was someone else.

By the time I arrived in Kwàmfà, I was spent. But I was more together.

Kee landed in a small field in front of a group of children. It had been a late morning. Some had been kicking a soccer ball around, others just hanging out socializing. Kee was so smart. He had purposely chosen an adult-free spot. No matter where he landed, I was bound to be food for the gossip mill. Best to have the gossip starters be children. They weave the best stories.

They all stared, grinned, ooh and aahed as I got off Kee. There were decently dressed boys and girls, all around nine years old. Boys *and* girls of this age playing together was damn near unheard of in Timia, Agadez, and just about every other place I'd traveled in the last four years. Kwàmfà was really a unique place. It must have been a rest day; otherwise, they should have all been in school.

One little girl grew bold enough to speak up. "Are you a jinni?"

"Sheza," one of the boys whispered, pulling the girl back. "Don't speak to him."

"I'm Dikéogu," I said.

The response was perfect. Whispers of surprise and wonder. I was remembered in Kwàmfà.

"We thought you were dead," one of the boys said.

I laughed. "So did I."

Kee took to the air and the kids gasped and laughed. Kee sent me a mental message letting me know that he'd find me later in the evening. I had nothing to give the children, but they didn't seem to mind. I think they were happy to be the first to alert everyone about my arrival. I rushed off.

I didn't go straight to where I wanted to go. If Ejii was here, I wanted to find her before the news of my arrival got to her. But I wasn't ready yet. I strolled to the market, where I bought a meal of lentil soup, fried plantains and fresh bread and a bottle of palm wine. I was once again glad for my veil. It hid my tattoos nicely.

I took my meal to the Hall. It was time to find Gambo.

The Hall was where all the council meetings took place. It sat in the middle of Kwàmfà, a grand sandstone structure. Inside, it was really just one huge round room with a super high ceiling. To make things even better, the ceiling had a large skylight. If there was a place I could tolerate being inside of, at least for a few hours, it was the Hall.

The floor was white marble, as were the supportive pillars at the room's perimeter. My sandals clacked as we walked in.

"Hello?" I called. "Master Gambo?" My voice echoed. "Master Buji? Master Jaa?"

The walls were decorated with Fulani-style ebony masks embroidered with thousands of tiny colorful beads, Wodaabe calabash bowls, large silver decorative Tuareg daggers, and leather amulets. To the side was a small bar stocked with several kinds of alcohol and the door to a kitchen. In the center of the room, after stepping down three marble stairs, were a bunch of black leather chairs and couches. Luxurious, yes . . . but everything was dusty.

I went to the back. Though it seemed to be growing wild, the garden, at least, was alive. There were all kinds of flowers in bloom, but just as many prickly-looking weeds, too. Someone had at least been watering it. Flowers like these don't just grow in a climate like Kwàmfà's. And the place was mad with butterflies.

This was where I slept before and it was where I would sleep now. Even with the nice skylight, I just can't stand the indoors. As if you haven't noticed this. I suspect it's this way with all rainmakers. We need to see the sky. But I also like to feel free. A roof over my head feels like having my arms and legs restrained.

I unwrapped my food and ate in contemplative silence. *Where is everyone?* I wondered. The Hall didn't feel abandoned, just unused. For years. Months. Everything else in Kwàmfà seemed normal enough. I didn't see many Ginenians. I still saw Changed Ones coexisting side by side with humans. Kwàmfà seemed bigger and more packed than other towns, and I noted the presence of a lot of foreign dialects, but nothing that worried me.

I needed to see Gambo. To tell him I was all right. I ate fast. I set my satchel down and folded my veil. I left the Hall and walked quickly north. People stopped and stared. They recognized me. I was the kid who helped Ejii save the world. I have no idea why they kept crediting Ejii and me with stopping the chief from invading Earth. It was more complex than that. Sure, Ejii and I had key roles in what happened, but so did Jaa, Gambo, Buji, and about ten others. The idiok baboons had come up with the idea for the damn nsibidi pact; they'd written it, too. People always want to simplify everything. *No one* can "save the world" alone.

People whispered but no one approached me. They must have all known where I was going. And since no one came up to me, and several people actually followed me, I knew that Ejii was home.

CHAPTER 13

Ejii

And there she was.

Waiting for me on the steps of her house. Golden, cat-like shadow-speaker eyes and onyx skin. She knew I was coming. She wore a wrapper and matching top made of some sort of red and yellow print material. She stood up. I stopped some yards away from her and stared. Ejii had grown, but was not much taller than when I'd left her three years ago. So she was not tall or short. I stepped up to her.

She stood there smirking at me.

"You look . . . different," I said. Honestly, I'm not one of those pig men who doesn't care about girls' and women's feelings. But this one time, I had to actually work hard not to look at her enormous breasts. I mean, my God, when did *that* happen?

"Oh, stop it," she snapped, rolling her eyes. "So do you."

"Yeah, but *you* look . . . *different*," I said, pointing at her chest. No reason to beat around the bush. This was Ejii. My friend.

Ejii laughed. "I *know*," she said. "I hate them."

"I don't."

"Oh Allah," Ejii said, shaking her head.

There was an awkward pause.

"I was going to come back to find you," I finally said. "But Gambo and Buji said you were gone. Then I was . . . side-tracked."

"I heard," she said. "I . . . I actually just got back. About a week ago."

Pause. How much did she know? Had she spoken with Gambo?

"So where *did* you go?" I asked.

She turned to me. Her face was beautiful. Tumaki's face swept into my mind. I felt a twinge of guilt.

"I haven't seen you in years," she said. She laughed and looked away. "Plus this is now. That past is the past."

There was a mountain of experience between us. You could feel it. What had happened to Ejii? What wasn't she telling me?

"Ejii," I said. "What . . ."

She took my hands. "I have a thousand things to tell you," she said. "But not today."

"Okay," I said. I was relieved, really. If she told me what she'd been up to, I'd have to tell her what I'd been up to, too. Killing Big Blokkus, all I'd seen on the cocoa farms, Tumaki, the lost year. My chest tightened. I didn't know if she was reading me or not. I didn't want her to know too much. She'd feel sorry for me, pity me. Then she'd hate me.

"Would you like to come in?" Ejii's mother asked, coming from behind Ejii.

"Certainly, ma'am," I said, letting go of Ejii's hands, glad to step away from her. I glanced behind us. It looked like half the town had gathered and everyone was staring. What-ever.

I remember that meal vividly. Couscous, fluffy rice and spicy red stew, roast mutton (which I didn't eat), sweet fried plantain sliced long down the middle, boiled eggs with a pinch of salt, sliced firm-but-sweet mango, juicy dates covered with caramelized sugar, roasted yam and peppered palm oil. Out of habit, I sniffed everything before eating it. The food was heaven. I ate like a horse under the heavy gaze of Ejii and the brooding gaze of her mother.

CHAPTER 14

Arif

I walked home in the dark with Ejii on my mind. After eating, we hadn't talked much. She'd taken me to the back of their house and introduced me to a strange friend. A giant bird, but nothing like Kee. When you look at Kee you can identify him. You think, "Goddamn, that's the biggest eagle I've ever seen."

Ejii called this weird bird Plantain. Yeah, like the large, delicious, banana-like fruit. Remember her camel, Onion? Yeah, Ejii seems to attract animals who like to name themselves after fruits and vegetables. I don't know what that's all about. Anyway, Plantain had brought Ejii all the way from some forest deep in Ginen called the Greeny Forest. No, let me correct myself, not brought her, traveled with her. Plantain wasn't just some creature. She was Ejii's travel companion.

"She's a mutatu," Ejii told me. "A land bird."

Plantain was shaggy brown with limp fuzzy feathers that looked more like soft hair. It looked like a tiny wooly mammoth, if mammoths had two legs with feet like an ostrich and a thick red-orange parrot-like beak instead of a trunk. Plantain eyed me with the wisdom of an old tree and then blew a piercing whistle that made me want to punch it in the head. Anything to get it to shut up. Oddly, the whistle came

out of a hole in the top of its head. It cocked its head back
and cawed in a way that sounded too much like laughter.

"She's laughing," Ejii said with a chuckle. "She thinks you're
funny."

"I'll show her funny," I said, sticking my fingers in my
ringing ears.

Plantain was one of those birds who didn't like men or
boys. Maybe that was why it acted like such an ass to me.
"She'll never let you ride her," Ejii said.

I shrugged. "Kee would have her for dinner," I said.

Ejii only laughed. She was excited to meet Kee. And Kee
would probably love her as much as Plantain did. Animals
always tended to like shadow speakers. Some shadow speakers more than others, like Ejii's friend Sammy. She'd told me
he could speak with any animal. Ejii could only talk to cats
and certain rodents. But that was more than any non–shadow
speaker. And Plantain and Ejii seemed to communicate just
fine.

After my introduction to Plantain the mutatu, we'd sat
on the steps in front of her house for a whole hour looking
at the sky and saying nothing at all. I wanted to tell her about
Tumaki. I needed to. It felt like a lie sitting there, drinking in
her presence, and her not even knowing about Tumaki. But
she had her secrets, too. After a while, I just got up. I looked
at her. I was about to tell her. I just knew she could see it all
in my eyes, feel it all, the way she felt things without your
permission. I suddenly grew annoyed. She was always pry-
ing. "I've gotta go," I said, looking away.

She got up. "Okay."

I walked away. No goodbye. No hug. I would have loved to hug her.

======

I walked around brooding for about an hour. Kwàmfà at night was safe, even with its lack of night lighting. Anyone stupid enough to try anything on me would be sorry. I was in no mood to have my thoughts interrupted, either. There was a war going on in my mind, and heart, I guess.

I missed Tumaki. It had been a year but it felt more like weeks. I missed her books. I missed her touch. Her feel. She was lean and muscular like a deer. She had the most delicate hands. I missed our talks that would so often verge on becoming but never became arguments. She always had something to say and I always had to have the last word. I missed Tumaki.

But I was remembering Ejii. Remembering how she and I had so much in common. We had gone into other worlds together. I remembered how much I admired and was amazed by her. I had seen her die and return from the dead. I had seen her push her abilities until, literally, her eyes bled. I'd seen her grab the sharpest sword in worlds with her bare hands in order to save an utterly selfish, terrible man. And I remembered what I had felt for her before we left each other. I had been too young and stupid to admit it to myself back then.

My head was full by the time I arrived back at the Hall. I pushed the two double doors open. I didn't notice that the darkness was thick here. Or that the air was a little warmer.

Or that I wasn't alone. I didn't bother turning on the lights. I was going to the garden, where I planned to get a little sleep.

It was when I heard Kee's soft warning chirp. Only then did I freeze. I was halfway across the large room of the Hall. Standing amongst the leather chairs. All thoughts of Ejii and Tumaki fled my mind. The air was too warm. The darkness was too thick. *The dark beast from the fields!* I thought just before they attacked.

They pressed in on my throat, knocking me backward. Whispering a thousand obscenities in my ears. Throttling me. I saw only black. Then just like that, they pulled back and were gone. I lay on the floor gasping and rubbing at my throat. Outside you could hear thunder rumbling. I was so angry with myself. I'd been so shocked, I'd panicked so thoroughly, I'd forgotten to defend myself.

I sat up, wheezing. Angry as hell. Ready to kill something. My eyes fell on a man standing a few feet away. WHAM! I blasted him through the open back door. The lightning I created would keep the darkness from returning. I jumped up, still seeing stars, and ran toward the garden to finish him off. Whatever he was. Before I could get outside, the blackness surrounded me like wasps, slapping me onto my back. This time, I called lightning to the ground, but the darkness didn't scatter as it should have. I felt panic returning as the darkness pulled back a little.

"Enough," the man shouted. I couldn't see him. He was lucky. I was charged up and ready. The only reason I didn't let it loose was a thought of the Hall. I didn't want to set it on fire. But I would have had I thought the blackness would come at me again.

"I'm sorry," he said.

That got my attention. As my eyes adjusted and focused, I saw him on the other side of the garden. His caftan and pants were a little burned and his turban had been knocked off, but that was about it. He wasn't a man, per se. All right, he was about my age. I don't consider myself a man, but I'm not a boy either. Let's say, I'm a guy. Anyway, so was he. I was pretty tall for my age, but he was a bit taller than me. Not as muscular, though. Lean muscular. Still kind of strong, but I could break him if I had to.

He wore his hair in long braids with copper bands at the tips. Wodaabe. Even in the near dark of the room, I could see that he had eyes like Ejii's. He was a shadow speaker. Well, not completely like Ejii, though. Her shadow-speaker eyes were golden, like all other shadow speakers I'd seen. His were a really weird violet. *So those were his shadows, not the dark monster from the cocoa farms,* I thought. I frowned. His abilities had obviously evolved differently from Ejii's. Who the hell was this guy?

"I . . . there are times when they are out of control."

"You can say that again," I snapped, sitting up and rubbing my chest. "You pull something like that again and I will not hesitate to kill you."

"They'll kill you first," he said, walking in. He passed me and sat in one of the leather chairs, sighing.

"Don't underestimate the speed of lightning, wind, and electricity," I said.

He only sucked his teeth. He got up when he saw that I was going to go outside. "I don't like the indoors," I said over my shoulder. I figured if he was going to try to kill me, he would have already. Plus I'd hear him if he tried to come up behind me.

"You're Dikéogu, I assume," he said.

"Who are you?" I asked. Kee walked up to meet me. He eyed the guy behind me with such intensity that the guy stopped.

"My name is Arif," he said. "I'm a friend of Ejii's." I turned around and he laughed. "Your bird doesn't like me."

"Obviously for good reason."

"He is lucky I have control of my shadows at the moment." I sucked my teeth and sat on my mat.

"What do you want?"

He just stood there. I frowned deeply as I really looked at his face. Okay, so this was the type of guy women would fall alllll over. He had that kind of face. Flawless, strong cheek-bones, and then those eyes. This guy was Ejii's "friend"? I didn't like him.

A detail popped into my head. Ejii's earrings. The large silver hoops she'd worn during our journey. She told me a friend named Arif had given them to her. No, I didn't like him. That's an insignificant detail to remember, but you don't forget stuff like that when it involves a girl you like.

"Well, first, I wanted to meet you," he said.

"Nice to meet you," I snapped, rubbing my neck.

He pursed his lips and then sat down across from me, the coppered tips of his braids clicking. Actually, he clicked a lot. He wore leather pouches around his neck embroidered with copper rings and beads. These were traditional amulets of the Wodaabe. Several rings on his fingers. And thick silver earrings. We frowned at each other. I was nervous about looking into his eyes.

"You can't control them?"

He sighed and rubbed his face. "It's a long story."

I wanted to know his story. Despite not really liking him, I sensed his pain. He seemed older than he looked. He and I had a lot in common.

"Okay," I said.

"What's your story?"

"You're really a friend of Ejii's?" I asked.

He nodded. "Since Jaa took off Ejii's father's head and Ejii was free to hone her shadow-speaker skills."

Ejii's goddamn father and his archaic laws. I've never been one for the death penalty, believe it or not. But in his case, I make an exception. If Jaa hadn't returned to Kwàmfà and killed him, Ejii would have been married off at the age of ten to a cook's lazy son. She'd probably have ten kids by now and be sloppy and sad. And from what I know, shadow speakers go crazy if they don't travel. So maybe she'd be dead.

"If you are so close to her, can you tell me what's wrong with her?" I asked.

"Yeah," he said. "That's actually why I came."

"Oh, really?" I asked. He was lying. Or at least, he was only telling part of the truth. I'm not stupid. He'd come to check me out, too.

"Have you seen her?" he asked.

"First person I went to see," I said, chancing a glance into his eyes.

"She look okay to you?"

"Oh, she definitely *looked* okay. More than okay." I laughed to myself.

He frowned. I could see him swallowing his words. "Dikéogu, did she tell you?"

"I just got here," I said. "We haven't had much time to talk yet."

I didn't like the look on his face. Like he didn't want to be the bearer of bad news.

"What?" I asked. "What is it?" I waved a hand. "Forget it. I'll just wait until she tells me tomorrow or something."

"She won't tell you."

"She will," I insisted.

"She won't."

"It's been three years, but Ejii and I are still close."

He sucked his teeth with annoyance. "It's not about that. I'm not here to bicker with you."

"Then don't," I snapped.

"Look," he said, more calmly. "I'm just trying to help." He caught my eyes. I glimpsed a yellow clear sky. He put the image in my head. I understood. He was telling the truth.

"Okay," I said, looking at my hands. "If you know where she's been, then . . . show me." I hated the idea of this, but it was the best way. "Do what she does. Can you do that? Or are you just good for siccing your shadows on people?"

"Why are you such an asshole?"

"You really don't want to take our conversation in that direction," I said, letting a spark tumble down my nose. The air darkened and warmed, his doing. I didn't care. I was ready to fight this guy to the death.

He backed off first, pulling his shadows in. The air cooled.

Then he just started talking. "This is what she told me," he said. "Not in these exact words, but close enough. We shadow speakers can communicate in deep ways, especially when we are close friends."

I bristled. Honestly. Who was he to act like he knew so much about her? I knew Ejii when her abilities had just begun to manifest. She'd been with *me*. He needed to remember that. Anyway, I wanted to hear about Ejii, so I let him talk as opposed to slapping and electrocuting him. Okay, so Arif knew a lot about Ejii, and by the time he finished speaking, I was glad he'd come to see me. Ejii would have never told me all this. She was too proud and private. Here's her story in a nutshell:

Life settled for Ejii after she returned to Kwàmfà. But soon Ejii realized she was in pain. Great great pain. Dying wasn't something a person easily got over, obviously. Not even when the person was a shadow speaker. Remember, she died the moment we all entered Ginen. It's a risk every shadow speaker takes when traveling. The farther a shadow speaker travels, the greater the risk. So imagine the risk Ejii took when she traveled from one world to another. The more I think about it, the braver I understand she was.

Ejii described to Arif what it was like to join the vast greatness of Allah, the Whole. She had told me about this, too. She said she left her body, flew into the sky, shed all that made her Ejii. She went on and on about the song the Whole sang. How lovely and pure and eternal that song was. Arif said that that song never left her. Even when she returned to her body and her life and continued on to help save the worlds at the Golden Dawn Meeting.

After returning, when all was said and done, when her mother felt it was okay to leave Ejii at home alone, it descended on her. "She described it as an emptiness deeper than the universe," Arif told me. "And it was haunted by that lovely song."

"I died," Ejii whispered over and over. When her mother got home that day, Ejii pretended all was well.

Over the next several days, she'd look at her hands and then her reflection in the mirror. She would catch flies under cups, pick them up, and psychically fall into them. She could see how soon the flies would return to the Whole. Flies only lived a few days. She grew so obsessed with this that eventually she started catching all sorts of insects. Grasshoppers, ants, mosquitoes, gnats. She would fall into all of these and see their fast-approaching deaths. She'd catch a brief glimpse of the Whole at the end of the insect's life. It was this instant that she craved. It was like a sip of the perfect palm wine, a spoonful of the perfect spiced soup, a moment of ecstasy. Then it would be gone. She'd envy the insects so much that she'd crush them in her hand. Then she'd cry.

Then came the day she caught a multiplying scarab beetle. It was shiny black with a blue sheen when it reflected the sunlight. Its wings were indented with hundreds of tiny circles that made it look like a detailed black golf ball. I've seen this kind many times. She fell into this scarab. But instead of getting a taste of the Whole, she saw something else. Something that blew her mind so completely that hours later her mother found her curled up on the kitchen floor.

"Infinity," Ejii whispered to her mother. "They don't die. How can they not die? Why won't they die?"

Her mother had called Jaa, Arif, Sammy, and Arif's

teacher Mazi Godwin to come help snap her out of it. When nothing worked, it was decided that Jaa would take the emotionally crippled Ejii on a journey back to Ginen. It was the very mutatu Ejii now rode that had taken her safely far far north, into the Greeny Jungle, to the Old Woman on the "forest-covered mountain."

After Arif finished telling me all this, we both sat back, pensive.

"So the woman cured her?" I asked.

"I guess," Arif said. "Ejii won't talk about her much."

I shivered. Everyone had his or her limits. Ejii had gone mad when she reached her limits. I had, too. I looked at Arif, wondering if he'd ever reached his limits, and what happened when he did.

"Let me get the palm wine I brought," he said. "Then I'll tell you."

I frowned, indignant. "Don't do that!" I snapped. "See, this is why I don't like shadow speakers. You people can't help rummaging in other people's heads like it's your right. It's not your right. Do that again and—"

"And you'll what?" he called from the Hall's kitchen.

"Burn every single one of your damn braids," I mumbled to myself.

We finished the whole bottle. He was well mannered, I'll give him that. I know if the roles had been reversed, I'd have brought nothing but myself. We were quiet as we gulped down the wine. It was sweet, barely alcoholic. Thank goodness. I don't respond to alcohol too well. It tended to heat my temper.

A half-full glass of palm wine in hand, Arif leaned forward. "So you're coming from . . ."

"Nuh-uh," I said, laughing. "You first."

He leaned back on his elbows and looked at the sky. "That's your bird?"

I looked up through the skylight. There was Kee, soaring in large circles. I laughed. He and Arif had definitely gotten off on the wrong foot.

"Not *my* bird," I said. "He's doing me a favor."

Arif grunted. We sipped our palm wine.

"Did you leave Kwàmfà?" I finally asked.

He sighed. "Yes," he said. "Not long after Ejii left the second time."

"How far did you go? Did you die?"

He looked at me and again our eyes met. I didn't look away. He showed me . . . I saw him. He lay in a windy field of green grass. Beside him stood a camel. Above him flew three large birds. The sun was high, thin clouds rushing by. The sky wasn't blue. It was purple. Agonia. He'd been in Agonia.

"I must have crossed into that place," Arif whispered, pulling me back into myself. "Then something descended on me. Like a giant bird. It was beautiful. I was taken from my body . . . My eyes must have changed afterward . . . at some point," he said. "That was about a year ago."

"What can you do now?" I asked.

"I can understand the shadows," he said. His face went dark. He shook his head. "You've basically seen how I can get."

"Yeah," I said vaguely. What was he hiding? Whatever it was was big. Between Ejii and Arif, the half-truths and hidden shame certainly piled up fast.

"Anyway, I almost died out there in the first week," he

said. "But even death would have been better than staying home with the Drive pulling at my soul like that."

He went on to tell me he'd joined a group of Arab men traveling to what used to be Libya and was now a vast shallow ocean whose bottom was peopled with the sweetest-tasting fish and the most fragrant water plants. He told me about his year and half traveling on a strange flat ship, seeing water monsters and demons, a Changed girl and her brother who could swim like fish, then his weeks in Agonia. The look of pleasure on his face as he recounted his adventures made me kind of like him. I think a shadow speaker who has traveled is one of the happiest types of people in all the worlds.

———

He could have gone home, but he stayed. We'd been up all night talking. I'd told him most everything. About the cocoa farms, learning from and then leaving Gambo, Tumaki, the lost year. Maybe it was the palm wine, but I told him so much. More than I'd told anyone. The guy was a stranger yet I spilled my soul to him. Maybe it was his shadow-speaker eyes.

Regardless, he didn't say much. He didn't judge. I appreciated that. He slept in the Hall on one of the leather couches. I admit, I was kind of glad. Arif was okay. Sure, we'd tried to kill each other, but we quickly got over that. Maybe it's a Changed One thing. And maybe others needed to take a page out of our books.

I didn't sleep much. Too much to think about. Plus there

were these butterflies that came to the garden at night that made this weird ghostly sound. They irritated Kee, too. Every time one of the butterflies would start its wavering singing, Kee would grunt and stamp his feet, making the butterflies scatter. As daybreak approached, you could hear Kwàmfà gearing up. Actually, the noise started even before the sun rose. People were arriving in noisy camel caravans, on loud scooters, a few trucks.

I'd arrived in Kwàmfà at a very busy time. The Gerewol Festival, the great Wodaabe celebration of beauty and life, just happened to be a day away. Kwàmfà was about to get really packed, to my annoyance. So that was mostly the reason for all the activity. But it wasn't just that. People were pouring in for other reasons, too. The disintegrated pact. It seemed many were fleeing to Kwàmfà for answers, guidance, and hope. So where was Gambo? And Jaa? Buji? Arif didn't know either. No one in Kwàmfà did. Something was going on.

"Hello?" someone said.

I sat up from my mat. She knocked on the door again. Arif was already up. He made it to the door before me but not by much.

"Oh, Arif," Ejii said, surprised.

There was an awkward pause as her eyes went from him to me and back to him. Now she knew that I knew all she'd been through. She narrowed her eyes at Arif and stepped inside.

"Has Jaa come by here?" she asked. She waved a hand. "Forget it. We'd have all known if Jaa was in Kwàmfà. Arif, have you seen Sammy? I went to his home; it looked deserted."

"You didn't hear?" Arif asked.

"That's your other shadow-speaker friend, right?" I asked, trying to get her attention a bit.

She ignored me and looked at Arif, irritated. "Arif, I've only been here a few days. What have I had time to hear?"

"Oh," he said.

"So where is he?" she insisted. "He's left, hasn't he? The Drive, right? I assumed . . ."

Pause. I looked from Ejii to Arif and back to Ejii.

"Ejii, sit down," Arif said. He glanced at me.

Ejii refused to sit down. She'd told me much about Sammy. Arif, Sammy, and Ejii had been best friends. Sammy was the one who could communicate really well with animals. He was also a pretty big guy and used to protect Ejii from her idiot half-brother Fadio by threatening to beat the camelshit out of him.

"Have you at least heard from him?" Ejii insisted.

"Just sit down and I'll tell you."

There was music outside. A parade was walking through the streets. A band played loud screechy Arabic music, and through the open door I could see people gathering to watch some men cartwheeling and flip-flopping down the street.

"Arif," Ejii insisted, looking panicked. "Where is everyone?"

"I don't know where Jaa, Gambo, and Buji are."

She looked at me.

"I . . . I don't know either," I said, shrugging. "I left Gambo . . ." I shook my head. "It's a long story, but I haven't seen Gambo in . . . in a long time."

"Please, Ejii," Arif said, taking her hand. She snatched it away, a wild look in her eyes. She was trembling. Slowly, she sank to the arm of one of the leather chairs. Arif sat across from her. What the hell was he about to tell her? He looked at me. "Sammy was our best friend," he said.

"Was?" Ejii said quietly.

Arif was still looking at me. He turned to Ejii and took her hands. This time she let him.

"Sammy was killed about six months ago," Arif said.

Ejii whimpered and moaned, pressing her face into her knees.

"Did he ever leave?" she whispered. "To give in to the Drive?"

"Yes," Arif said. "About two weeks before me. He came back about eight months ago. Oh, you should have seen him. Any creatures that were around would treat him like their chief. Flies would clear dust from his path. Lizards would bring him sand pearls. All kinds of birds would watch over him. Butterflies would land in his hair and spread their wings. They wanted to be his shade and jewelry."

Ejii didn't move, still pressing her face to her knees.

"It was the cats and dogs who loved him most," Arif said. "Especially the cats. He told me about spending a lot of time with a tribe of sand cats just after leaving here. They knew you, and . . ."

Ejii quickly stood up, wiping her face with her hands. I noticed her face was dry.

"Did it happen here?" she asked, her voice hard like stone.

"Yes," Arif said.

"In Jaa's town? Kwàmfà? New Mecca? Who would kill a Changed One?"

New Mecca? I thought. *That's a new one.*

"There was a young woman. People knew her around here. They called her Lifestyle. She was one of the winged ones and she was also very beautiful. She was also very . . . fast. She liked attention, she liked men. And she did not want to marry, not even multiple husbands like Jaa."

"Marriage is not for everyone," Ejii mumbled.

"No, it's not," Arif agreed.

"Go on," Ejii said.

"They broke her wings," Arif said. "There was a boy who saw them do it. He ran away to get help. This must have been when Sammy came up the road. He was always patrolling the streets at night. Ever since the Day of Reckoning, when your father's wives and their people tried to take over Kwàmfà while you all were in Ginen, it was something that Sammy did. He saw some things during the Day of Reckoning that he swore he would never allow to happen again. When he returned from his travels, he continued doing it.

"He walked around with a group of cats and dogs as escorts. He could speak to them. When he saw Lifestyle dead on the ground and those men standing over her, he attacked. There were five men standing there over Lifestyle's body. All of them had knives and plenty more violence in them. Sammy attacked, blind with rage. There were too many of them. They killed Sammy . . ."

"Oh Allah," Ejii breathed, sitting back down.

Arif continued. "Then the dogs and cats killed the men. When it was all over, there were seven dead. There was an uproar. Some people wanted justice for Lifestyle's murder. But she was a Changed One and she was known for being promiscuous. So, many felt she got what she deserved. They wanted justice for the five men killed by Sammy and his mob of wild animals.

"This town's dark side came forward," Arif said. "Kwàmfà is a great place, but it is *not* perfect, and as it evolves, well, so does the disease it's had since its creation. The Changed and human live together here, but not in perfect harmony. There is love but there is hate, too."

I needed to get out of there. Goddamn it. I didn't care if it would piss off Ejii or Arif. Even back then I could feel it. Impending doom. Definite destruction. Imminent disaster. Let those two wallow in it for a while. I needed fresh air. I needed to clear my head.

I stalked down the street, pushing past the crowds. Ignoring the stupid parade. Gerewol. A beauty contest when tragedy was right around the corner. Stupid! The nsibidi pact for peace was gone. There would be war. But even before all that, a war was already going on. A quiet war of discrimination with genocidal highlights. Ugly, ugly. I wanted to kick all the revelers in the backside, slap all the laughing children.

There was a deep bass in my head. It went *DOOM! DOOM! DOOM! DOOM!* Like a senseless masquerade was fast approaching. A harbinger of my own negative destiny.

Ejii. Arif. Tumaki. Sammy. Me. And where the hell was Gambo? Where was this town's Red One Jaa? Where was her other husband, Buji? You could read it in the sky. This would come to no good end. I eventually returned to the Hall in the late evening. Ejii was gone. Arif was gone too. Ejii had left me a note. "I'll see you tomorrow. Don't desert me again."

CHAPTER 15

Gerewol

It was the weirdest spectacle I'd ever seen. And I'd seen a lot. It was so weird that it made total sense that this tradition known as the Gerewol was hundreds of years old. I was glad that I arrived late. This was *not* my kind of thing. The crowds. The music bands. Hausa men using their useless old guns to shoot blanks. Dancers. The noise of people talking, roaring Tuareg camels and braying donkeys, the grumbling of Wodaabe long-horned cattle. Too much body heat. A thousand types of perfume, incense, and scented oils. And then you had the contestants.

They lined up in the center of the square. They were all dressed up in long leather tunics embroidered with colorful thread, beads, and copper rings. They put on necklaces, leather amulet bags, and white wrappers. Their heads were wrapped in white and black turbans with long black feathers stuck in the middle.

They clicked and clacked with colorful beads, silver crosses of Agadez, zippers, talismans, and cowry shells. Some even had watchbands, old keys, empty printer cartridges, e-legba parts, and locks sewn into their clothes! It was wild. And trust me, my descriptions aren't doing it all any justice.

Everyone's outfit was personalized; there were a hundred variations.

Men carried spears and mirrors. They lightened their skin with yellow paint. They blackened their lips and the rims of their eyes with kohl to bring out the whites of their eyes and whiteness of their teeth. They shaved their hairlines to make their heads look longer. They drew black lines from their foreheads to their chins to show the symmetry of their faces and make their noses look lengthier. They decorated their cheeks with patterns of dots and circles and lines.

Then these overdressed guys jumped, made exaggerated faces, crossed and rolled their eyes, bared their white teeth, and danced. I said I'd be honest, so I will say this: Yes, they were attractive. Minus all the makeup, they were tall and that slim kind of muscular that women like. Perfect faces and whatnot. But goddamn, what was with all the makeup and vanity?

There were a few Changed Ones competing. One was a winged man. No doubt, the guy stood out. He'd adorned his enormous white-feathered wings with cowry shells and tiny bells. He probably wouldn't be able to fly until after the contest. There was also a windseeker who had the nerve to levitate as he danced. These were the Changed Ones whose physical attributes were associated with beauty. Let a plant-worker, who is typically very short, try to compete. The judges probably wouldn't even let him near the line of competitors.

The Wodaabe people traditionally *despise* "ugly" people. To them, if you have any kind of deformity, like an asymmetric face, bad teeth, beady eyes, a round head, or a scar, you'd better invest in some magical objects to offset your hideousness. I think, for them, Changed Ones fell on both sides of attractiveness. Shadow speakers apparently were glorious to them. Obviously, it was the eyes.

A group of three young women slowly made their way up the line. Ejii said they were supposed to be the most beautiful women of the guest groups. I don't know about the most beautiful, but they were certainly pleasing to the eye. Especially the tall one.

They wore huge, clunky brass anklets that reached their knees, many gold-hooped earrings in each ear, and wide black veils. And they wore bead bracelets and these huge clicking necklaces made of cowry shells. They also had similar indigo facial designs. Two of them held a red umbrella over an ancient-looking woman carrying a bunch of decorative white horsetails. According to Ejii, the girls were the judges and the old woman was the head judge.

"You okay?" Ejii asked me. She was obviously enjoying my discomfort with the whole thing.

"This is some weird camelshit," I said.

She smiled. "It takes some getting used to, sure."

"I don't think I'll ever get used to this."

"Oh, relax," she said.

We were sitting under a special tent with the Kwàmfà council: Ejii's mother, the muscular old shadow speaker named Mazi Godwin, and a windseeker named Boniface. I sat in Gambo's chair and Ejii sat in Jaa's red chair. It just worked out this way. With all three of them still missing, Ejii's mother thought it best that we occupy at least two of the seats.

"How much longer is this going to go on?" I asked.

"Wait for the head judge to give the finalists each a white horsetail," Ejii said, grinning excitedly. The judge pointed at the first finalist, a tall slender man, and the crowd went wild.

"Yes!" Ejii said, standing up and clapping. I frowned. Ejii obviously favored this guy. Two of the women advanced toward the man, demurely laughing and smiling. Ejii sat down, now looking annoyed. I smiled. It was custom for the winner to have a gleeful night with one or more of the chosen girls. I guess Ejii just remembered this.

"Arif *naawdo!*" one of the girls suddenly shouted.

"Purple eyes! Purple eyes!" the crowd chanted, laughing and pointing.

I blinked, noticing his eyes. *No, it can't be*, I thought. It was. Arif. I hadn't recognized him, he was so made up.

"Just perfect," I grumbled.

Then I noticed something . . . He'd painted a red line from the middle of his forehead to the tip of his nose and another line across his forehead. He'd put white dots on each side of the red line. He'd imitated my tattoos! He glanced our way and winked at me. I had to grin. I got up and clapped. In that moment, I knew I could trust Arif with anything.

The crowd went wilder when Arif broke into what I can only describe as a happy dance. I think Arif had just been told that he looked good enough to eat. He flashed and rolled his strange violet shadow-speaker eyes. Even from where I was, I could glimpse the power in his weird eyes. Anyone who loved him would be crazy to look into them. I wondered what Ejii saw when she looked in them.

I looked at Ejii and saw that she now looked thoroughly pissed. She mumbled something, but I couldn't hear her.

The chanting swelled and all the contestants began to dance more vigorously. Two more finalists were chosen. Both were attractive, tall, and crazy looking, but neither was Changed. The three finalists stood in front of the judges, waving their horsetails as they moved. People in the crowd pointed and shouted, jeered, gestured. If people hadn't been smiling and laughing, too, I'd have been sure they were about to start rioting. It had been a while since I'd been in the midst of unleashed joy.

Even with their leaders missing, the whispers of genocide of the very people Kwàmfà folk made room for, the pact gone and war just over the horizon, the Chief of Ooni looming, these people could generate such happiness. Of course, I didn't really feel a part of it. I was too heavy with other things, I guess. Maybe that was why I noticed the very tall, dark-skinned man in the white kaftan and pants. Maybe that's why Ejii did, too.

He seemed to appear out of nowhere, standing right behind one of the contestants on the far end of the line. He walked slowly toward the center, slipped to the front, and stood behind the finalist who was probably Arif's strongest competition. Still no one seemed to notice. Except Arif. He'd stopped dancing and was staring at the man.

He looked at Ejii and me. I couldn't hear him over all the singing and laughing, but I understood his lips. "Who is . . . ?"

Ejii and I got to our feet.

"No idea!" I said.

It happened fast. The tall man in white opened his mouth to the sky. His fangs were sharp, white, wet. His eyes were wide. His long-fingered hands like claws clamped on the young man's neck and shoulder. I gasped. All of this happened in broad daylight, before hundreds of smiling joyous people.

Gerewol was an ancient tradition. It celebrated the shallow, fleeting thing called beauty. Ejii started running forward. I followed. Too many people. The man with no eyebrows bit the young man's neck. There was a splash of blood. People started screaming, running.

"Oh Allah!" Ejii gasped, as she tried to move forward. "What kind of camelshitting . . ."

"Ejii, get back!" I barely shouted.

There were fireflies appearing from both sides of the contestant line now. Even in the sunshine they glowed, orange like small suns. Then in the crowd, more figures wearing white, grabbing and biting.

I stopped. There were too many innocent people running around. No way I could use a blast of lightning. I'd have killed everyone around me. I briefly wondered if I'd killed Tumaki when I blasted lightning in her library. *No,* I knew. *She was already dead. Then they took her.* I shook my head. I had to concentrate. *A lightning storm,* I thought. I'd have to take the chance. I looked around. Already several contestants lay shriveled and dead.

Adze were attacking the most beautiful Gerewol contestants. Locking their fangs on necks and sucking them dry. A few started on audience members. A woman kicked at a female Adze, but her kicks didn't seem to elicit even the slightest pain, and the Adze just kept sucking. A man was trying to smash the head of another. Another man drove a dagger into an Adze's sides. No success. When they were feeding, they could not be moved.

But when they were done and had thrown the husk of the contestant aside, that was when they became violent. I saw a man slapped in the face by a freshly fed Adze. The force of the slap sent the man flying. A woman was crushed to the ground under an Adze's foot.

I wanted to just stand there screaming. I wanted to vomit. I wanted to curl up and die. Give up. Wait for an Adze to come at me. I didn't want to bother fighting back. I was so tired. Nothing could stop all this. Nothing could stop the chief from having Kwàmfà destroyed by these creatures. Destroying all Changed Ones. Enslaving Earth.

There wasn't a cloud in the sky.

"Nothing but darkness," I said aloud. I saw it. A darkness in the daylight sky. It loomed and rolled just above me. Threatening to swallow us all. A terror like you would never know fell on me and I nearly dropped to my knees. This was the end of the world that was supposed to happen during the Great Change. This was it.

Then I heard clicking and clacking. Not from far away. Just above my head. When I opened my eyes, I was staring into the face of the giant fish woman. The creature I'd seen in the Aïr Mountains during my teachings. The goddess. She was all bone and sinew. She was silver scales and brown skin. Black eyes and fins. Her every movement sent a painful popping crack through my brain. Like knuckles cracking, painful yet sweet. She spoke to me in Igbo. It had been a while since I'd spoken my first language. It instantly calmed me.

Her voice was wet and guttural. "If you do not remember

where the rain started to beat you, you will not remember who gave you the towel with which to dry your body." *What the hell does that mean?* I thought, confused. Not the best time for confusing godly proverbs.

Then a strength was flowing through my body that nearly lifted me off the ground. I blinked and she was gone. "Okay," I whispered, the image of her still strong in my mind. The smell of the ocean, the lake, the spontaneous pond, the rain in my nostrils. My clothes were soaking wet. I had to pull in the moisture from far away. As I did this, I saw Ejii. Still running toward the tall man in white, the one who'd started it all. He stood in the middle of the chaos.

She snatched something from under her shirt. A seed shooter! She was shoving people out of her way. Trying to get a clear shot. He stood where he was with the contest finalist still in his arms, his mouth clamped to the young man's neck. People ran away from and around him, like he existed in a different space and time. No one touched him. No one tried to stop him.

Ejii aimed. Moved closer. Someone roughly grabbed her arm. Ejii stared at her.

I located the moisture I needed and my mind clouded. I imagine that my eyes became the color of mud, but how can I know this? As I faded, I let my eyes focus on the woman holding Ejii's arm.

She wore a purple dress. Not a wrapper and top. A full dress, made of thick material, but it did not fall heavily. It moved with the woman's body. A strange cloth. But it was not clean. The dirt looked like dust, from traveling. Far and long.

Rain, come, I said. Everything went fuzzy. Silent. Then screaming and chaos around me blasted back in, loud, clear. My eyes refocused. The woman was still grasping Ejii's arm. Her nostrils flared, a sheen of sweat glistening on her dark skin. Purple eyeshadow.

"You won't kill him that way!" the woman shouted. "You cannot kill him! Not any of them!"

Ejii shook her off. The young man was dead and limp in the hairless man's arms. Ejii fired at the hairless man. Her aim was perfect. The eyes of a shadow speaker can see for miles. A seed shooter's aim is most accurate in the hand of a woman. A seed shooter in the hands of a female shadow speaker is the recipe of death.

The seed embedded itself in his cheek, blowing out the flesh there. Flaps of skin hung. No blood. And the man didn't seem to feel a thing. He threw down the dead finalist like a sack of millet. Then I was pulling and pulling and drawing. My clothes grew wet with sweat and moisture. My skin was cool. The sky began to darken. A rumble of thunder from nearby. Then the storm was upon us. *Crash!* The lightning was huge and robust. It struck a building nearby, setting it on fire. The Adze screeched in the light. Many fled. Thank God.

I looked for Ejii. Same place she was before. She shot at the head Adze again, gnashing her teeth with rage. She ran at him, letting more shots fly. She hit his arms, belly, chest. Holes appeared in his clothes. Still no blood. And he did not fall. Finally, right before her, his eyes boring into hers, he disappeared. She found him easily and shot at the tiny firefly he'd become. The seed knocked him sideways, but he soon caught himself and zipped away.

"Fucker!" she snarled, looking around for the first time. She met my eyes. I focused on her nose.

"Well done," I said with a quick nod.

"Your storm is working," she said.

"Not completely," I said.

Several weren't so afraid of lightning.

"Don't follow me, Ejii!" I said as I ran into the crowd. Forget the danger. I could hear the static popping off my hair, my clothes, the sand around me. I charged up. I was breathing heavily. If I was to control the electricity I was producing, I *had* to control my breathing. I was dizzy as I struggled with my lungs and diaphragm, which only wanted to take more oxygen to my brain. I aimed for the first one I saw. She'd just grabbed a little boy of about thirteen. She shook him about like a rag doll, laughing madly. She held him to her, grabbed his head and shoulders, and bared her teeth.

I let loose a wave of electricity and both of them went flying. The Adze woman caught herself in midair. She disappeared. I ran to the boy. He looked up at me, stunned but unharmed except for the cuffs of his pants, which were smoldering. I patted out the small flames with my tough feet.

It started to rain, lightning crashing every two seconds. I'd brought the storm right above us. The screams of people mixed with screeches of fleeing Adze. I looked ahead and my eyes grew wide. Arif—and there were about five Adze on him. *How is that possible?* I wondered. I could just barely see him as he grappled with the Adze. The air around him was heavy with smoke. But smoke didn't hover in the same place. Smoke didn't become sharp edges and pierce the undead like hundreds of daggers. Smoke wasn't alive.

"Shadows," I whispered. But not like the darkness that I had seen in the field. This darkness was full. This was the darkness that made things grow. This was darkness that defended life with unmatched violence. This was the bad thing I sensed Arif was hiding. I understood why he'd hide it. Who would go near him if they knew he was capable of this?

Right before my eyes, I saw what I had yet to see Adze do. As they tried to flee, blood oozed from where the shadows touched them, bright red and glowing a hot orange. As they struggled, they became wet with it, spattering it and flinging it everywhere. They grew wetter and wetter, but they did not die. Vile.

Arif crouched there, an angry look on his face. A look I knew, too. He was torturing these terrible creatures as I had tortured Big Blokkus. But Arif didn't have time for this; he was needed elsewhere. Most of the Adze had fled, but a few people were still under attack.

"Arif," I shouted.

His blank eyes shot toward me and I stepped back from their intensity. Not far from him, an Adze took down a young woman.

"Let them flee!" I said. I pointed at the young woman under attack. "Look!"

Slowly, too slowly, he turned his head and saw the screaming woman moments away from being bitten.

I ran around him and let loose a blast of lightning. Both the Adze and the woman went flying. Then the Adze changed into a firefly and zipped away. The woman got up on shaky legs and then fell back down, sobbing. All the hair on her head was gone. At least she was alive.

I turned to Arif. The Adze he'd been torturing were gone, leaving pools of blood in the sand. Arif straightened up. He was covered in Adze blood and glowing bright orange. His embroidered tunic shined with it, his amulets and necklaces and cowry shells dripped with it. The feather in his turban drooped with it. He looked like a demon or a god. Unworldly. And unhinged.

"Don't come near me!" Arif bellowed. His voice was not his own. His violet eyes glowed.

A deep voice spoke from behind me in a language I didn't understand. I whirled around. The tall Adze who'd started the attack smiled, his face and body unscathed. He turned and spoke to the few Adze left. Ejii came running, her seed shooter up. He changed into a firefly as she shot. The seed just barely missed him. All the others changed and flew off with him.

As quickly as it had begun, it was over. The Adze flew into the air, a small galaxy of orange stars ascending into the dark rainy sky. They zoomed off as a bolt of lightning crashed above.

Arif stood there, his shoulders curled in, his hands clenched in fists as if trying to hold something in. I asked the rain to stop. It did. Ejii stowed her seed shooter back under her garments. We were damaged people, us "advanced Changed Ones." That's what I call those of us who took our powers to that next level, regardless of the consequences. Ejii with her seed shooter. Arif with his murderous shadows. Me with my storms. *It's not hard to understand why the chief believes we are a disease*, I thought. People lay all over the place, in the wet sand. Some moved, too many did not. Somehow I'd found myself in yet another war zone.

All the Gerewol contestants lay dead, except Arif. The contestant with the white wings lay nearby, dried up, his face frozen in a pained death mask. I guess he hadn't been able to take off with all those cowry shells and tiny bells hanging on his wings. His wings were each broken in three places. As the wind blew, more of his feathers sloughed off with it. The skin underneath was that dry, even after the rain.

Ejii and I slowly walked to Arif.

"Don't touch me," Arif hissed, turning away. He knelt down.

"Arif," Ejii whispered.

"Were those . . . those were what you spoke of?" he asked. His voice shook as he spoke.

"Yes," I said.

"You could *smell* their age," Arif said. "Thousands and thousands of years." He shuddered and spat to the side. He still glowed the strange orange color.

"You've seen those before?" Ejii asked.

I nodded. "They're called Adze," I said, looking around. I noticed someone's veil lying on the ground. I picked it up and brought it to Arif. When he made no move to take it from me, I knelt beside him and on instinct began to wipe his face. It was a weird thing to do but I did it. He didn't stop me. "They were sent by Chief Ette," I said.

Both of them flashed a look at me. Trust me, it isn't pleasant to be under the gaze of two advanced shadow speakers. I swore I was about to turn to stone or melt or burst into flames or something.

"Maybe," Arif grumbled, frowning.

"Definitely," I said.

Ejii cursed as she looked around. But no tears. That was so strange. The Ejii I knew would have shed tears as she tried to make things better. None of us cried, but how angry we must have looked. I wiped Arif's forehead, cheeks, and then neck.

"Thank you," he said, not looking at me.

I grunted, wringing out the veil. A mix of Adze blood and rainwater.

"Arif," Ejii said quietly. "What was all that?"

"It's what I can do," he said. "My shadows are . . . more lethal than most. I'm not a man of peace anymore." He looked at me. "Can you bring more rain? This blood stings."

CHAPTER 16

Stormbringer

It took hours for Kwàmfà to regain any semblance of order. Ejii's mother, Mazi Godwin, and two other elders helped round people up. So many bodies, so many suffering from shock, no one knew what to do, no one knew what to say. This year's Gerewol was supposed to settle people's minds so that they could properly prepare for war. Now what? And what of the absence of Jaa, Gambo, and Buji?

Men, women, and children walked around sobbing, weeping, wailing. A lot of men and women went to the mosque to pray for hours instead of helping to clean up. Some wandered about stunned. Hands shook. Tempers flared. I saw a bunch of men refuse to help with the cleanup, choosing to sit in circles guzzling palm wine and talking about the end of days. Those of us who cleaned up had glazed or wet eyes. We would never forget the sight of the shriveled bodies of one hundred and one Gerewol contestants.

Most people avoided Ejii, Arif, and me. Our confrontation with the Adze hadn't gone unnoticed. Me? I just wanted to laugh at it all. Like in that classic novel, *Things Fall Apart*, everything was falling apart: the world, Kwàmfà, my life. Everywhere I went, there was terrible trouble. Or maybe I brought it wherever I went, like my storms. As I helped move bodies, a memory from my lost year bubbled to the surface. Some woman who had given me a dried fish when I was homeless had called me "Stormbringer."

"People like you are followed by dark clouds, Storm-bringer. You stay in one place long enough and you will bring a storm. May Allah help you find dry land." I tried to remember why she'd say this to me, but I couldn't remember anything else about her. Was I cursed? Rainmakers were supposed to bring good fortune. At least I was alive. But I liked the name Stormbringer. Yes. I liked it a lot. It suited me well.

———

When I next saw Ejii she was like stone.

Arif and I walked back to the Hall for a little sleep, where we found her waiting for us. Arif didn't want to return home. Rumors were already flying about him being the only contestant to survive. Being a Changed One, even in Kwàmfà, lent him to only negative suspicions. He feared most for his family's safety. "Best to stay away," he said.

I was kind of glad for the extra company. Kee tended to hunt at night, and needless to say, the day's events had spooked me to the bone. How did we even know the Adze weren't still lurking about?

Ejii met us at the door. She grabbed my hand and then Arif's. "We need to talk," she said in a tight voice. She squeezed my hand.

"What . . ."

"Inside," she said. Her hand was shaking. Her face was

strained from the stress of holding in whatever she needed to
say. She shut the doors behind Arif and me. Then she sank to
the floor and went silent as a desert cat. Neither Arif nor I
knew what the hell to do. At first I thought she'd fainted, but
her eyes were wide open. Her face was full of pain.

"What now?" I moaned.

Arif knelt down and I knelt beside him.

"I just spoke with Mazi Godwin," she whispered. "She's
dead. He's dead." She glanced at me and quickly looked away.
I frowned deeply and cocked my head, straining with everything that I had to understand what the hell she was talking
about. I didn't want to ask her. I just wanted to know. She
wouldn't meet my eyes.

"Who?" Arif asked.

"Jaa, Buji," she said. "Mazi Godwin just told me. He heard
from some sand-dune cats who'd witnessed it."

"They don't lie," both Arif and Ejii said together.

Ejii whimpered. "I needed her. That's why I came back."

I was listening and processing, but it was like my mouth
was glued shut. It was like my blood had become glue. Like
my skin had become glass.

"What happened?" Arif asked.

"They were on their way here," she said.

"Right," Arif urged. "Coming from a meeting in Agadez."

Ejii nodded. "That's what Mazi Godwin said. Somewhere
in the desert between, they were attacked by over a hundred
Adze. The sand-dune cats say they took Buji first. Then, in a
rage, Jaa took down many of them with her great sword.
Gambo with his wind and lightning. But they eventually got

her, too. They got Jaa the Red One of the New Sahara. The
cats described a tall male Adze as the one who grabbed her
when her back was turned."

"No bodies left?" Arif asked.

"No . . . but the cats saw . . . Buji and Jaa are dead."

Silence. No tears.

"And Gambo?" I finally asked, forcing my petrified throat
into use.

Ejii opened her mouth but then closed it. Arif was grasping his head like there was too much noise in the room. The
air grew darker. None of us cared. *Let his shadows end us,* I
thought. *I can't take any more loss.* It started raining outside.
Fine, it was me. Ejii grabbed my arm. I yelped, then I saw *blue
sky, blotted out by the brown sand heavy winds of a great storm.
The winds did not roar, they sounded like a thousand women
screaming. Shrieking. Destroying. Consuming. Hot with rage. Full
of terrible darkness.*

I managed to yank my arm from Ejii. I jumped up. If I
didn't move away from her, I'd slap her. I'd have slapped anyone too close to me. Anyone close to me. I was about to bolt.
That was my first reaction. That's always my first reaction.
Run. Kee was outside. I could jump on him and we could be
away from this place.

But Arif grabbed my arm. And though I was stronger
than he was, much stronger, though he risked me socking
him in the face or electrocuting him, he managed to keep me
there. No, not him. His shadows. They crowded me like pillars. I let out some painful currents. His shadows didn't react
to my electricity. I was trapped.

I sat down beside Ejii. I held my head in my hands. I let

what Ejii had shown me sink in, as opposed to fleeing from it. Every bone in my body ached. All my still-tender wounds, physical and mental, throbbed. Now this. My mentor, my teacher, the man who was like a father to me, the man who was so much like who I thought I'd be, had become an Aejej. A living storm whose only purpose was to rain terror on people. When Ejii showed me what he'd become, I saw deep into Gambo's heart. It had been infected by the dark beast from the cocoa farms. What had that thing been? I knew now. It had been Gambo's and my destiny. Our fate.

There is nothing worse than realizing that the path you've been set on ends with something so terrible. I was indeed cursed. How could I explain this to Ejii and Arif? They would have understood, but what good would that have done? As I settled and came to terms with things, I understood one other thing: I'd stop the chief before it happened.

Minutes passed. "Are you all right?" Ejii asked, speaking into my ear. I shivered, feeling the brush of her lips. Yeah, I was okay. As much as I could be.

Arif made tea. He made it Tuareg style. The ceremony of it was soothing. Twice, Ejii had had to go outside to be alone. Arif and I watched her go. We were worried about her, but we didn't say anything. Sometimes you have to just let things happen the way they will and hope that the worst doesn't happen. Sometimes. Thankfully, Ejii returned to us a few minutes later. She didn't shoot herself in the head with her seed shooter or hang herself with a piece of rope.

As we drank the last cups of the tea, Ejii told us what else she'd learned. Ejii's mother had alerted her that at the crack of dawn, elders and councilmembers from all over the Sahara would arrive at the Hall for an emergency meeting. This meeting had originally been planned to happen in two days.

"My mother is councilwoman, but people will expect me to act in Jaa's place as leader," Ejii said. "I want both of you there with me."

"I'll be there," I said. Anything involving putting an end to the chief, I wanted to be part of.

"You sure you want *me* there?" Arif asked.

"Very," she said.

The room was naturally cool. We each lay back in the leather couches, rested our heads back, and sighed. Not thirty seconds passed before we heard the large doors open. A girl of about twenty, wearing a heavy purple dress, stood in the doorway. Her dress was filthy with mud, as if she'd been helping to bury the dead. I recognized her from earlier.

"Where is Ejii, successor to Jaa the Red One?" she asked like she herself was a queen.

I bristled with irritation, thinking, *What now?*

"I am Ejii," she said, standing up. "How do you know about—"

"I've come a long way to speak with you," the woman said, still not coming in.

Ejii looked at the woman for a moment and then gasped. She turned to Arif and me and whispered, "I know her!"

"Me too," I said. "She tried to stop you from shooting that Adze."

"No," she said. "I've seen her even before that."

"Where?" Arif asked. "Is she dangerous?"

We looked at the woman. She seemed content to wait for us to finish talking.

"I don't think so," Ejii said. "Dikéogu, remember when we were in Ginen, just before the Golden Dawn Meeting? Before everything started happening?"

I nodded.

"I remember gazing at the Ooni Palace and seeing a woman looking out one of the windows, crying. I later saw that woman in the palace. She was one of the chief's wives." She nodded toward the woman. "That's her!"

"Oh," I said.

"Ask her in, then," Arif said.

I wasn't so sure. Anyone who was married to the chief had to have something wrong with her.

"Please come in," Ejii said. She turned to Arif and me. "Come on, you guys," she said, looking us both in the eye, her hand on her hip, close to her seed shooter. She didn't trust this woman either. "Greet her with me."

The first thing I noticed upon a closer inspection was that the woman's long dress was tight fitting. And she wore vine bracelets similar to the ones Buji wore. And she had the saddest face I'd ever seen. All I could wonder was what she had suffered. But everyone in that room had suffered, so that didn't make her special, and that didn't make me automatically trust her either.

"Have you come with Adze, too?" Ejii asked the woman.

"No," the woman said.

Ejii gave her an intense look. The woman didn't flinch, though she looked afraid. "Take my arm, Dikéogu, Arif," Ejii said.

"Oh, not again," I groaned.

We each took hold of an arm. Ejii then took the woman's hands.

I felt Ejii grab me. I grunted. I heard Arif grunt, too. We all fell in. It doesn't get better the more you do it. Even when you know it's about to happen. This time, it was like swimming in her mind, her memories, and her being at the same time. As a man, it was utterly jarring. As a human being, a non-shadow speaker, it was awe inspiring.

Perfumed, purple silk and cloth. She hated them all. They'd sold her out. They'd sold her away. Because she was trouble. Because she was abnormal.

. . . She let her hair grow and grow and she twisted it into spirals, helixes, and trained knots. Like the clumpy locks of African windseekers. She used palm oil, kaolin, the juice from an indigo flower on her skin. She painted beautiful things. People thought she was a witch because her art was bewitching. People would come and look at it for hours.

. . . She preferred the beads of the southeasterners to the mirrors of the northerners. Though she was a northerner—the most traditional, strict, and narcissistic of the Ooni people.

. . . Scented oils, breasts, lips, softness, she liked women. The chief had heard of her. He had his soldiers come to collect her. She was only sixteen years old then. Her family was glad to be rid of her. Shame to honor in a matter of seconds. She was added to his collection of wives. She was dragged from the home she shared with the woman named Shola, the most special woman in the world.

Months later, while she was in her chambers, the chief sent her a box. In it were Shola's nose, two fingers, and left breast.

She grew plants in her chambers and drew murderous paintings of the chief.

. . . He would demand her presence in his purple rooms. Once every three months. He covered his heaving body with scented oil . . .

By this time I was fighting it. I saw where it was going. I'd already seen too much. Was this what Ejii saw when she fell into people? The nakedness of what was revealed! It was beyond embarrassing. I glanced at Arif. He gave me an appalled look. "I know," I mouthed to him. I could still feel the woman's pain. She would never ever have to explain to me why she ran away from the chief.

Ejii and the woman were looking at each other. Ejii's face was wet with perspiration. "J . . . Jollof," Ejii whispered. "That's your name."

"Like the rice?" I asked. I laughed nervously, a bitter taste in my mouth. I still couldn't look at her. She might as well have been standing there naked.

She nodded, but she didn't laugh. The hard look on her face said that she wanted the chief dead just as much as I did. I knew for a fact that she did. Ejii walked up to her and gave the woman a tight hug. Jollof sobbed into her shoulder. "Come," Ejii said softly after several moments. "Sit down." Ejii coughed and cleared her throat. "Dikéogu, can you please get her some tea."

"Do you want sugar in it?" I asked Jollof. I don't know. What else was I supposed to ask?

———

I took my time. I needed to get out of there. At least until what Ejii had shown us wore off. So I prepared a full meal. We all needed it. The last time I had eaten was early in the morning, hours before Gerewol started. Arif seemed to feel the same way, for he came in a minute later.

He opened his mouth, about to make some half-assed excuse. I held up a hand. "No need to explain."

He laughed and sat on one of the stools, running his hand over his short hair. I put some water to boil and found some food in the fridge. Maybe Ejii had put it in there—some leftover roasted chicken and . . . jollof rice. Arif and I looked at the large pot of rice and burst out laughing. We laughed and laughed. It was desperate, hysterical laughter. It was the laugh of shock from seeing the death of beauty, the death of a town, evil within ourselves, and ill omens all in one day. I wondered if it was the last time I'd ever laugh again. This made me laugh harder, which made Arif laugh harder.

I squatted on the floor, trying to calm the cramps in my belly. Arif started laughing again. The room flickered to a darker shade. Arif's shadows. I laughed harder at this, imagining an evil, ridiculous mix of rain, thunder, wind, wild evil shadows, roasted chicken and spicy jollof rice, all here in the kitchen. A micro universe of chaos in the kitchen. We were freaks.

"I . . . I mean, what kind of woman likes women?!" Arif managed to ask.

That sent us off again.

"Imagine having to lie under . . . under that goddamn chief," I wheezed. "She's lucky to be alive!"

I had to lie on the floor. Arif was on his knees, snickering and wiping his face. I felt like crying. But all that came were more laughs.

Eventually, we calmed down. We got up and prepared the food in silence. One look at the jollof rice and we were laughing again.

By the time we came back out with the food, I felt better

than I'd felt in a long time. Ejii looked at the rice, then at the smile on my face, and then smiled and rolled her eyes. Arif handed Jollof a cup of the sweet milky tea he'd prepared. He handed another cup to Ejii. I looked at him and then decided to be obnoxious, spooning the rice carefully into Jollof and then Ejii's plates. Arif took my cue and extremely carefully placed pieces of chicken on their plates. Like slaves.

"What is wrong with your husbands?" Jollof asked. "Is this how men are here?"

Husbands?! All hints of laughter flew from me like a flock of startled birds.

"Oh, they're not my husbands," Ejii quickly said. She glanced at me and then Arif and then looked away. I wasn't about to look at Arif, either. *Ah ah,* can you imagine?

Jollof looked at the three of us, then laughed to herself, picking up her teacup. "Okay. If you say so."

"None of us is married," Arif said.

"Okay," Jollof said.

"And I don't want a husband," I added. How stupid did that sound?

Jollof laughed. "Okay," she said again. She didn't sound convinced at all.

Thoughts tried to creep into my head about Ejii, me, and Arif and Jaa, Gambo, and Buji. I pushed them away. I had enough on my plate to think and go crazy about.

"So how did you get away?" I asked.

"The Ogoni ants who guard the plant palace and the white owls who live at the top, they are my friends," she said. "The owls took me away and the ants made it so that no one could follow me."

"I didn't know those ants cared about anything but that plant palace," I said.

"Once one becomes an Ooni wife, she becomes part of the palace," she said.

"Jesus," I grumbled. Women had it rough everywhere. Even in the most technologically advanced human civilization anywhere. What camelshit. *"Part of the palace" indeed,* I thought. But then again, they *had* helped her get away. So she wasn't exactly prisoner to the ants.

"I came in with a caravan of people with faint skin and black hair like mutatu feathers," she said.

"Arabs," Ejii said, smiling.

"Yes, Arabs. Very kind people," she said.

Ejii cocked her head. "You stretch the truth."

Jollof looked hard at Ejii, then looked away and quietly said, "I don't speak of that."

I frowned, knowing I'd probably missed something in the vision Ejii had shared with Arif and me. Really, I didn't want to know what it was that I'd missed. Judging by the look Ejii and Jollof had just exchanged, it was something pretty bad. I wondered if Arif had picked up on whatever it was. He was too busy not looking at me for me to tell.

"I respect that," Ejii said. "But please, no lies. We all know that it's not easy out there. The land is wild and people can be harsh."

"But mostly people are kind," Jollof insisted.

"Maybe if you are not a Changed One," I grumbled.

"Granted," Jollof said with a nod. She sighed. "I left Ginen with some travelers, and all along the way I met kind people everywhere. People are exploring, discovering each other. Yet all the chief wants is to destroy that with war."

"Not if we can help it," Ejii said.

"That's why I came to you," she said. She cocked her head and said, "Let's say the three of you did marry."

I opened my mouth to speak, but she held up a hand. I don't know why I shut up. But I did.

"The chief would see your union as an abomination, as he sees the fact that I prefer to bed women as an abomination," Jollof said. "To me, I see the three of you and it is natural. But he believes only a man can marry many women. Even worse, he would see a marriage of Changed Ones as blasphemous. Your very existence is an affront to nature because you were created by the crimes of your people. The very crimes that caused all the five worlds to become one."

She paused. I waited. What I had to say was no longer so important.

"He has to be stopped," Jollof said.

Ejii looked at Jollof. Jollof gazed back at her. "Dikéogu, Arif, take my arms again," she said. We both did. "You might want to brace yourself," Ejii said.

"What do you . . ."

We fell over the edge again . . .

Jollof stood behind the door, peeking into a large room. The chief lay on a massive bed in the middle of the conference room. Behind him was an enormous window that opened on the great city of Ile-Ife. On the wall was an elgort trunk, the black thick wrinkly skin shriveled with age. The chief had not been the one to kill it during the hunt. The man was so large that he could barely walk.

His eighteen-year-old son had killed the beast. And that very son was currently tied to another smaller bed beside the chief. Three old women and two old men stood around them.

. . . The room smelled of frying palm oil and strong curry. They took off the chief's clothes and slathered him with palm oil.

. . . His son begged and pleaded. "Let me go! Papa, I don't want to do this! I've changed my mind." He thrashed against his restraints. The vines on his arms and legs tightened. He stopped thrashing.

. . . They brought out a small pestle and ground up a live scarab beetle. As it died, it multiplied into two living beetles. These ones were ground up too. They multiplied again. The same was done. Over and over, and each time, they were ground up. Finally they let the remaining scarabs fly away. The mash was fed to the chief. Jollof saw all this clearly from where she hid. She shuddered with disgust.

. . . They spoke words over the chief and his son. The chief looked excited, the son looked terrified. Herbs were burned. Some strange plant was brought out of a sack. One of the female elders planted it in the floor. It had green needles for leaves and a large pod-like bulb. As the ceremony wore on, the room's atmosphere shifted. The pressure dropped, the air took on a silvery sheen, the smell of curry intensified. Jollof was about to flee. Then one of the women brought out a knife and slit the chief's throat. The chief looked glad, had even offered his neck . . .

Jollof ran for her life. Her scream thankfully caught in her own intact throat . . .

I came back to myself, fighting the urge to vomit. I leaned forward. Arif and Ejii were also gagging. I ran to the bathroom and threw up everything I'd eaten. The smell of palm oil and curry was still in my nose. He'd offered his own neck. I threw up some more.

"That sick camelshitting son of a . . ." I lost my breath, leaning my head on the toilet. Tears squeezed from my eyes. What had the chief done to himself? To his son? I had been sold into slavery, witnessed genocide, child slavery, seen the girl I loved sucked dry by Ghanaian vampires. But this by far was the evilest thing I'd ever seen. It was just one man dying and by his own choice, but there was something so repulsive about it, so fundamentally wrong, so essentially sick.

When I returned to the main room, Ejii handed me a warm washcloth. Arif also had one pressed over his face. Jollof sat beside him, her back stiff, knees together, hands clasped. A picture of unease. But Ejii seemed perfectly fine.

"Have some tea," she said, handing me a cup. It wasn't the sweet milky tea. It was bitter and minty with only a hint of sugar. Exactly what I needed.

"When I was with the Old Woman in the Ginen forest," Ejii said, "she taught me this trick to help deal with extremely . . . unpleasant moments. Imagine being in a cave full of bat dung with no shoes. It's cold, dark, and damp. Smells awful. The dung is slimy and crawling with cockroaches and beetles. The wet squelching sounds."

I felt my gorge rise and took another big sip of the bitter and refreshing tea. I wanted Ejii to shut up. "Your point," I asked, irritated.

Ejii smiled. "Ten times she brought me there. Eventually, the Old Woman and I could sit in that nastiness and happily eat mangoes. Why? Because we could successfully block out all that was around us and only smell, taste, feel, hear, see sweet sweet bright orange mango." She became serious. "Even though I can do that, what I just saw made *my* stomach turn."

"Goddamn," I whispered.

"The chief is dead, isn't he?" Ejii asked.

"No," Jollof said. "He's not."

Ejii blinked. "But . . ."

"I just had a feeling," Jollof said. "It was night. Late. I don't sleep much because I have bad dreams." She paused. "I heard whispers in the conference room. Sometimes I go there before daybreak when it's quiet and all you can here are the crickets singing and the cooing of the doves who live in a bush there. That big window is where I sit and look out at Ooni."

Maybe that was the window where Ejii had seen Jollof crying in the night before the Golden Dawn Meeting. It would make sense.

She sat back, her shoulders curled. "I saw them kill him. But he's not dead. His *son* is." She wiped away her tears. "For the last two years, the chief's body had been failing him. He was just too unhealthy. His heart and other organs just couldn't take it. Healers did all they could, but he was dying. What I witnessed was the corruption of reincarnation. It was Chief Ette pushing his son's spirit from his son's body so that he could take it over. It's an old old old practice."

I felt the urge to gag again. I grasped my belly and shut my eyes.

Arif looked disgusted. "How could . . ."

"The chief's medicine women and men can do many things," Jollof said. She sighed. "Poor Ikemefuma."

"*That's* his name?!"

She nodded.

I almost laughed. Tumaki had had a super old auto-graphed copy of *Things Fall Apart*. In the book, the main char-acter, Chief Okonkwo, sacrifices a boy who was like a son to him. The boy's name was Ikemefuma and the chief's stupid actions essentially led to his downfall.

"I was very close with Ikem," Jollof said, her eyes misting. "He . . . he was my only friend."

"Why would the chief *do* that?" Ejii asked. "Why not someone else?"

"It doesn't work with just anyone. Plus, he felt it was his right," Jollof spat. "He refuses to die until he has done away with Jaa . . . and you, Ejii. And until he knows his kingdom is secure and settled. This was a month before the pact crum-bled. He wanted to be strong when it was time for war. Since he could not do anything warlike, he's been campaigning in Ooni, trying to regain support. Ooni's sentiment has changed. Dikéogu, if you and Ejii go back there now and someone rec-ognizes you, they will kill you.

"I don't know how Ette befriended the Adze, but he sent them to kill off all Changed Ones, starting in this part of Earth you call Western Africa. The chief also plans to quickly restore your world to normalcy and repair your environment. It is what Ooni people do best. It comes naturally to us. He already has people putting out the flames in your New York City. In Dubai and Israel, there are openings to these places in Ooni. He will clean the air. The water. Changed Ones will become a rarity. He will bring back predictable life.

"This place is still mostly desert, but it won't be for long.

Jungle will slowly roll across it. Food will grow. Animals will come. The spontaneous forests will stay and flourish."

It sounded almost beautiful and for a moment I was lost in the thought of the world growing again. Normal. Then the moment passed. The ends do not always justify the means. And there was never any excuse for genocide. Never.

"He has special plans for Kwàmfà," Jollof said. "He sent the Adze to suck your town dry of beauty, to kill its spirit. That is the first phase."

I slammed my fist on the table, spilling my tea. Jollof jumped; Ejii and Arif didn't. "Goddamn it!" I shouted. I had nothing else to say so I said it again. "Goddamn it!"

Rainmaker

I don't know how much longer I can keep telling this fucking story. It only gets worse from here. It's only more darkness. Mostly. There are bright spots but mostly darkness. We're traveling faster now. By camel. Camels that look like they've been fed on the dead and drunk of the living. Camels that would follow ants into an anthill. Camels that have danced with masquerades to the beat of an awful song. They sweat, they salivate and slobber and roar. Their fur is like harsh mold. They're the color of dusk.

Yet here I am. The Prisoner. No, I don't think I can tell this story, but I will. I must. Or else the darkness will consume me. God damn my father. Allah never forgive my mother.

Even now I can smell a storm. Close. Not on the horizon yet. But close. With some rest, I'll continue.

CHAPTER 17

Honor Code

Eventually we all went to sleep wherever we felt comfortable. Ejii and Jollof slept in the main room on the leather chairs. Arif settled himself at the kitchen table, a bottle of beer in hand, where he eventually nodded off. I retreated to the garden. I must have been asleep as soon as I lay down on my mat. I still wore the same clothes I'd worn while I helped to move dead bodies. Disgusting, I know. But I was so exhausted, mentally, physically, spiritually.

I had no dreams or nightmares, praise Allah. About two hours had passed when I opened my eyes. I could tell by the location of the stars and moon. I heard spirited whispering from inside. I got up and went in through the open back door.

A tall guy about my age stood before Ejii. He was light-skinned and had the face a Wodaabe woman would fall in love with—perfectly symmetric, long narrow face and large eyes. He also had a head full of long thick hair that fell to his shoulders in thick braids. He could have easily competed in Gerewol and given Arif a run for his money. Maybe that was why Arif was standing there looking like he wanted to murder the guy. I didn't like the guy's body language either. He stood too close to Ejii. He was looking into her eyes.

"I don't believe you," Ejii whispered angrily.

"I . . . I understand," the guy said. "But please. I'm here. Anything you need or are planning. I'll stake my *life* on it. You have to believe me." He looked away, grinding his teeth, his fists clenching and unclenching. I knew this type of guy. Whatever he was apologizing for, he hated doing it.

"What's going on?" I said, stepping in. Jollof was still on the couch, snoring.

"Fadio," Arif said, motioning toward the guy. "Ejii's camel's ass of a half-brother."

"Ah," I said, starting to understand. I cocked my head and took a good look at him. Ejii had told me plenty about him. He was a year younger than she. The first son of her monster of a father. A son by a woman closer to Ejii's age than her mother's. Before Chief Ette brought purpose to the art of hating Changed Ones, Fadio had made a sport of it just because.

"He's suddenly decided that Changed Ones are not the scourge of the Earth," Ejii said, narrowing her intense eyes at Fadio. "Yeah, all it took was for his mother to give birth to a baby who disappears and reappears whenever he feels like." She laughed. "Welcome to the dark side, Fadio."

I saw the change on Fadio's face. It was like something had switched on. And that "something" was ugly and mean and angry. Arif sensed it too. We both moved closer to Ejii. Fadio wasn't intimidated, as he stepped very close to Ejii, using his height, weight, and gender to intimidate her.

"Your goddamn mother has stripped my family of most of what we had. I am the only son of the chief left here. With my mother. All my siblings have moved to Agadez with the other wives. Your mother has shamed me, shamed everyone. All we have is our house and what the council gives us to live on." He spat to the side. "Do your worst, witch. Camelshit is camelshit."

Ejii stared up at him, back straight, face hard. Fadio didn't understand what he was dealing with. The girl he knew had changed. She took out her seed shooter and pointed it in his face.

He looked at me now. "Tell your woman to stand down," he said. He looked at Arif. "Or is she yours?"

Ejii looked as if she was going to go crazy with rage.

"Fadio, I think you need to shut up," I said. I stepped up to Ejii. "What are you doing?" I calmly asked. Arif sucked his teeth loudly and plopped himself on a couch. "Shoot him or not," he said, with a wave of his hand. "Makes no difference to me."

Ejii didn't move. Fadio took a package of hemp sticks from his pocket. Back home, kids called these *gbana*. He arrogantly proceeded to light and smoke one—all the while, looking Ejii directly in the eye. It all seemed like silly harmless bravado on both their parts, but I swear to you, Ejii was *not* bluffing. She was going to kill him. Her eyes had gone blank, she was tired, and she was very, very angry.

Fadio took another drag from his *gbana*. He blew out the smoke. "Put the seed shooter down."

"No."

"You're still a bitch," he snapped.

"As you are," she said.

He slowly turned his back to Ejii and looked up at the skylight. Ejii cursed and brought down her seed shooter. "Where did you learn the Ginenian honor code?" she asked. Her voice was slightly shaky.

"'Plant no seed in a man's turned back,'" he recited, his back still turned. "Isn't that how it goes?"

She said nothing, replacing her seed shooter and leaving the room.

He turned to me. "Want some?" he asked, offering me his hemp stick.

I shrugged. I'd never tried one. No better time than now. It tasted like soil and made me feel like my feet were an inch off the ground.

Ejii came striding back into the room. She walked up to Fadio and grabbed his arm.

He frowned, asking, "What are you . . ." His eyes grew wide. A minute passed. She didn't let go. He whimpered and blinked as if that would stop what she was showing him. Ejii's jaw was set and she held his eyes with hers. I stepped away from them. I could see images in my mind. Faint. He dropped his hemp stick on the marble floor.

When she let go, he let out a piercing scream and stumbled back, his back to the nearest marble pillar. Jollof jumped up, fully awake. Ejii smiled, very satisfied. Arif smiled too, nodding at her.

"Now he is ready to join us," she said, a hard look on her face.

Fadio looked at her with stunned watering eyes. "I . . . I didn't . . ."

"*Now* you understand," she said.

There was a knock at the door.

"Oh my God," I said. "What now . . ."

POW! The noise came from blocks away.

We all stared at each other. Jollof started putting her sandals on and grabbing her things.

I'd only heard that noise once in my life. When I was with Ejii, Gambo, Jaa, and Buji in the middle of nowhere. Somewhere near Biafra City. Not long after, Ejii's camel Onion had died from being hit with stray bullets.

"Who the hell would be dumb enough to fire a gun?!" Ejii shouted.

I didn't know anyone even had guns anymore.

A woman screamed. The sound of something shattering. The knocking on the door grew more frenzied.

"Who's there?" I shouted.

"Open up!" a female voice shouted back. "Please!"

There suddenly seemed to be chaos outside. A swell of confused and panicked voices, screams, shouts, pleas, all from close by. The scuffle of feet, the roar of camels. Someone turned up very loud highlife music. Arif looked out the window to see who was at the door.

"Just a woman," he said. "Open it." Then he turned to look out at the street and froze. Ejii joined him at the window. I opened the door.

The woman was about eighteen, short, and chubby with skin dark like Ejii. She wore a colorful yellow and black wrapper and a black T-shirt. Though worn out, her clothes did not look like the clothes of a poor woman, or a thief who lacked skill. Like me, she had no use for shoes. A traveler. Despite whatever the hell was going on outside, she looked calm and had a pleasant smile on her face, as if she'd just gone for a stroll.

"You all better grab what you can," she said, stepping in. "The Adze have come to finish what they started."

=====

The next half hour . . . it all happened so fast. It's a jumbled mass in my head.

The woman's name was Lifted and she was from Ghana, the same homeland as the Adze. She'd come a long way. She'd planned to present herself at the meeting that was supposed to happen in the morning.

"I can kill them," she said, stepping in and closing the doors.

"Camelshit," Arif said. "Those things do not die."

Someone screamed outside. We all looked toward the door.

"We need to leave," Lifted said.

"I'm going to get my mother," Ejii said, stepping toward the door.

Fadio was already moving.

"I suggest you stick with me," Lifted said. "You're dead the minute you walk out that door. Trust me. And you can't help anyone when you're dead. At least not in the way you want to."

Fadio paused, indecisive.

Arif grabbed his head, shadows darkening the space around him. I think he was straining to keep from running out the door, too. Once in a while, in certain situations, it's good to have no family. This was definitely one of them. Otherwise I'd have been struggling to stay, too.

Suddenly, Ejii bolted for the door. I kind of saw it coming. She had a look on her face. I ran after her. She was fast, but I'd reacted just in time. I grabbed her arm and put my other arm around her waist. She was smaller than me and I was pretty strong. I didn't think I'd have a problem, but she reacted with such strength and force that I almost went flying back. I held on, though. We fell to the floor.

All I could see was her shriveled-up body. Seed shooter or no seed shooter, those Adze would eventually have their way with her. Just like they did with Jaa and Tumaki. All it took were enough of them. And who knew who else was out there? I suspected I'd find Ginen soldiers, too. I couldn't let this happen to her. Not when I knew what I was up against this time.

It was like wrestling with a giant scorpion. She was powerful and she punched, slapped, scratched. Then she was like an electric eel, her electrical charge being horrible images. She blasted and blasted me with them.

Sitting in a stinking cave with a maggoty beetly floor.

Being manhandled by a group of Tuaregs.

The burning sting of a scorpion.

"Abid!" he spat at her. The hateful word traveled to her soul.

The bite of a large beaked bird on her arm as she slept.

It was like it all happened to me. I could feel what she felt. The pain, fear, terror, rage, hopelessness. She inundated me with those images one after the other, lightning fast. So it was like feeling it all at the same time. On top of this, she gave me a hard punch in the gut, knocking the air from my lungs.

My brain clouded. I passed out.

═══

Ejii was screaming.

I was on something. Something moving. Alive. I cracked my eyes open. Still night. The night that would never end.

But someone had a glow lily, for I could see everyone in a sort of dim purple light.

I was on a camel. Where was Kee? Maybe flying above.

Ejii was screaming. She sat on her mutatu Plantain with Lifted. I couldn't quite see Ejii's face. I didn't think I'd want to. I'd never heard such a sound. Well, yes, I had. Once. Back in Timia. From my own mouth.

Lifted sat with her. Keeping her from falling.

Behind her Arif and Fadio rode a white camel. It practically glowed in the night. Arif was stiff as a statue. Staring straight ahead. Fadio's face was streaked with flowing tears, his eyes red, his body softly shaking as he quietly sobbed.

Everyone was dirty with dust. I looked at myself. I was, too.

"Keeeee!"

I looked up. There he was. At least there was that.

"You all right?" Jollof asked in my ear. She was sitting behind me, her arms around my waist. She was holding me up.

"What happened?"

"The worst thing I've ever seen."

Ejii let loose a soul-ripping shriek that must have carried hundreds of times farther than her shadow-speaker eyes could see.

━━━━━

Ejii's mother was dead, Arif's family was dead, Fadio's mother and baby brother were dead. Kwàmfà was no more. If it hadn't been for that mysterious woman who showed up at the Hall right when it started, we'd have all been dead, too. She could produce and control a terrible light that killed whatever it touched. Even when that thing was undead. She'd blasted all attacking Adze into a fine dust. When we encountered Ginenian solders, where Lifted could not use her light, Ejii and Arif had used a seed shooter and deadly shadows. In this way, we escaped Kwàmfà.

All through I'd been unconscious from whatever the hell Ejii had done to me. So I didn't see Ejii witness her mother sacrifice herself in an attempt to save some running children. I didn't see what was left of Fadio's mother and brother when we got to their house. Or what was left of Arif's parents, siblings, uncle, and four aunties at his house. I didn't have to. I could imagine.

We didn't know where we were going and we didn't care. We just kept fleeing. When it grew hot, we stopped in the shadow of a large rock and set up camp. Nobody spoke. We had food and only the camels, Kee, and Plantain. We slept though the rest of that day and night.

I had many dreams that night. Of the sky. Clouds, soft, fluffy, cool, damp. Below was the desert. Rainbows, well-being. I felt the hardness of Kee's beak against my cheek and slowly I woke up. "Keeee," he whispered. I heard the flap of large wings. *Where's Kee going?* I wondered groggily.

When I opened my eyes, I was eye to eye with a large kola-nut-colored owl.

CHAPTER 18

Return

Kola returned to me.

She was healthy. She smelled like flowers. And she had a tiny red beaded anklet on each leg. Everyone was still asleep. I was glad for this because I needed the silence and mental distance.

I got up and she flew onto my shoulder. We walked some yards away from the camp and sat down in the sun. It was still morning but it was already getting hot. An arid heat. For miles and miles there was nothing but tall craggy stones like the legs of petrified giants. A black beetle scrambled across the sand past my foot. Kola and I eyed it as she leaned against my cheek.

"We're like that beetle," I told her. "Just trying to get by."

She didn't think so. She thought we had much more to do than get by. She told me so. In her own way. In the way of one chi to the other who was her chi.

She knew of what I had been through up to the moment after Tumaki was killed. Then she'd lost me. She told me she hadn't been sure if I was dead or alive. She'd thought I was dead. As I've said, in a way I was. But in a way I was very much alive.

Kola had traveled far. She had joined two of the giant

white owls who normally protected the Ooni Palace. They'd joined other birds and traveled to Agonia, a land dominated by sentient birds of all shapes and numbers. A great confluence of birds, Kola called it. They'd all just known to go.

And what came out of the meeting? She could not explain it to me, not all of it. She said that Ejii, me, the chief, and many others were discussed. The coming war was discussed. The war would lead to Earth's destruction, the elders proclaimed. But the main message was that there was a man that was a bird who all birds knew of and who knew birds. It was the same message I'd gotten from the Desert Magician. Dieuri. Find Dieuri.

At some point, during the time that she thought I was dead, she'd mated with one of the white-owl males. I didn't want to think about how that had worked, the size difference and all.

"There are four," I said. "Aren't there?"

She clicked her beak. All female, all the reddish brown of the outside of a kola nut. All who'd grow much bigger than her.

Dieuri. How was I going to get the group to get it together and help me look for this man?

I heard sobbing not far from me. Ejii. In her tent. I considered going to her, but the sobbing was hard. From the gut. I didn't go to her. Okay, I was afraid. Maybe she needed to be alone and maybe she didn't, but I wasn't going to risk it just now. I wasn't going to risk her again doing whatever she'd done to me in Kwàmfà or worse.

I took my e-legba out instead. Kola flew into the sky. She wasn't going far. Just to get something to fill her belly. I had a weird feeling, I kid you not. A flutter in my belly. I looked

around. Ejii had come out of her tent and was splashing her
face with water from the capture station. Still sobbing, she
brought a bucket of water to the camels. Then she went and
buried her face in the hide of that giant bird of hers.

Arif was peeking out of his tent. He got out and went to
her. I bristled as he took her in his arms. *Dammit,* I thought.
Then I cursed again because there were worse things to worry
about and both of them had just lost their families and everything had gone to camelshit. No room for jealousy. How
could I even *feel* jealousy? I didn't even want to touch Ejii.
Not when she was crying and upset like that.

I shook my head and trained my eyes on my e-legba. Better to concentrate on an annoying episode of *Felecia at Large.*
My eye fell on the mysterious files on the screen. I still didn't
want to open them. Those were ghosts I didn't need to un-
leash. Especially not right now. I rubbed my forehead. My
head was so full.

The new episode was titled, "A Very Old Man With Enormous Wings," and highlighted as "hot," which meant it was
one of the top most-viewed items online at the moment. I
clicked on it and enlarged the image box and turned up the
volume.

My mother was standing with a microphone in hand in
what looked like the bush. Behind her was a mob of people
shouting and talking at the same time. My mother had to
speak loudly to be heard. She was all grins and wide eyes and
nostrils, like she was trying to eat, see, and inhale everything
around her. She wore a traditional Igbo blue wrapper, matching top, and head wrap, as opposed to her usual expensive
European-style business suit.

"Today, you witness history, ladies and gentleman," she said. She spoke in English as always, but below a link flashed, advertising translations into Yoruba, Igbo, French, Arabic, Efik, Japanese, Turkish, Ashanti, German, Spanish, Chinese, Russian, and at least another twenty other languages. Did the transmission of her show even reach as far as where those languages were spoken? I didn't care.

"We have a special treat for you on so many levels," she said. Her brow was damp with sweat. For her to allow that meant this was serious indeed. This had been recorded live. A man came running up behind her. He laughed like a damn monkey and shouted something in a language I didn't understand. He shook his fists at the camera and shouted "Yaaarr!" and then ran off.

My mother looked at him with disgust and then remembered she was on camera. She smiled her well-known inviting smile. "Behind me is something that will save us all." She started walking toward the mob. When people saw the camera, they quickly moved out of the way, staring at my mother. The mob was mostly men but some women, too. All in various types of Nigerian attire with a European mix. Colorful textiles, caftans, bubas, dashikis, jeans, shorts, T-shirts, even suits.

"My husband Chika Obidimkpa is a brave man. Not only does he make sure our networks run smoothly, but he has greater aspirations." The mob had hushed, the trees blocking the sunshine a bit as she walked toward wherever she was going. "Like me, he is dedicated to the old ways," she continued. "To keeping our Earth *Earth*."

Then she stood back as the camera came upon one of the

worst sights I'd ever seen. He was tied up against a giant bao-bab tree. Like a butterfly pinned in a glass box, except he was alive and he was more like a bird. A rope around his waist and another holding his legs down. His arms were held out and in place with ropes tied to metal pegs. And then there were his enormous wings. Brown like those of an eagle, each nearly the length of two cars! They had a curved white claw on each end like those of a bat.

This was why Kola and the other birds knew of him. He was practically one of them.

I stared at Dieuri, the man who had tried to save the Earth by inventing and then launching Peace Bombs. My mouth hung open. Winged people were always magnificent-looking. They looked like angels, if angels existed, which I didn't believe. I'd never seen a winged person who wasn't pretty or handsome. They'd always been young. Winged people seemed to only be born, not instantly made as many were when the Great Change happened.

Dieuri was old, according to his wizened face. Maybe eighty. He was a rich brown, not a dark brown. He glared into the camera with disgust and rage. My spirits lifted a tiny bit. At least he wasn't done for. Not yet.

"With the help of Chief Ette's soldiers, we've managed to capture someone you've all heard of. The man who destroyed the world!" She laughed. The urge flew through me like light-ning. Only the thought of Tumaki and the fact that this de-vice was all I had left of her kept me from smashing it.

"Well, he is no longer a man. He is a rat with wings, a giant bird or a bat or whatever he is. An aberration. And how should aberrations be handled?"

The crowd shouted back various responses, all of which involved violence.

My mother smiled triumphantly, looking into the camera. "The mad scientist known as Dieuri, the Haitian maker and detonator of the infamous Peace Bombs, has been captured right here in Lagos. We will clip his wings in seven days at seven p.m. at the Mobolaji Johnson Arena on Lagos Island. Tune in and be a part of it. The Chief of Ooni from the land of Ginen will give a speech afterward. We're on our way back to normalcy, my friends. This is *Felecia at Large*." She made the peace sign and grinned. Then the screen went black and the Obidimkpa logo popped up on the screen.

Rainmaker

There's no question that there is a god. Or gods. Or God. No doubt. There is something. How could you possibly be an atheist after living through the Great Change? The Great Merge? Witnessing all this?

CHAPTER 19

Allah's Great and Glorious Design

I showed them Kola. Told them what Kola had said. Retold them about my encounter with the Desert Magician. And then I showed them my mother's show. Fadio and Lifted weren't convinced that I was an Obidimkpa, which was understandable. So I showed them my parents' goddamn interview, which featured the clip of me a few years ago.

Fadio had spat to the side. "I knew that woman was crazy."

Lifted just stared at me with new eyes. I knew what was going on in her head. She was realigning who she thought I was. I was shifting from "slave boy" to "rich boy fallen on hard times." She really didn't have to do that. I was the person she knew, not the person from that interview.

Eventually Fadio, Lifted, and Arif were convinced. We had nowhere to go. We needed direction. I gave them something concrete. I gave them a purpose. So we all took it and ran with it. That night, we looked at a map on my e-legba to determine the best way to get to Lagos.

In two days, we arrived at a small town, where we sold the camels for a ride to Lagos on an old oil truck inhabited by a sparkling lizard. I handled the haggling, despite my slave tattoos. I looked the oldest and strongest, and I knew I'd be the best at it. Fadio was too spoiled. Arif's shadows might attack the driver if the driver did something stupid. And men from these parts didn't take well to negotiating with women.

The truck's driver wore a thick pair of lopsided glasses and spoke very proper Hausa. He switched to Igbo when he heard my accent. This really threw me off. We had traveled east. We were nowhere *near* Nigeria. All people spoke around here were Hausa, Arabic, Fulani and other variations of those languages.

"You know this thing here," he slapped a hand on the side of his truck, "It is Allah's great and glorious design. You'll be traveling with the best, the safest. No breakdowns on the road."

"That's what we heard," I said. "There are six of us . . ." I paused. We'd rehearsed the story, but it still felt awkward in my mouth. I pointed to Ejii. "She is my wife." I pointed to Arif and Lifted. "Those two are married." I pointed to Jollof and Fadio. "And those two are married." Ejii, Lifted, and Jollof had donned veils. Ejii wore one that covered her entire head, to hide her shadow-speaker eyes. Arif had discreetly turned away so the driver couldn't see his eyes.

He squinted at each of us, then a smile spread over his face. I didn't like it. It was a greedy smile. *Dammit, we didn't dress shabbily enough,* I thought. No matter. I launched in with my first bid. He laughed at me.

"You must be kidding me," he said. "Didn't I tell you this moto is run by a sparkling lizard? Honestly, can you say that you've ever ridden in such a moto?"

"Sir," I said, trying to look puffed up, dark, and mysterious. "I've eaten sparkling lizard for lunch."

He looked into my eyes. When his face changed, I knew he'd seen what I needed for him to see. I wasn't kidding. And I wasn't about to let him rip me off. After that, the haggling went more smoothly. The price was still high but reasonable.

"Call me Eyeglass," the driver said, holding out a hand to close the deal.

"Call me Dikéogu," I said. Yeah, I used my real name.

"What is that thing?" he asked, pointing at Plantain.

"It's a bird," I said. "She is kind."

"Will she agree to sit with the cargo on top?"

I nodded, though I had no idea.

"And it won't drop feces on everything I pack in there?" he said.

"No." This I knew. Plantain was possibly more private about her private business than even Jollof. She'd disappear far away behind sand dunes, bushes, rocks, when she had to go. I think she even dug a fairly deep hole first.

"She is light?"

I shrugged. "Well, she's a bird, so I guess." Though she was also flightless. Most likely she was pretty heavy.

"Okay," he said. "Count yourself lucky. Usually the largest animal I'll carry is a chicken."

"I appreciate it, sir," I said. As if he was going to give up our business. I didn't bother telling him about Kola. She'd follow us in the air and land on top of the bus when she needed a rest. Not a problem.

Eyeglass claimed he'd made the trip from Lagos to the northern cities and towns of Niger over fifty times. I didn't believe him. But I believed he'd done it a few times. Still impressive. I wanted to ask him how he navigated the spots of weirdness, but I didn't want to open that can of worms. Next thing you know, he'd be looking too closely at Ejii or Arif or noticing that Lifted's odd glow wasn't just from her healthy, flawless brown skin.

He'd installed seats inside the truck and windows on the sides. But it was still hot and bumpy inside. And don't get me started on the static. Since learning from Gambo, I'd gotten my own static problem under control. But the sparkling lizard made static a problem for everyone. You couldn't move without causing a crackling sound. And you didn't want to brush up against anyone either.

The six of us sat in two rows close to a window. None of us was in much of a mood to talk. There were about twenty other passengers, too. A few babies, a few mouthy kids, one little girl who wouldn't stop staring at me, Ejii, and Arif. Thankfully, she wasn't much of a talker, so she didn't bring any added attention to us. She just kept peeking between the chairs.

We didn't talk to anyone and they didn't talk to us. It was a pretty quiet ride. I think people were a little scared, too.

———

Eyeglass would speed up when things stopped making sense. That's what I noticed. I sat at the window and I watched the landscape. For an hour it would be cracked dry earth, then we'd hit grass and you'd feel the truck start going a lot faster. I mean a LOT faster. When the land went back to hardpan, we'd slow down. Sometimes we'd go at high speeds for ten minutes, other times over two hours. During one of the two-hour stretches, we drove through what looked like a very mountainous region.

After an especially long stretch of speeding, we finally slowed down. Outside, the land was no longer desert. It was savanna. We were near the Nigerian border. I turned and met Ejii's eyes. She nodded.

"That driver lied to you," she said. "There's a lot more to this truck than he told you."

———

We were at a rest stop at a large cluster of stunted trees. Enough to provide some privacy. It also gave us a chance to stretch our legs. Our last break had been hours ago.

Somehow Ejii and Fadio got to talking. They were speaking in Arabic, so I couldn't understand what they were saying. I watched them as I leaned against a tree. Arif had wandered a few yards away, looking out at the field of dry grass and trees. Though in the sun, he was shaded. I wouldn't have gone near him for anything.

Lifted and Jollof had their backs turned as they had their own discussion. Ejii's mutatu was off stretching her legs and snacking on some blades of grass. Kola was perched on her back. I didn't like the way Fadio was looking down his nose at Ejii. Or how Ejii's hand had suddenly migrated too close to her hip where her seed shooter rested. Neither was smiling as he or she spoke; their voices had dropped low.

Then Fadio's voice suddenly rose, his face twisting. The only word I caught in the rapid Arabic he spat was *"abid."* I

moved forward. That word meant "slave," a derogatory word
that the Arabs liked to use on Africans. Even I knew that. A
distant fuzzy memory wafted through my head. I'd heard
that word many times in my lost year. Those who had called
me those names did not fare well.

"Uh . . . Ejii," I said as I approached. I let out a breath of
relief as she lifted her hand from her side. Then, *smack!* with
her full hard-callused hand across Fadio's face. He stumbled
back, glaring at her. I grabbed Ejii's hand as she brought it
back again, rage in her eyes. Fadio only looked at her, not
even touching his face. *Good man,* I thought. I knew too many
men who would have returned the slap with five times the
force and then not stopped there.

"What the hell are you doing, Ejii?" I asked. I motioned to
Jollof and Lifted to stay where they were. They nodded. Several of the other passengers were watching us, too. By now,
people had realized that Ejii and Arif were shadow speakers.

"Everything all right?" Eyeglass asked, peeking from under the hood of the bus.

"All under control," I assured him.

Ejii just glared at her half-brother. No, let's get it straight.
No one has that kind of hate for a mere half-brother. Different mother or not, Fadio was her *brother.*

Fadio only turned and walked away. For a moment, I
wasn't sure what to do. Then I took Ejii's hand and led her in
the opposite direction, which happened to be toward Arif.

"What was that all about, Ejii?" I asked.

She said nothing. Arif turned around. I almost jumped
out of my skin. For just a moment, *just* a moment, he looked

like a monster. His face was black like the beast in the cocoa field. A bottomless pit of darkness. Then it was gone. Leaving me looking right into his strange violet eyes.

We were both infected with whatever it was. And we understood that now.

"What happened?" he asked, his voice rough. He coughed to clear his throat.

"She won't say," I said.

"Neither of you would understand," Ejii whispered.

She sat right there in the sand. She looked up at me. "You, Dikéogu," she said. "Maybe you would." She rubbed her forehead and face with her veil. "I don't know what possessed me to," she said. "I don't know why I told Fadio."

We sat down on both sides of her. Ejii was one to pick and choose what she let you know and see. She was an expert shadow speaker and her control of this was near perfect. You never saw what she did not want you to see.

We waited.

"Oh Allah," she said. She looked up. "Arif, I know you. You've never known love. You've only known many women. Winner of Gerewol, the mysterious shadow-speaker traveler." She scoffed. "So many female conquests. You're free to do that because you're a man. Travel and know many women."

Arif didn't know what to say. Hell, *I* didn't know what to say. He was only nineteen or so. To have that kinda record. Impressive. But not really. Nothing compared to what I had with Tumaki. Or what I wanted with Ejii.

"He was telling me about Aabirah, his girlfriend," she said. "She was . . . in Kwàmfà, too."

"Oh," we both said, looking away and understanding that Aabirah was dead.

Ejii frowned and closed her eyes, rubbing her forehead again. "So I told Fadio that I'd been in love once, too," she said.

My eyebrows went up. "Oh? With who?" I asked.

"You fell in love with a windseeker, didn't you?" Arif asked.

"Did the shadows tell you that?" she asked.

"Just answer my question," Arif said.

I don't know what came over me, but I started laughing. "You're kidding! Now I see why you're so upset." I laughed some more. Stupid thing to say, stupid reaction, I know. Sometimes I can be really stupid.

"What was his name?" Arif asked softly.

"Ahmed," Ejii said. She glanced at me. "He was Arab."

Oh, shit, I thought. Now I understood Fadio's use of the word *"abid."* I suspected that he wasn't necessarily insulting Ejii. He was probably referring to what this Ahmed guy had thought of her. How could Ejii be with both a windseeker and one who was racist, at that?

"Did you know he was a windseeker?" I asked. "Or did you just wonder about the fact that it was always breezy whenever he was around you?"

"Shut *up!*" she suddenly shouted at me.

I put my hands up. "Okay. Sorry."

"I knew what he was the day I met him," she said.

"Go on," I said, begrudgingly.

"I . . . can't," she said. "I want to, but . . . it's just so . . ." She sighed.

"You can't tell us?" Arif asked.

She shook her head. "And I'm not about to *show* you, either."

"I have an idea," I said. I brought out my e-legba. Though I was yet to listen to the recording of myself, I had figured out the record mechanism that Tumaki had added. I was considering recording my recollections of all that had happened. But I hadn't found the time or peace of mind to do so. "Why don't you record yourself and then Arif and I can listen to it later?"

She thought about it and then nodded. She took my e-legba and wandered off.

Here is the file . . .

Translating . . .

Ejii File, recorded October 13, 2073

This audio file has been automatically translated from the Arabic language.

Dikéogu, first I want to say that you are a real idiot for what you said.

But you're sort of right.

I should have known better.

But then again, some things are beyond our control, Dikéogu. You should know that just as much as I do. Arif told me about your girlfriend, Tumaki. I'm sorry you lost her . . .

Maybe I should have let Jaa impale Chief Ette. I should have let her do him in and spare my hands the scars from her sword. You know, the scar tissue on my hands is so hard that I can put out a flame with the centers of my palms and not feel anything. Not very ladylike, huh?

If I'd let Jaa kill the chief, she'd still be alive. Buji, m . . . my mother, Mazi Godwin, Arif's family, Fadio's family, his girlfriend, all of Kwàmfà, all those who've been killed in the genocide.

Anyway, on to a lighter subject. Ahmed. It was about a year after I'd left the Old Woman. I was alone, except for Plantain, my mutatu . . .

By this time, I didn't fear traveling alone, though I knew what the land was capable of. Allah bless us, we've all been through so much, you, me, and Arif. Lifted and Jollof, too. We're like elders and we're not even twenty yet. Even back then, I was mentally old. I had yet to meet another Aejej, but I'd survived plenty of sand and heavy thunderstorms. I knew what it was like to almost die of thirst. Plantain, all mutatu, are like camels. They can go for long periods of time without water. She'd had to let me drink her blood or I'd have perished. And I had learned what it was like to kill a human being. Many times, actually. You all know these lands and their people have become rough. Many are full of murder. I don't know why.

So at this time, I was just wandering. Seeing. Thinking. Plantain is in many ways like me. She left Ginen with me because she suffers from wanderlust, too. Before she left her home, which happened to be the Old Woman's home, too, I'd first had to ask her. When she gave me an enthusiastic "yes," I had to then ask her herd. For three days, they made me eat fennel seeds with them and sleep in their field under the stars. Whistling and chirping amongst themselves. It was like I was jumping through the hoops of a traditional marriage. When they finally let us go, Plantain and I ran nonstop for over thirty hours. She was that happy.

When we entered the Sahara, things got dry, tough, and angry.

When we came across the spontaneous forest in the middle of nowhere, I was so relieved. We were out of water and there were no clouds in the sky, so our capture station was useless. And we had been traveling all day and were miles and miles from any type of civilization. Plantain ran to the small pond and started drinking. I cupped some of the water in my hand. I know what bacteria and the type of microorganisms that will make you sick look like. Another thing the Old Woman taught me.

The water was fresh, so I started drinking like crazy. There were several palm trees and some other smaller bushier trees. Shade. Respite. It was very very hot this day, the sun high in the sky. Plantain started munching on some of the plants. I laid my mat under a tree and quickly fell asleep.

I woke up hours later to Plantain's soft whistling. It was dusk. I heard someone humming and splashing. I listened harder. It sounded like one person. I slowly sat up. He wasn't far from me. Only a few yards, standing in the small pond wearing only his blue pants. As he walked deeper into the water, he hissed as if something was paining him. I could see in the dark and he could not, so I wasn't worried about him spotting me. His things were on the dry ground, closer to me than him. A satchel, a tattered blue shirt, and a silver, very sharp-looking dagger.

Where is his camel? Or scooter? Or vehicle? I wondered. *How did he get here?* I stood up. He still didn't see or hear me. I walked up to the water, stopping next to his things. That was when he froze, up to his shoulders in the water. He whirled around. Before I realized it, he flew at me. Fast like a hawk! I leapt to the side, snatching his satchel.

He landed, and snatched another small dagger from his pocket. He eyed me with such rage and disgust that I stumbled back. He addressed me in Arabic. "Filthy *abid* bitch," he

spat. "I'll slice her belly open just for touching my things."
His wet face was scratched up and I could see many cuts on
his arms and his chest. He leaked blood like a sieve.

I was so appalled by his condition and his words that
I just stood there. He took this as further evidence that I
couldn't possibly understand him.

"Ugh, Allah protect me," he said, taking a step closer.
"Will my day grow worse?"

He was much taller than me and strongly built, but he
looked our age, about sixteen years old. He had skin the color
of milky tea and the hint of a beard capping his chin. He had
the usual windseeker features, somewhat large wild eyes,
and his long, onyx-black hair was braided into seven large
braids with copper bands on the ends.

"What is wrong with you?" I snapped, in Arabic. He froze,
shocked that I could speak his oh-so-sacred language. "Where
do you come from that your mind is so twisted?" I continued. I
looked him up and down. "There are no slaves in these lands."

"Hand me my things," he demanded. "*Now.*"

I immediately read him. I smelled turmeric. Tasted sweet-
meats. He was from the country that used to be called Iraq.
He flew this far? I wondered as I swam within his past. *What
must he have seen?!*

He came from a lavish home. He was one of five sons and
four daughters. His father loomed large as I read him. His
father did not smoke or drink, and prayed five times a day.
His father hated spontaneous forests. He also hated the fact
that the way to the nearby village was never the same whenever he walked there. His father hated the foreigners who
came through his village, with their black skin and burned

hair, the new *abeed* he called them. He hated how the quality of the air was different. He was an important man in the crumbling government. Too important to have a windseeker born into his household. His son knew his father thought him ruined.

As I looked into this young man, I heard him step toward me, ready to grab his things from me while I was in that strange state I get into when I am reading someone. I was helpless. I had to see. One day, I will learn to read and not be so vulnerable. The Old Woman could not teach me this trick, unfortunately.

Looking into him, I was surprised to find poetry and gentleness. The boy before me loved salty olives. Curvy women. The beaded necklaces around the necks of the strange black-skinned women who came from the new world. The open clear sky. The drums in music moved him. His quiet mother, whose hands were always writing strange fantastical stories in the notebook she hid from his father. Open land . . .

It came as it always did. In fragments, details, like a puzzle.

The day his father drove him away was the day of the dinner. Golden-sequined organza curtains. The walls were covered with brocade wallpaper. Plush red velvet couches. Gold and green beaded lampshades. Shisha pipes at every table. It did nothing for him. His breeze blew the curtains around, caused lampshades to click and clack. Made people move away. He and his father had argued over his breeze and it had turned vicious . . .

A windseeker must fly . . . not even his father's heavy hand could change that.

"You *abeed* are the lowliest of all mankind. Always have been, and always will be!" he said to me.

"If you hated your father so much, Ahmed," I said, "why do you speak like him?"

His motions, again, were so quick. My seed shooter was at my hip. I wouldn't hesitate to use it. My reflexes were normally on point. But something about him slowed me down. Before I realized it, he'd reached into his pocket and was flashing a flashlight in my face.

I shielded my eyes. He clicked it off. "Give me my things," he said, with a sigh. I threw them over to him. He glared at me and then slowly walked to the other side of the forest. I went back to Plantain. "That boy is poisoned," I said, gathering some sticks to build a fire. "Thankfully, he'll probably be gone by morning, as this forest most likely will be."

Come morning, the forest was still there and he was in the water again washing his wounds. I sat up from my mat and watched him, amused. He deserved all his pain.

He groaned as he submerged himself. He'd obviously been attacked by a flock of carnivorous hummingbirds. They like to attack windseeekers. I'd seen it happen before. They moved lightning fast, so once attacked, you were going to get pecked. They can kill when especially angry, but they usually just jab. And their beaks carry some kind of poison that leaves their victims in pain for days. I chuckled to myself as he emerged. I went to my things to get breakfast. I had plenty of food. Once I filled my water bags, I'd be fine until I got to the next city. I had no idea where I was. Possibly somewhere in what used to be Libya. I'd planned to stay at this oasis until it disappeared. If he would just go away.

"The water will only make it worse," I said to him. "You should stay out for the rest of the day."

He didn't reply. He ignored me the whole day. So I ignored him, too. This was fine with me. He didn't take another bath in the water. Not until the next day.

We coexisted on the oasis for a week. It was as if the forest thrived on us, for overnight, it grew a mango tree and stalks of sugarcane, and the water remained clear and fresh and even began to have fish in it. Cicadas sang in the trees at dusk. I'd heard of this happening, spontaneous forests almost having a sentient existence when people they like stay in them. But this was my first experience with one.

All around us, however, was desert. As there was between the two of us. He would never go near the water when I was in it. He avoided the mango tree, as I tended to sleep underneath it. But every so often, I'd catch him watching me. When he saw that I saw him, his face would twist with disgust and he'd walk away.

Each day I wished he'd be gone. Arab racism was an old old old practice. The practice of slavery is never easily forgotten or overcome, and there had never been a civil rights movement in the Middle East or North Africa. There was no incentive for change. I learned much of this the hard way in my travels. I know you don't speak Arabic, Dikéogu, so I'll explain the root of the word to you. *Abeed* is the Arabic word for "black" or "slaves" or black people, Africans. *Abid* or *abd* is the singular form.

Ahmed did not fly away. After a while, it felt like we were competing. This place was so wonderful; neither of us wanted to be the first to leave it. The sugarcane was sweet, the mangos were sweet, the fish were tasty. All was plenty. The peace and quiet. The isolation from the rest of the world. It was a paradise.

We stayed there for a month. Plantain had never been so happy. The forest grew a little garden of fennel, to her delight, and each day, what she'd eaten grew back. Once in a while, she'd trot into the desert for exercise. I spent most of my time writing in my journal, thinking, sleeping.

Then one night, I woke in the middle of the night to Ahmed crouching over me, a raised rock in his hand. It had been a long time since I felt that kind of terror. My scream caught in my throat, every part of my body flexed, but I stayed still. He had a wild look on his face of someone about to do something terrible in the name of those who raised him. I stared at him, willing him with all my might to look into my eyes. *Look*, I demanded with my mind. If he didn't, he'd kill me, I knew . . . and it was not going to be a painless, quick death. I strained for his eyes. *Look, now!*

He looked into my eyes. He looked for a long long time. His face went from intense to slack to troubled. He got up, dropped the stone beside my head, and walked off. I rolled over and wept. I threw the stone in the pond, where it landed with a thick plunk. It was a heavy stone. I didn't go back to sleep. But not out of fear of Ahmed. I had seen something in his eyes, too.

That morning, he brought me stalks of sugarcane and a fish he'd carefully roasted. And that was when we started talking. We talked all day. He told me how a jungle had started to grow in his Iraqi village. I wonder if the Ginen people had started invading around there, too. It was likely that they had planted that jungle. He told me about all the places he'd been. He'd even been to America! Ah ah, to be able to fly! I don't know how he could carry his racism for so long as a windseeker, one who travels, a Changed One. But he did.

Nonetheless, somehow . . . I cured him.

By the next day, some of the trees in the forest had disappeared. We shared what we had. By the next day, all the sugarcane was gone. We left together the next day, when the pond went foul. We traveled together for six months.

You and Arif know about windseekers. I didn't at the time. All I knew was that they were people who could fly. After about nine months, we were so close, so . . . in love. We saw so many places, met so many people, learned so much, loved so much. But he was haunted by "her," his chi. For windseekers, this is the person they are destined to be with. It is written, many say. Or more thoroughly, an old man who saw me with Ahmed once said, "They can't stay with anyone for very long. Always yearning for their chi, whether they love someone else or not. Ah, they're a miserable lot." I wondered if he too had once loved a windseeker.

No matter who a windseeker loves, it is written.

Ahmed would see her standing above him whenever he and I were . . . together. He would see her around corners. In his dreams. He grew depressed and restless. He didn't believe anything he didn't write should be written. But he wasn't stupid, either. One day he just flew off when I was asleep. We'd been together for so long. It must have been a new record for him. But then again, Ahmed had a high threshold for pain. He left this ring on my finger. This jade ring fits my pinky perfectly.

Translating . . .

Dikéogu File Series continues

*This audio file has been automatically
translated from the Igbo language.*

CHAPTER 20

A Moment

We were two hours outside of Lagos. Which meant we were two hours from my parents and the place where they'd strapped up Dieuri like some sort of birdman Jesus. He only had to die to make the world a better place, right?

We were only a few hours' drive from my home in the southeast. Arondizuogu, Nigeria. I might as well have been home. The land was consistently moist, red soil, populated with green. No desert. How long had it been? Years now. I was seventeen.

I listened to Ejii's recording when we stopped for our last rest at a vehicle stop. Then I gave my e-legba to Arif. As he walked off to listen, I went to find Ejii. Before I could say anything, she said, "So Arif told me about your girlfriend, Tumaki."

I bit my lip very hard. "Arif has a big mouth."

"Why didn't you tell me about her?" Ejii asked.

I shrugged.

"Can I see her?" she asked.

I thought about it for a moment.

"Can I see him?"

I let her take my hand. I hated seeing him. Always a breeze around him. Always his thick braids blew. He had keen eyes like those of an eagle, toffee skin, and a great intensity. I could see why she loved this guy. How could I compete with that?

When she let go, she stepped away. Her brow furrowed, unsaid words obviously on her lips. Did she feel the same way? How much did she see of Tumaki? She'd only shown me what he looked like. Ejii only let you see what she wanted you to see. She had perfect control. As for me, well, who knows what she saw of Tumaki and my time with her.

I looked at the ring on Ejii's finger. It was light green jade, carved in the shape of a bird. She was right. It fit her perfectly.

"Did he ever tell you what he saw in your eyes?" I asked.

"No," she said.

"*Abid*. I *hate* that goddamn word."

"Me too," she said.

"I . . . I think he did, too," I added. "Eventually."

"Yeah," she said.

I took her hand. The one with the ring on it. I pulled her to me and hugged her. She sighed deeply and buried her head in my shoulder, also quiet, never crying, but so so sad. I knew her sadness wasn't only about Ahmed. Her mother, her mentor, herself, her hometown . . . all gone. I tightened my arms around her, lifted her chin and kissed her. She opened her eyes and looked up at me. She kissed me back. Then we were kissing each other.

She pulled back, touched my face, smiled at me, and walked away. I just stood there. For once, there was nothing else on my mind. For the rest of the day it was like this.

CHAPTER 21

Lagos

"Satan *na* **Lagos's brother,"** a man said.

He was like a ghost as he pushed his barrel of homemade flour from his flour factory down the road. He was covered from head to toe in the stuff. This was his response to my saying, "Hello." Lagos is Satan's brother. I laughed because I agreed.

I'd been to Lagos many times with my parents. They had a second home there. Only in my last year of living with them did they agree to my pleas to leave me behind in Arondizuogu when they went. I knew they were embarrassed by me and I used this to my advantage.

I hated Lagos. The place was dirty, chaotic, full of criminals and shysters, and clogged with way too many people. Bad air and garbage. Area guys and 419 scammers. Loose women and mad men. Whole neighborhoods were built on swamps because of the lack of housing. These places don't exist to super wealthy people like my parents, who usually lived right next door. Only in Lagos would you see dirty slums and palace-like homes existing right beside each other, the only thing separating them being a creek of dirty water and a heavily guarded wall topped with broken glass and a charged wire.

"THIS IS LAGOS. POPULATION: ?? AND GROWING," a large metal sign read. It was tilted to the side, probably by the Harmattan winds. As soon as we entered Lagos, I started coughing and had to close the windows. As we traveled south, the air quality grew progressively worse. By the time we reached the truck stop, it was so bad that if you inhaled too deeply, you had a coughing fit. The air of Lagos was absolutely abysmal. This place was the type of place that Ette would want to wipe off the face of the Earth. This was the kind of place that made Ette okay with committing genocide. Still, despite it all, we'd made it to Lagos. Thanks to Eyeglass and his magic truck.

"What does that thing really do?" I asked him. He'd unloaded all his passengers and was walking over to a small restaurant.

He looked around before responding. It was just the two of us for the moment. He leaned toward me and grinned. "I have no clue," he whispered.

I laughed.

"The thing cuts through places like hot knife," he said proudly. "That sparkling lizard is only icing on the cake." He paused, looking closely at me. "It's something I do, I think." He touched his chest. "It's me."

"You?"

He nodded. "You know what I mean."

I blinked and then I understood. He was some sort of Changed.

He smiled and nodded. "Eh-heh, you see now." He stepped closer to me. "You and your friends watch your back. I see you. Lagos is better than where we just came from, but no place is safe for people like us."

"We will," I said, slapping and grasping the man's hand. He patted me on the back.

"You're a strong boy," he said. "I know who you are. You give your parents hell when you find them. Make them face their bullshit."

My stomach did a backflip and I must have looked ridiculous with shock. Eyeglass grinned, knowingly laughed, and walked away.

———

We headed on foot to a nearby hotel that Eyeglass recommended. We didn't carry much, so walking a few blocks was nothing. Plus it gave us a chance to stretch out our legs.

So much movement. The roads were gridlocked with people on camelback, cars, a few trucks, and so many scooters and bicycles. People shouted, laughed, cursed, and spit at each other. On the sidewalks, people jostled past one another. Some shouted on "people-to-people," those small round gadgets that allowed people to communicate with small networks of individuals. I've only seen these gadgets in Lagos. They came in all kinds of colors. Others stared at e-pals, somehow managing to not walk into anyone. A beggar who had no arms and whose dirty brown rags barely covered his privates walked up to Ejii and stuck a dirty hand in her face, forcing her to stop.

"Please," he said in Yoruba. "Do Christmas for me, *abeg*."

He froze, noticing Ejii's eyes. He stared into them for a long time. He put his hands down, startled, and quickly turned and walked away, looking over his shoulder as if he expected Ejii to come after him.

"What was that about?" Jollof asked.

Ejii and Arif looked at each other, obviously sharing some kind of inside joke that wasn't funny.

"I already hate this place," Fadio mumbled. "Full of barbarians."

Lifted laughed. Ejii took my arm and we all started walking.

"That man is a murderer," she said, a distant look on her face. "He was a kidnapper and murderer of especially small children. You want to know more?"

I nodded, feeling cold and sweaty. I wanted to turn around, find that man, and send a lethal current through his system. Yes, execution style.

"He would sell their body parts to people who used them in dark rituals."

"Trash," Lifted said.

"This is Lagos," was all I could say.

"Let's stay focused," Ejii whispered.

Ejii stopped walking and looked back. I turned with her. "You see him?" I asked.

"Yep," she said. "Clearly. To his very cell." She ran off.

"Go," Arif said to me. "We'll wait."

I ran after her.

We almost lost him in the crowd. Almost. She grabbed his arm. He turned, stunned and ready to strike back. If he'd laid a hand on her, or even tried, I'd have smashed his face in the way someone should have long ago.

His mouth hung open, his jaw slack. He stared into her eyes. The look on her face was cold and harsh. Tears welled in his eyes. His shoulders curled. He held his belly as if he'd been angrily punched there. His face collapsed into deep deep sobs. Ejii let go.

"Come on," she said, turning away from the man.

Ritual killings of children had been a problem in Nigeria for decades. Poor children snatched off the street, not to be made slaves but to be brutally murdered, often to have eyes and ears removed, sold to the insanely evil medicine men and women, performers of dark arts. I should have kicked him while he was down.

CHAPTER 22

Freak House

Before we got to the hotel, someone tried to sell us a toilet bowl, a sewing machine, a people-to-people, a can of fuel, hair extensions, a broken capture station, strange-looking mushrooms, and a bag of bootleg bush hoppers. Jollof was nearly hit by two scooters that zoomed down the busy sidewalk. They had their handlebars turned inward, adapted for such tight squeezes. Lifted almost used her light to kill an overly aggressive man who thought she was the most beautiful woman he'd ever seen. Fadio almost got into a fight with a group of area guys who wouldn't shut up about his long wavy hair. And we'd had to make our way around three street fights.

When we reached the small but clean hotel, there was no one behind the counter. Or so we thought . . . until he seemed to materialize right before us. A disappearer. Now we knew why Eyeglass had so eagerly recommended this hotel.

"Welcome," he said.

We got two rooms. Lifted, Ejii, and Jollof in one and me, Fadio, and Arif in another.

"Plantain will be okay here?" I asked Ejii as we took the elevator to the seventh floor.

Ejii nodded. "She says there's a safe spontaneous forest

about a mile from here where she can stay," she said. "Kola
will stay with her."

It was a good idea. If we needed them or they needed us,
Kola and I could communicate no matter where they were.

"Still, I hope no one tries to steal her when they see her
walking alone," I said.

"Once, someone tried to steal her when I'd stopped for
some direction in a town in Chad. She whistled so loudly
that the men's ears started to bleed. She headbutted another
guy in the chest. He was still unconscious when we left."

Dikéogu laughed. "Your peaceful bird did that?"

"She's peaceful until there's a reason not to be," Ejii said.

The rooms were plain but nice. And we had a balcony.
Thank God. If we hadn't, I had planned to go stay with Plantain and Kola. You think I'm kidding? Then even this far in
the story, you don't know or understand me. The stars are
more of a comfort to me than any bed or pillow. Haven't you
been paying attention?

―――

The hotel was full of visiting Changed Ones. It was a real
freak house. And I say that with love. I'd never seen so many
of us. Windseekers, rainmakers, disappearers, metalworkers,
shadow speakers, shapeshifters, growers, mindreaders. There
was a woman who could see through walls and a man who
could walk through walls. The best thing was that there was
an unspoken agreement. People respected one another. The
man who could walk through walls didn't go around stealing
people's things. The mindreaders stayed out of people's heads

as much as they could. Stuff like that. Of course, most of these people weren't very skilled with their abilities. So there were slips, spills, and accidents. Whatever.

Most of those here were under twenty-five, as most of the Changed were young, born that way. The thing is, none of these people were on vacation. Everyone here was basically hiding. Hiding until the day after tomorrow. Arif and I learned most of this by hanging around the lobby talking to folks.

Fadio refused to come down. "I'm fine up here," was all he said. An old cat always keeps his spots, as my father used to say. Fadio's baby brother had been one of the Changed, he'd just traveled hundreds of miles with four of the Changed, he'd seen terrible things happen to innocent people who happened to be Changed, he knew it was all wrong and wanted to stop it . . . yet and still, he remained prejudiced against us. In a way, I forgive him. It's just what he is. But in a way I don't. No one is "just" anything. At some point, we all make a choice. Lifted, Ejii, and Jollof were in their room having some deep discussion. Lifted and Jollof were holding Ejii's hands and Ejii wouldn't look at us. Arif and I left them alone.

The lobby was full of people drinking palm wine, beer, Fanta, and juice, but mostly beer. Arif and I sat kind of to the side and just listened to people. It was best this way. I didn't need anyone recognizing my face and Arif didn't need to get in any altercations with drunk Changed. Not with his wild and angry shadows. Everyone in the lobby was talking about the same thing. "I think if they kill Dieuri, we all gonna die," we overheard a windseeker woman say.

"Oh, please," another woman said. "What sense does that make?"

The windseeker shrugged. "Just seems possible, the way things are."

"Well, whatever happens, you can believe you won't find me anywhere *near* the arena," a young man said. Several grunted in agreement. I didn't blame them. Once a mob got a taste for blood, that taste only intensified. A group of men spoke in hushed Arabic near a corner. Arif had his head tilted in their direction as he listened intently.

"What are they saying?" I mouthed.

"Shhh," he said, frowning.

I sucked my teeth and looked away. I met the heavily made-up eyes of a shadow-speaker woman. She was wearing a very tight red European-style dress, and though I couldn't see her feet, I was sure she was wearing heels. She looked Igbo. *Ah ah, could she be any less discreet about why she's here?* I thought. She smirked at me and winked. I shook my head and looked away. Last thing I needed was to look into the eyes of a lady-of-the-night shadow speaker. Of course I'd have nothing to do with that kind of woman in the first place, but imagine what one who's a shadow speaker could do!

Suddenly Arif got up. "Stay here," he said. He walked over to the Arabic-speaking men and seemed to introduce himself. I wanted to really pay attention to Arif's shady-looking conversation, but then that shadow-speaker sex worker had the nerve to come to my table. She couldn't have been older than twenty and was probably closer to seventeen. *Ugh,* I thought. *Lagos.*

"What's your name?" she asked in Igbo, her voice sultry, her head blocking my view of Arif and the three men.

"Nobody to you," I replied, annoyed and moving to the side to see.

Nothing seemed to deter her. Not my refusal to look into her eyes, nor my obvious lack of interest.

After several minutes of attempting small talk, she got frustrated. "What is wrong with you?"

I looked away from Arif and actually looked at her, though not in her eyes. "What's wrong with me?" I laughed. "I'm not the one throwing myself at some random guy!"

"A girl's got to . . ." She blinked and then stared at me. She cocked her head.

"Don't say it," I growled.

"But you . . ."

"Yes."

"But they said you were dead."

"My parents say a lot of camelshit."

She sat back, a big grin on her face. "I used to pretend you were my little brother. I wanted your parents to be my parents so bad. Wow, I don't know how I didn't recognize you sooner."

I shrugged.

She sat back, her entire body language shifting. She was no longer on the job. I relaxed a bit. "You going to go tomorrow?" she asked.

"Are you?"

"What? So they can kill me after they kill Dieuri?" She waved a hand. "I won't even be near the place." She turned her gaze back to me.

"I'm not going to look you in the eye," I said. "I have a

close friend who's a shadow speaker. I know what you people
are capable of."

"Relax," she said. "I'm not a prostitute. I'm a fortune-teller.
I just want to tell your fortune."

I laughed loudly. She was totally lying. She was too flirty
to be just a fortune-teller. "Listen, girlie," I said. "I wasn't born
yesterday."

She smiled big. She knew she was caught. "Okay, well,
right now, I just want to tell your fortune."

"I don't have money to spend on something I'll eventually find out anyway," I said.

She humphed and rolled her eyes. She had lipstick on her
teeth. I chuckled, glancing over at Arif. He was still in deep
discussion with the three men. They all looked so serious.

"So you're going to go, I assume," she asked after a moment. "To meet up with your parents?"

I frowned at her. "Look, I'm not here to do *anything*."

"Now who's lying?" she said, laughing.

I started to get up. The last thing I needed was to have
some idiot lady running to the press or, worse, my parents, to
tell them that I was alive and in town. She grabbed my hand
and an image of sweet-smelling flowers flew through my head.
I sat down. Thankfully, she meant me no harm.

"Relax," she said.

"Don't do that to me again," I snapped.

She looked around and then looked right at me. "I can't
understand the shadows very well. But they pointed you out
to me. That's why I came over. I thought they were telling me
you'd offer me a lot of money. Now that I see who you are, I
realize they pointed me to you for a different reason."

One of the men Arif was talking to took out a pen and drew something on a piece of paper for Arif. It was hard to listen to this woman and pay attention to Arif's conversation at the same time. "Huh?" I said to her, watching Arif.

"There's a place," she said. "They're calling it Atlantis. I hear it really is the real deal."

I grunted, barely listening.

"It's where many Changed are fleeing to. It's where Dieuri has been staying."

That got my attention. "Huh?" I said, this time looking into her eyes. For a moment, she held me with them and I saw a large green island.

"It's where Dieuri has been living," she said. "And it's where I hear his great laboratory is. People are saying he's created something that will bring the Lord Jesus Christ back to the world." She was earnest in her words. I rubbed my temples. The woman was talking nonsense. Jesus had nothing to do with this. Nigerians always mixed religion into things at the most inappropriate times.

"You don't believe me?"

"No," I said.

"I've been there."

"Where?"

"Atlantis," she said. "I lived there for months. It's beautiful. Stone buildings, humans and Changed living side by side in peace, plenty of food . . ."

I sighed loudly and rolled my eyes. "So why'd you leave?"

She laughed. "I'm a city girl. There's a fortune to be made here in Lagos for girls like me."

Okay, that sounded rational and pretty honest. "Atlantis, though?"

"I know, it sounds bizarre, but what's bizarre these days, really? Forget the name of the place. Fact is, a huge island has risen out of the sea just off of the Nigerian coast. And amazing things are happening on it." She leaned forward and lowered her voice. "But look, if you can, if you are not here alone, if you are here with some powerful eager friends who have an agenda, *save Dieuri. Biko*, please, save him, *o*! The only reason he came to Lagos was because the Ooni chief extended an invitation to discuss peace. It was a lie, a trap. Free Dieuri so he can finish his work."

I just stared at her. I mean, one minute she was a prostitute, the next she was talking irrational nonsense about Dieuri bringing Jesus back, and then she was convincingly begging me to do what I'd just traveled across the Sahara to do.

"W . . . where is this Atlantis place?" I asked, trying to sound like I didn't care.

"He will show you, if you free him, I'm sure," she said. "Those who don't know speak of a great wasteland off the coast, where the water suddenly dries up. Where everything ends. Those people have no idea. Please, save that man! I saw him fly by once . . . there can be nothing evil about someone like that."

She had tears in her eyes as she abruptly got up and left me sitting there. Her words connected well with what the Desert Magician said. Maybe this was why we were to find Dieuri. But Atlantis? Sounded like something out of one of those Indian animated films.

"Ugh," I mumbled. "Shadow speakers are such a weird bunch."

Arif came back over.

"Well?" I asked. "What was so urgent that . . ."

He waved a hand. "Just some guys talking about selling some upgraded people-to-people devices at the Dieuri execution tomorrow. Two of them are disappearers and one is a windseeker. They wanted me to join them. Even wrote out the potential profit numbers, hoping to convince me."

I'd learned more from a young fortune-telling sex worker than he'd learned from a group of well-dressed businessmen. Not for the first or last time, I needed to realign my way of thinking.

That night, we all stayed up for a bit talking. I told them about what the woman had said about a so-called Atlantis, and Lifted corroborated the story, saying that she'd heard someone speaking about such a place, too.

"Well, we need to free him first," Ejii said. We all agreed.

I knew the city and the location of Dieuri's so-called execution best. The Mobolaji Johnson Arena on Lagos Island. I used the back of a brochure to draw a diagram of the place. Soon, we had a plan. A shaky plan, but a plan nonetheless.

CHAPTER 23

The Very Old Man with Enormous Wings

"**Some of these people are** going to have to die," Lifted said.

We were just outside the arena in the parking lot. It was our last chance to really talk without being within earshot of anyone. We had about an hour.

"No," Ejii snapped. "I *told* you I can do this."

"Ejii," I said. "Be realistic. Look at all these people. And you know the chief will have his soldiers in there, too."

Jollof nodded. "He will," Jollof said. "He's been waiting to catch this guy since his root workers mentioned his name."

"If Ejii says she can do this, then we have to trust her," Arif said. "That's the plan."

"I'm just saying," Lifted said. "There are a ton of people in there. And none of them want to see this man freed. I've seen you use your gift many times now. But this is a lot of people we're talking about. And you have to hold back every single one."

"We'll do our best, Ejii," I added.

"Oh, and Lifted's light is such a delicate instrument," Ejii hissed. "What if it touches a child? What if as it's hitting oncoming soldiers and police it washes over a big group of people behind or beside them? Are you guys *really* ready to watch fifty innocent people die?"

"I can control the intensity," Lifted angrily said. "I can just make people sick, too."

"Not always," Ejii said. "Not when you're scared for your life or super upset or being attacked. Remember that startled desert fox?"

Lifted kissed her teeth. She had taken tons of lives, but she'd wept when she'd accidentally killed the furry creature that startled her in the night.

Fadio shook his head. "Ejii, which do you want? A few people dead, or millions in some huge war of the worlds?" he paused, frowning. "How would Jaa have handled this?"

Ejii laughed cruelly. "You mean the woman who chopped off our father's head?"

"Ejii!" I said.

Pause.

Fadio held a hand up at me and I quieted. "I've had a lot to consider in the last six months . . ." He swallowed. ". . . since my little brother's birth. Jaa did it right before us, yes. You and I watched our father beheaded. Our father who would have probably eventually seen to a smaller version of what the chief is doing. He'd have seen the Changed disposed of in some way. He'd have made it happen. Jaa did what she had to do. For the greater good. No hesitation." He paused. "Shouldering these kinds of burdens is the job of leaders."

Wow. A complete one-eighty. And who would know Ejii's father's mind better than Fadio, who had been a smaller version of him for so long?

"No," she said after a moment's thought. "I've walked in

her shoes. They fit, Fadio. They fit too well." She paused. "You all need to trust me on this. Just give me a chance. I'll do it so that we make it *peacefully* to Dieuri, free the man, and escape before anyone knows what's happening."

———

The parking lot was packed with camels, scooters, and people drinking beer, palm wine, and that mystic mango juice and smoking cigarettes and *gbana*. It was all the atmosphere needed, a bunch of drunk and high people. You could feel the charge in the air. The thought that the arena would be packed to capacity nauseated me. The Mobolaji Johnson Arena could hold thousands.

The military was out in full force. This didn't set me much at ease. They looked scared or nervous. And all of them, surprisingly enough, had seed shooters. When did the damn things get so popular? Probably when Chief Ette decided to get involved with the Nigerian government. Let's see how that was going to upset the balance of what was left of Africa. Seed shooters, the new gun. What really didn't help was that *all* the military soldiers were male.

In the large milling parking-lot mob, you didn't see one obvious Changed. If there were any, they were incognito, as Ejii, Arif, Jollof, and I were. Ejii and Arif both wore sunglasses. It was a very sunny late afternoon, not a cloud in the sky, so they weren't the only ones. My facial tattoos brought a few stares but nothing more. Plenty of Yoruba and Hausa people had tribal markings.

One of the books I read in Tumaki's library was about the

United States of America decades ago when the country was having so many problems accepting their African citizens. They used to snatch up these people, and hang them by their necks until they were dead. Lynchings. It was "jungle justice" in a land of no jungles. I'm not sure which is worse, having your head chopped off or being hung by your neck until you died from suffocation. For some reason, this place had the feel of what I imagined the Ku Klux Klan rallies from America used to have.

There were dozens of vendors selling suya, boiled eggs, akara, small bags of peanuts, cashews and orange juice, oranges, fried plantain. Most of the sellers were girls. I always wondered how they could carry their foodstuffs on their heads, navigate the camels, donkeys, scooters, and cars, and quickly count money at the same time. Some had set up alongside the road, selling more elaborate meals like ikokore and jollof rice.

There was a general overabundance of birds hanging around. Tons of hawks and eagles circling in the sky. A flock of noisy pigeons milling about in the rafters. Several snowy egrets standing on top of cars and camels. The few trees in the area were heavy with birds! Those doves that laugh all the time, some blue-purple white-eyed birds, owls, green parrots, all were milling about at the roof of the arena.

Kola, who'd maintained her distance above, landed in one of the trees, and the cheeping, cooing, whistling, cackling, tweeting, head nodding, beak clicking, and wing flapping increased.

"Does anyone even notice the birds?" I asked.

"People are preoccupied," Arif said.

You could hear the noise of a ton of people inside the arena.

"Yeah, they're focused on something with much bigger wings," Ejii said.

I'd been to this arena once, when my father took me to a soccer game during a visit to our house in Lagos. The arena was a big place, though not so well kept. Like many places owned by the government, it was slowly falling apart from a lack of regular maintenance. The Nigerian government was always putting money into great big projects and then forgetting it had to later maintain the damn things. Look at the city of Abuja. Perfect example. Of course, the overabundance of spontaneous forests popping up there didn't help, either.

We had to elbow our way into the arena. The perimeter of the soccer field was surrounded by more skittish-looking soldiers, all toting seed shooters and all still male. *Someone is stupid as hell,* I thought. I remembered the two female N.B.I. agents back in Niger, who could not only shoot straight but could handle themselves like warriors even without the seed shooters. Discriminating against women remained one of the dumbest practices ever.

A stage was set up in the center of the soccer field. All around it, high curtains hid what was probably Dieuri strapped to some stupid apparatus of torture. I felt like I'd entered one of those ancient Roman arenas where they killed people and animals in front of a slobbering mob. There were no seats left, which suited me fine. You didn't sit down amongst people riled up like this.

"I hope they kill that king of cockroaches, prince of disease," a man spat to no one in particular.

"Cockroach go see peppa today," another man said beside him. They both laughed and slapped and grasped hands. Everyone was in good evil spirits.

We'd come such a long way. What we wanted was on that stage. All we had to do was act now. We settled in our seats and waited for seven o'clock p.m.

━━━━━

The sun set. The lights came on.

On the hour, a gong sounded seven times. The audience quieted down, everyone looking to the stage. Nothing happened. Nothing happened for another two hours. We should have known. Everyone should have known. African Time. These were different times, but some things will never change.

As time passed, people went to go get something to eat or stretch their legs. So we were able to move closer and closer to the front. Now we were only two rows away. It would have been stupid to risk it, but no one ever said that Fadio wasn't sometimes stupid.

"Dammit," Fadio said, getting up. "I've gotta eat something."

We all looked at him.

"Can you get me some . . . uh, jollof rice?" Jollof finally asked.

We all burst out laughing. A mix of hunger, fear, and two hours of anticipation will make anyone a little giddy. Fadio wasn't gone for two minutes when the arena lights went off, putting the crowd in darkness.

"Prepare to witness history," a deep female voice said, echoing around the arena. My mother. I shivered, remember-

ing this very voice so much softer, less mean, telling me stories at bedtime and nagging me to do my homework. All
before the lightning began to strike.

"He was born Jean-Pierre Toussaint in the affluent hills
of Pétion-Ville, Haiti. Yes, people, this man was born with a
silver spoon in his mouth. Both his parents were engineers
who graduated from the American school of MIT. His parents spent winters in Boston and summers in Pétion-Ville.
Young Dieuri lived year-round in Haiti, spending winters
with his mother's parents in their large house.

"These two elders had an affinity for sorcery, black magic,
witchcraft. Imagine this man's twisted upbringing of science
and the mystical. You see how it all began? Young Dieuri
eventually attended MIT and studied engineering and physics like his mother and father. And he too began to live in
two places.

"'Evil genius' is too kind of a description. For his doctoral
dissertation, the man created the very microprocessor that
causes e-legbas to continue to be able to pick up signals from
across this strange Earth. He also claimed that it could pick
up signals from other places. An *evil* device that could com-
mune with maybe even hell itself."

People in the audience whispered and kissed their teeth
and grumbled. It was camelshit. I rolled my eyes. Where she
was embellishing was obvious, as was where she was flat-out
lying. But parts of this story must have been true. I wondered
how she'd gotten this information. Maybe she'd forced it out
of Dieuri.

"Those who knew him were not surprised when the man
later became a terrorist," she said sharply. You could feel the

audience surge with energy at her words now. "With his *terrorist* organization and his *terrorist* thoughts and his *terrorist* actions, he became a great threat to the world!" The sound of her kissing her teeth echoed through the arena. "He was an *anarchist*, a god of chaos. He wasn't concerned with all the recent strange phenomena that were happening. Anyone remember the talking baboons?"

The audience practically shouted assent. "Yes," she said. "Animals suddenly speaking, evil things happening, then you had climate change, heat waves, the floods, drought, famine, islands and coastlines disappearing. Even his homeland was slowly sinking under water. Maybe that was why he wanted to destroy our Earth. He tried. Oh, he tried. He *almost* succeeded."

No, the nuclear bombs *almost succeeded,* I thought. Were these people crazy? Dumb? Deaf? Blind? Under some sort of really messed-up juju? A lot of these people were the ages of my parents and older. They were *there* when it happened. It *wasn't* Dieuri's Peace Bombs. *Those* kept the Earth intact!

"When the American president and North Korea started posturing, this man couldn't keep out of it. He is the reason our fine Mother Earth is going haywire, for all this evil. He brought Satan back to Earth!"

Everyone burst into cheers. The roar was deafening and I had to close my ears. Shouting, yelling, laughing, jumping, pounding feet, pumping fists, cursing. At the very same moment, the lights came on at full blast, blinding us all. When my eyes adjusted, I looked at the field. The curtain was gone. Cuffed to a grand, rotating metal apparatus was Jean-Pierre

Toussaint, also known as the mad scientist Dieuri. My father stood above him, brandishing what looked like a huge sword.

"Oh Allah," Ejii said from beside me. "He's magnificent."

He was too far for me to see him clearly. He looked to be wearing blue pants and a long blue caftan. And his wings were held down by something, stretching them out to their full length.

"What do you see?" I asked Ejii.

She leaned close to my ear, her lips grazing the tips. I stood very still, trying not to move. I could see Arif looking at me from beside Jollof, clearly annoyed.

"His wings are bound with chains," she said. "His wrists and ankles are cuffed with metal shackles, too. He doesn't look angry or scared." She paused. "Your father is carrying a sword with a jeweled hilt. It looks very very sharp."

"And now, we will vanquish Satan," my mother announced as she strutted onto the stage. Prickling with embarrassment, I looked at Ejii as she took in the sight of my mother in person for the first time. I couldn't tell much from Ejii's expression.

"Look there," Jollof said, pointing below. The soldiers had all turned from the audience to the stage. Even the ones from Ginen. *Shoddy work*, I thought.

"Now," I said.

"But Fadio!" Ejii said.

I got up, as did Arif, Jollof, and Lifted. Lifted was softly glowing as she stood. Arif nearly disappeared as his shadows sprang from him. I brought in a swift breeze and pulled in some clouds. I wanted to be able to bring rain when I needed

it. The sky was already happy with wind and moisture and it
complied with no argument.

"He'll have to find us," I said.

We made it to the wall of the field when two things happened. "Wait! Ejii!" Fadio shouted. I could just barely hear his
voice over all the noise. Only I must have heard, because I
turned just in time to see five men in purple come running
up from behind Fadio. Then, *swip! Swip! Swip!* I specifically
remember hearing that sound exactly three times. My hearing
was so sharp. Maybe it was due to my connection to the sky.
Maybe adrenaline. There was a scream from behind me. When
I turned around, I met Ejii's wide eyes. Jollof stood behind her
a little to the left. Everyone around them was scrambling away.
One arrow stuck out of Jollof's chest, and as she stumbled and
turned around, I saw two more planted in her back.

They knew not to bother with seed shooters. They had
one target and one target only. We'd been so stupid. So focused on rescuing Dieuri that we'd traipsed into an arena full
of Ginenian soldiers and not once considered the fact that
one of the chief's rogue queens was with us. Not once considered that we'd been spotted and followed long ago. Not once
considered that the chief had been giving his soldiers pictures
of Ejii and me, too.

Then the birds started attacking and going nuts. Flying
into the air and diving at soldiers and civilians alike. Angry
as hell. I saw a tiny bee-eater zoom at a soldier and peck at
his face, dangerously close to his eyes. Another soldier was
attacked by a crow. A pelican slammed its body into a woman's head wrap, knocking the woman's black wig off. Then
some hummingbirds started pecking at her bald head.

"Ejii," I shouted. "Do it!"

But Ejii was staring at Jollof.

Jollof was falling. Behind her, Arif's eyes went violet.

"Look out!" I heard Fadio shout. He had been in front of me when the soldiers had come. I whirled around just in time to see it about a foot from my face. Tall, black-brown smooth skin, bald head, white white dress, her fangs bared. She was bent forward, her mouth aiming right for my neck. Then the Adze went shades darker as Arif's shadow came right between her and me.

All this happened in seconds.

His shadow blew a soft breeze against my face and felt like hot damp silk. It smelled like smoke and flowers and dirt. The smell traveled right up my nostrils and suddenly I could taste it, too. And I could hear it whispering its ancient ethereal language.

I will never ever forget that veil of shadow and the shocked Adze's expression as pin-sized pricks of blood began to spread across her face. Arif's shadows were damage personified. Repulsed, I fell backward and scrambled away as the Adze thrashed and screeched in pain, spraying its glowing red blood. There were others coming, too. And Arif's shadows happily took care of them.

Fadio leapt over the now empty bleachers and threw himself over the wall. Lifted and Ejii were already running, too. WHOOSH! Several Adze to my left were there and then were not, blasting away into huge puffs of dust as a sickly yellow-green light shined. Lifted. Her light was a solid yellow beam that burst from her with such intense power that looking at it hurt my head. It was my first time witnessing her in action.

I got to my feet, taking a glance at Jollof's body. She lay between the bleachers, unmoving. Dead. Poor Jollof. She didn't deserve to die like that. Though she must have known. Why didn't she speak up?

I took off.

All I was thinking as I ran was, "Oh my God, oh my God, ohmyGod!!"

You can never understand the terror of such moments until you're wrapped in them. Behind me, Arif and Lifted held off several Adze. Soldiers were running onto the field from all other sides. People were screaming and running and trampling each other, their secret fears of chaos coming true as the birds finally took their anger out on them. I imagined Kola leading them in the attack like a symphony composer. Ejii seemed too stunned by Jollof's death to do what she needed to do to everyone.

As we ran toward the stage, I could see my parents watching us approach. I wished I could see their facial expressions. But why weren't they fleeing? Why weren't the birds attacking them? Two large eagle-like birds seemed to have landed on Dieuri's apparatus. Even with the help of the angry birds, there was no way we were going to get out of this alive. I shoved away these thoughts and concentrated on bringing down the rain and lightning.

I ran faster. *Swip! POW!* A seed from a seed shooter flew by me some feet away and exploded in the grass, leaving an ugly hole. Birds kept falling to the ground as they sacrificed themselves to flying seeds and arrows to assure our safety. Some sort of duck, many pigeons, a falcon.

Arif's shadows extended to the other soldiers, causing

them to stop and cower. The brave ones shot through the shadows. These soldiers were the ones taking down the birds. The Adze had stopped behind us, too. Once they got a taste of the pain Arif could inflict and the shock of death from Lifted, they hesitated.

It seemed like we ran forever. Everything had quieted now. The soldiers. The Adze. The birds stopped attacking. The audience members stopped stampeding, now watching the spectacle, still hoping to see blood, as long as it was not their own. What must they all have thought of those damn Adze? From what we'd heard, the genocide hadn't spread to Nigeria yet, let alone the far south.

When we reached the stage it was nearly silent. Ejii reached it first. She climbed on and exchanged some words with my mother, who was still holding the microphone, covering it with her hand. Then they seemed to start arguing. I couldn't catch any of it. Ejii grabbed my mother's arm, my mother tried to snatch it away. My mother slapped Ejii hard across the face. Ejii didn't let go.

My father, who'd been standing guard over Dieuri, left his post and went striding toward Ejii and my mother. My mother's face had gone slack. I jumped on stage. My father stopped. The shock on his face as he stared at me was delicious. His wide eyes, his mouth hanging open. He stumbled toward me a step, a weak finger pointed at me. With my head of fast-growing, thick reddish-brown dreadlocks. Four years later. The man still instantly recognized me.

"What the hell are you doing here?" he whispered.

"I'm here to free Dieuri," I said, stepping up to him. "You know how us cockroaches stick together." I stood eye to eye with him now. His hair was its usual black (which he dyed; it was really red brown like mine), cut low, his beard and mustache perfectly trimmed; he was the opposite of me with my dreadlocks, unkempt short beard, and red-brown hair. How afraid he looked as thunder rumbled from above. I laughed.

"You don't know what you're doing," he said, glancing at Lifted and Fadio as they climbed on stage. His eye stopped on Arif. "You don't want to get involved. There is a great chief from—"

"Chief Ette?" I asked, looking disgusted. "Yes, we've met. Didn't like him. Would do anything to disrupt any plans he has." I cocked my head. "So, Papa, why the hell did you let Segun do it?"

"Do what?" he asked.

"Ladies and gentlemen," my mother said into her microphone. "Be calm. We have a bit of a . . . situation here." She laughed casually, but looked unsteady. "It seems Mr. Dieuri still has a few . . . terrorist friends."

People in what was left of the audience started to boo and protest. She smiled. "Changed Ones, at that."

The boos grew louder. Some shouted for blood.

"Sell me off!" I hissed to my father. "Uncle Segun sold me off!! Why'd you let it happen?!"

"What?" he asked.

Lifted, Arif, and Fadio ran to Dieuri and were trying to remove his metal chains and cuffs.

"Don't play dumb, Father," I said. "I'm too old for that camelshit."

My father laughed at my words. "You've been running around in the sand, it seems. The term is 'bullshit.'"

I glared at him.

"Douglas, are we still filming?" my mother asked, into her microphone. A man from the far side of the bleachers flashed a white light.

"I heard that that's where you'd gone," my father said.

"Yeah, because you *sent* me there!"

"I didn't *send* you anywhere," he snapped. "You ran away like the little shit you are."

I stared at him. "But Segun . . ."

"You clubbed him over his goddamn head and stole his car, we know," my father said. "He came back looking like shit! There is a warrant out for your arrest! My own son!"

"That's not what happened!" I said.

"Dikéogu," Lifted said sharply. "Help us!"

"That's not what happened," I said, turning and walking away from my father. I quickly turned back around and sent a small but sharp current at him. It zapped his wristwatch. *Plink*, the watch's glass face exploded. "Fuck!" he yelped, and stared at me.

"Jerk," I grumbled.

I was shaking when I got to Dieuri. Was my father lying? Did they really just think I ran away? I had good reason to, with the whole town coming after me for accidentally zapping my neighbor's goats. But then again, my parents hadn't exactly tried to find me. But even if they had, would they have known to look for me all the way in Niger on a cocoa farm? God, it was weird to see his face, though. He looked the same as when I left him.

I looked up. Dieuri. To see him up close was overwhelming. His wings looked bigger than they had when I'd seen him on

my e-legba. And my e-legba didn't translate the intensity of
his face.

"Move fast," he said, in a gruff voice. His accent sounded
slightly French. "You think these people will hold off much
longer?"

I nodded, looking at the sky.

"Don't bring that rain down yet, young man," he said.
"Wet wings are no good for fast flight."

"Understood," was all I could say. "Everyone move back."

Lifted, Arif, and Fadio stepped back.

"Sorry if any of this pains you," I said. "I've never done
this to metal against anyone's skin before."

I sent the current through a link on the chain around his
waist. It turned to rust and the entire chain fell away. The
cloth from his shirt smoked a bit, a brown ring where the
metal had been. At least I hadn't burned his skin. Well,
not yet.

The crowd went wild with rage. I didn't look up to see
what was happening. I moved right on to the cuff on his
wrist. I was as careful as I could be. When it had turned a
reddish orange and looked brittle enough, I said, "You okay?"

He pulled his wrist through the crumbly rust. He grinned.
"Just fine." But the skin on his wrist was quite red.

I quickly did the other cuffs and stood back. Slowly he
got up. When he stretched his wings, I laughed. They were
the biggest wings I'd ever seen. They had to be over fifty feet
in width. As he stretched them, their wind almost knocked
me over. Yet they were silent as the wings of ghost owls. Kola's wings were like that. Even when she took flight, she didn't
make a sound.

Lifted ran to the front of the stage. "Tell them, Ejii!" she shouted. "You didn't want all-out bloodshed. You better make them stop!"

There were audience members running at the stage. Arif's shadows had pulled back and the soldiers began to move forward. The Adze would have been upon them if Lifted hadn't run to the front of the stage.

Ejii grabbed the microphone from my mother. "All of you stop where you are! This woman here is one of the Changed!" She pointed at Lifted. "A . . . a . . . a cockroach to you. She can produce a light that will kill you all where you stand! Stop now!"

Lifted stepped before her. Ejii moved back as Lifted increased her glow and stood before everyone, turning three hundred and sixty degrees for all to see her face.

There had to be a thousand people on the field now. *No way for us to get out of here*, I thought.

People stopped, but then they started moving again. A seed from a seed shooter popped not far from Ejii's feet. My mother was staring, my father looked angry as hell. The seed shooter must have done it. Ejii got really really angry. She pulled Lifted back. Yes, she touched Lifted right when Lifted was glowing. Her hand went right through the light. But . . . she didn't die. Her hands didn't die. There was a darkness around Ejii now. Her shadows or Arif's? I remember days after we escaped from Kwàmfà. One night I saw her sitting with Arif in the desert. Both of them in darkness, their shadows mingled. That was how I knew Ejii still communed with her own shadows. I guess every shadow speaker must.

Now, she sat down. A seed exploded beside her, making a hole in the stage. She didn't react. She opened her eyes wide. Behind me, Dieuri took off in a hail of wind. Then I remember nothing but absolute brightness the color of the ocean.

======

Water blue. Warm and salty. It ebbed and flowed. Ejii swam up to me. "Come out," she whispered.

I blinked. I was standing where I'd been when Ejii did whatever she did. Lifted, Arif, and Fadio were standing where they'd been, too. Only Arif didn't look bewildered. I don't think she'd taken him under at all. Maybe fellow shadow speakers couldn't be taken under like that.

The entire arena was standing there, like statues. Even the birds had fallen out of the sky or were standing dazed. Ejii still sat at the front of the stage, her eyes wide. A dove stood in front of Ejii looking up at her.

"Let's get out of here," Lifted said.

"Do we just pick her up?" Fadio asked, rubbing his face.

"Yes," Arif said. "She can hear us." He paused, looking at Ejii. "She told me she'd done this once before to an entire village that tried to kill her. But in that case, she broke all of their brains. They all convulsed and died."

Wow. I bit my lip and asked what I'm sure Lifted and Fadio wanted to know. "Will these . . ."

Arif shook his head. "She's got better control now."

Something made me look up at the fat clouds waiting to produce rain. Dieuri was circling above with several birds, apparently out of Ejii's range. I hoped Kola was up there, too.

I walked over to my parents. "Can everyone here still hear us?" I asked.

"Yeah," Arif said.

I picked up the microphone and tapped on it. The sound resonated deeply. No one moved. "You people are standing here as if you are brain-dead. It matches the way you have been behaving." I laughed. "From what I have heard about you Lagosians, this is pretty strange for you. You are the last people I'd expect to be manipulated by that goddamn camelshitting asshole of a chief from Ginen!"

Lifted tapped on my shoulder and whispered, "We have to go."

Arif had picked up Ejii and was climbing down the stage.

"Just a minute," I said, putting my hand over the microphone. I turned back to my captive audience. "Do you know what is happening in the Sahara? These Changed Ones you all hate so much, these people, people like me and my friends, and anyone who tries to help or support them are being killed like . . . cockroaches. I know you are all afraid and angry. I know you want things to go back to what they were, but they won't, and we Changed are just *people*, too. Do you remember slavery? The Holocaust? Rwanda? Kosovo? Sudan?"

I paused. They just stood there. But maybe they were hearing me, too.

"My girlfriend . . . the sweetest girl in the world. Kind, smart, ambitious, the chief's people killed her. Right before my eyes. She was nothing but a shell by the time they were through . . ." I was shaking, tears streaming down my face. Lifted had taken my hand and was trying to pull me off the stage. Arif was carrying Ejii through the audience. Fadio was standing on the field looking back and forth between me and Arif, unsure whether to help me or him.

"You support the chief of Ginen, then you are supporting mass murder. Period," I said. "And by the way, I am the son of Chika and Felecia Obidimkpa, the great goddamn Obidimkpa duo, West Africa's bringers of news and entertainment. My name is Dikéogu Obidimkpa and I am *very* much alive. I've never *had* malaria. You ask my parents what the hell happened to me. If my name is too long, simply call me the Stormbringer, because wherever I go, you will most likely see storms soon."

At that, I called on the sky to do what it was waiting to do. Lightning and thunder flashed simultaneously, ushering down a deluge of rain.

Before I jumped off the stage I had one more task. I ran to my mother and whispered in her ear. "Uncle Segun picked me up not far from the house. He sold me to slavers who took me to Niger to work as a slave on the cocoa farms. If you really care, now that you know, you'll have the man punished for his crime."

To my father I said, "If you really cared, you'd leave me be. Don't come after me. And don't be an asshole, tell the truth. Change your fucking message, Papa. The world is changed. You can't stop shit. But my friends and I will do our best."

CHAPTER 24

People are Strange

Dieuri couldn't stop looking at Ejii.

That's what I remember most about the odd moment a half hour after escaping that arena. The five of us had run for minutes and then spotted a crowded bus. We'd bickered and argued about getting on it. Most people had e-legbas. And it was pretty accurate to say that most people had been watching my mother's show live.

"We'll get torn apart if we get on there!" Fadio shouted as I hailed the bus to stop.

"Trust me," I said.

"No!" Fadio snapped. He was sweating heavily, his arm around Ejii's waist as he held her up but tried not to make it obvious. Ejii was pretty alert now, but weak. She'd pulled herself out of it when we were about ten minute away from the arena. Arif and Lifted were watching for anyone coming after us.

"Just shut up or something," I said as the bus stopped. "I know what the hell I'm doing."

People are strange. All hell could be breaking loose live on TV and people will choose to sit and watch the TV to see what happens next as opposed to look around them and see for themselves. Hey, I was the child of news people; I knew *some* things about human nature.

The bus stopped and the door opened. The driver barely glanced at me, an e-legba mounted to the left of the window that he listened to and watched as he drove. And everyone on the bus was the same. Eyes glued to their tiny screens as if Ejii's power had reached them right through their devices. Not one person looked up at us.

Some people sniffed and wept as my mother told the world that Dieuri had escaped and many were dead. And to look at the dead, many of whom had been turned to dust by "that most-lethal Changed One." She ranted and raved about how soldiers managed to kill one of the "terrorists." I had to shut off my e-legba when the camera showed Jollof's dead, still-bleeding body.

"Where?" Arif asked me in a low voice.

I shrugged as I looked outside. "Beach, maybe?"

Ejii shook her head. "Too open."

I glanced out the window and looked in the sky. Just barely, I saw the pinprick that was Dieuri flying high. Kola was with him, too. I didn't need to see her to know this. My connection with her was completely restored. She might as well have been right next to me.

"Well, look at all the buildings and the people out there," Lifted said. She wrinkled her nose. "I hate Lagos."

We ended up getting off minutes later near a spontaneous forest. Across the street were some office buildings and a closed-down gas station.

"You sure this is where you want to get off?" the bus driver asked, his eyes still on his e-legba.

We all said yes. Ejii and Lifted were already standing at the bus door, Arif behind them, then Fadio and then me at the end.

"I'd stay on the other side of the road, then," he said. "That forest is very unnatural." I could hear the broadcast replaying my words before I left the stage and I itched to get the hell off the bus before the guy or anyone else recognized us.

"We'll be fine," I said, pushing Fadio forward. The bus driver opened the door and we piled out. I breathed a sigh of relief when the bus pulled away. We scrambled across the street and walked right into the noisy spontaneous forest. I mean, honestly, it sounded like the place was full of millions of wind-up toys all chattering at the same time. What a racket! I used my e-legba's flashlight and Ejii brought out two tiny but efficient glow lilies. She gave them to Lifted and Fadio while she leaned on Arif.

I could see why people thought this place unnatural and why the office building and gas station across from it looked abandoned as opposed to closed down. As if the owners had just left these businesses, no packing up, no nothing. The forest must have sprung up one night and never left.

Even before we entered, the ground grew occupied with green tree frogs. We had to tread carefully. The last thing you wanted when entering a spontaneous forest was to kill its creatures as you entered. The trees were mangrove-like trees and every single one had a trunk occupied by singing tree frogs.

We walked in silence for several minutes. In my head, Kola spoke to me.

"South is that way," I said, motioning forward. "We keep going and we'll come to a pond. Dieuri and Kola will meet us there."

The muddy forest was full of amphibians, arachnids, crustaceans, and reptiles. Anything that loved moisture. Geckos, frogs, snakes, skinks, crayfish, spiders, pill bugs, crabs, large, small, of every color of the rainbow, not the kind of place I liked to hang out in. They were in the trees. On the ground. In the bushes. If you stopped and stood there for even two minutes, something bug-eyed and wet would start climbing up your leg.

Fadio had it the worst. He kept getting smacked in the face by gliding frogs. They liked his smell. Served him right for always drowning himself in perfumed oils. It was something men from Kwàmfà liked to do. Fadio had kept up with the habit even as we traveled south. He must have stashed ten bottles of the stuff in his things. Arif did it too, but not so much. Anyway, this weird type of gliding frog loved the smell.

We'd be walking and *SMACK* a dark green frog the size of my hand would fly and stick to Fadio's face. Then it would tilt its head to his skin and inhale. I've never seen a frog sniff anything. Some even licked him!

We reached the pond just as something large grunted and slithered into it. Thankfully, I didn't see what it was. The place was busy with mosquitoes, too. *Great,* I thought as I slapped a mosquito that had the nerve to try to bite me on the chin. *All we need is to catch some weird form of malaria to top things off.* More frogs, tiny red crabs, and some kind of wet-looking red lizards hopped, scuttled, and scampered about in the mud. The air here was so humid that my clothes felt like I'd just come out of the water.

Within a minute, Dieuri flew down and landed with a soft squelch. The wind from his wings blew the trees around us, knocking frogs and geckos from their hiding places. Kola landed on my shoulder. She leaned against my cheek.

I took a moment. It was different encountering him free, unshackled. I couldn't believe this was him, Dieuri, the man who changed the world, who basically saved *humanity*. If it weren't for his Peace Bombs, we'd have all been wiped out by the nuclear explosions. As he folded his enormous wings, he said, "I am sorry about your friend."

It was the first moment we had to process Jollof's death. I shuddered a bit as the fact of it settled into me. None of us could find words. He stared at Ejii with great intensity. She still leaned on Arif, but she was looking back at him with an equal scrutiny.

"You are Ejii," he said after a while.

"I am."

"The birds have told me about you."

"Have they?"

He lowered his voice and stepped toward her. "And I know the Old Woman."

Ejii stepped back, frowning. "Really? H . . . how?"

He smiled mysteriously, "She instructed me when I created the Peace Bomb."

"What??" Ejii said, shocked. "How?"

He shook his head and held up a hand. "It's not important now. We have lots to do and there's little time." He looked us all over. "I was ready to die." He sighed, looking sad and very old. "There comes a time when you get so old that you know the war at hand is not yours to fight. That it's for the next generation." He straightened up and stretched out his amazing wings. "This is still true. But apparently this old man still has some things to do." He looked at Ejii. "You," he said. "There's something you must do."

"What?" Ejii asked, quietly, taking another step back.

"Actually, all of you, it's important that you all come to my home on Atlantis." He paused, frowned, and then grumbled something in what must have been Creole. He looked at me. "I hate that name. Sounds silly," he said. He shrugged. "Anyway, the chief, his soldiers, the Nigerian police, and the Adze will be looking for you, and I suspect they will know where you are going. There is a dock not far from here. Follow the road south and you will see it. Wait there. Be quick and keep out of sight."

CHAPTER 25

Atlantis

The dock's fishy smell was making me nauseous. Or maybe it was just exhaustion and hunger.

At any moment, the chief's soldiers could show up. Or the Adze. I don't think any of us cared much, at this point. Come what may. Ejii stood at the very edge, looking out at the water. Who knew what she saw. Arif stood a ways off, looking at the deserted buildings behind us, his black shadows whirling around him. He seemed to be letting them loose more and more. Fadio and Lifted stood on the other side sharing a stick of *gbana*. I stretched out on the dirty wooden floor, listening to the water rush in and out below.

I looked back at Ejii, taking a moment to really think about her. Things had been moving so fast that I hadn't had a chance to think about the kiss we'd shared. If I walked up behind her now and took her hand, she'd probably inundate me with images of terror and then shoot me with her seed shooter. I missed the Ejii I knew from our journey to Ginen. The Ejii who wasn't so spiritually wounded yet. But then again, she'd probably say the same about me, I guess.

I allowed our kiss to flood my mind. Her lips had been soft and warm, she'd had a smile on her face. When she'd looked up at me afterward, in that moment, nothing burdened her. I got up and went to her. She glanced at me and then resumed looking at the horizon.

"I can't see *anything*," she said.

"That doesn't mean nothing's there."

She nodded. "It's funny," she said. "When I was a little girl, I always wanted to come to Lagos."

"Oh yeah?" I said, smiling.

"I knew it was too fast for me," she said. "But everything seemed to happen in Lagos. Celebrities were always making appearances, the greatest variety of Changed came from there, and the weirdest news always came out of there. I figured I'd always be entertained and I'd fit right in."

"In many ways, that's true," I said.

She shook her head and laughed. "No, I was only dreaming. This was when my father controlled my life. Back then, I knew I'd never leave Kwàmfà. Then after Jaa came along, everything in my future pointed to her. Even when I didn't know it." She paused. "Now she's gone. Now my mother's gone . . ."

We were silent.

She leaned close to me. I could feel her breast on my elbow, her warm breath in my ear. Every part of my body crackled like fat in a bonfire. "I've never told anyone this," she whispered in my ear.

"Not even Arif?"

She shook her head.

"Told anyone what?" I asked, feeling lightheaded and suddenly nervous.

She grabbed my arm. I tried to pull away. "No," I hissed. "It's the best way," she said. "She showed this to me."

═══

Then I could smell saffron, red pepper, cardamom, and warmed honey. And I was feeling red silk over my face, over my arms. High-pitched laughter twittered around me like a flock of small birds, birds with sharp beaks made for stabbing. I looked around, I stood in a desert, before a pyramid. The wind blew dust and more of the sweet spicy smell. I inhaled it and felt rejuvenated.

Then I was more Ejii than me. At least in mind . . .

Ejii had many visions of the future, since the Old Woman had opened her up to them. They took her without her permission and they always showed her things that mattered. But this was different. Was this the past, present, or the future? Her visions only took her to the future, as when she fell into people only took her into the past and present.

"*I died a wonderful death,*" a voice said. With each word, blood-red flowers of all shapes and sizes fell to Ejii's feet. "*A warrior's death, Ejii. I had to get out of your way so that you could play. When death comes, embrace it. It will come soon,*" Jaa said. A pile of red flowers was piling before Ejii as Jaa spoke. "*Three hundred trained, armed monsters.*" She chuckled. "*They put my sword to the test.*" She laughed and several small red and yellow canary-like birds flew into the sky. "*Dikéogu's illness is Gambo's. As is the cure.*" Jaa paused. "*Don't fret about me, Ejima-*"

for." Her voice grew harsh with rage. *"But you best kill that chief, that corrupted spirit of the bush."*

———

I came back to myself hearing a sound like the foghorn of a ship. I tried to focus on the water. Had someone come? No. The sound was coming from me. I was groaning, my mouth hanging open, saliva dribbling down the side. I closed my mouth and smacked my lips. My mouth felt dry and cracked.

"'Jii," I slurred. "You 'ave to stop that."

The look on her face sobered me up instantly. I'd never seen her look so nakedly terrified. She glanced at the others and then at me. "I fought like hell to stay alive," she whispered. A rose fell to her feet.

Both our mouths fell open.

"Has that ever . . ."

"No," she said, kneeling down to pick it up. She held it to her nose and then held it to mine. It smelled strong and fresh and felt like silk against my nostrils.

"After all that's happened," she said, "I don't want to die yet." She threw the rose into the water, where it floated. Bobbing up and down, slowly taken out to sea.

"Who said you . . ."

"Didn't you hear what Jaa said? *'When death comes, embrace it. It will come soon.'* I'm afraid to go to this place, Dikéogu."

I couldn't argue with her there. And what was all that business about me being ill? I didn't know what to say. I didn't want to go either. But behind us was only more trouble. If anything, I just wanted to be exactly where I was at that moment. I hesitated and then took her hand. She looked up at me and moved closer, resting her head against my chest as she looked back out at the horizon. Behind us, I could hear the whisper of Arif's shadows. I didn't dare look back.

"Something's coming," Ejii said.

I sighed. And I didn't ask her to tell me what, either. Whatever it was would come regardless. After about a minute, Ejii laughed and let go of my hand. She turned to the others. "Get ready," she said. "He's coming."

"What's so funny?" I asked, despite myself. One minute she's near tears and now she was laughing. That's a woman-thing that continues to confuse me. I mean, was I supposed to be afraid or relieved? Annoyed? I chose to be afraid. Our ride was coming. That meant the journey to what I was sensing to be a horrible end was continuing. I also sensed, as Ejii did, that we were almost to that end.

I grabbed my backpack and then looked around as if there was something else to do. Lifted and Fadio took some remaining puffs from their *gbana* before throwing it in the water, where something large and pink snapped it up. Arif came striding to Ejii and me, a dark look in his eye. He looked at Ejii for too long. She didn't look away. His shadows whirled around her, blowing the hem of her garments, but that was it.

"What is it?" Lifted asked.

"A fishing ship," Ejii said. But she was still smiling. She'd also taken Arif's hand and pulled him closer to her. What was Ejii playing at? What was Arif's problem? Even after all we'd been through, some things still mattered. Like choosing.

Arif met my eyes. There was nothing in them but triumph. Honestly, I didn't know I was competing. I didn't know I *had* competition. Hell, I *didn't* have competition. She'd kissed *me*. But then I thought about the earrings. She still wore them. A fishing ship was coming on the horizon to take us to goddamn Atlantis and this was all that clouded my brain. It would have been refreshing, if I weren't so angry. Still, my moment of normalcy didn't last long. It essentially lasted up to the moment I saw the fishing boat.

I don't know anything about fishing, but to my eye, the boat seemed big enough. I'd bet about thirty people could stand on it without it having any problems. It had a roof made of a shiny, metallic pink cloth, and on the hull in big black block letters, it said, "Mami Wata's Step-Brother." A powerful motor whirred at the back, swiftly bringing the boat right up to the dock.

"So you've made it!" the Desert Magician proclaimed, standing on the very edge of the boat.

I groaned, rubbing my hand over my bushy hair. I was in no mood to deal with this guy or whatever he was. It always seemed to come back to him. The goddamn camelshitty Desert Magician. We are nothing but pawns. I've always felt this way. Even when I was back home, I felt something greater at work. Something that couldn't care less about me as an individual. Something more than part unhinged.

He nimbly hopped off the boat and stood there for a moment staring at us. At least I thought he was staring at us. Who could tell what someone was looking at when he had dreadlocks covering his face? But I had a strong sense that this was what he was doing. And for that moment, I felt a sort of horror. You could feel his sight probing deep into you.

"You should have expected me, the keeper of the crossroads, dweller of borders," he said. "You always need me to grant you access. To translate." He didn't move, slightly leaning forward. "You've lost so much, the five of you," he said. "The princess Jollof made a choice. She was not surprised to meet death." His words touched my ears and heart. It was the first time he'd *ever* sounded completely serious. "When a fire starts from the shrine, no precaution can be possible." He nodded and looked at me. I was sure he was looking at me. I stepped back from his gaze. "Your owl sends greetings."

"She . . . she's with Dieuri, right?" I asked, grappling with the fear bubbling in my belly.

"She sits at his table as we speak. Tearing apart a mouse whose destiny will be different the next time around," he said.

I stood up straighter. "Will you take us to Atlantis, magician?" I asked.

He chuckled. "Doesn't it sound ridiculous? Atlantis. Not far from the Pillars of Heracles, according to the great white man, Plato. The great island containing a great civilization. Of course I will take you. It's not far. Come aboard my ship and rest a bit."

He pointed to Arif. "But you, my boy, come, let us talk first."

We all got on, except for Arif, who walked toward the land to speak privately with the magician.

"Can you hear what they are talking about?" I asked.

"No," Ejii snapped. "My ears aren't like my eyes."

"That's not what I meant," I said.

"I can't read him, either." She seemed panicked and I wasn't sure why. "The magician is like a universe," she said. "If I tried to read him or anyone near him, I think I'd die."

When the magician and Arif returned to the boat, Arif took Ejii's hand and took her to the far side of the boat. They put their heads close together as they talked. Honestly, Arif had always had a kind of nerve that really angered me. He had this habit of not explaining himself and just doing. Even if I stood next to them, I probably wouldn't have heard all they shared. Two shadow speakers together are like having identical twins with organically dueled e-legbas. They communicated on so many levels, you couldn't possibly keep up.

Anyway, what was peculiar was that Arif seemed to shine. In light. No shadows. The sun touched every part of him. I remembered the last time Ejii had met up with the magician. Her shadows hadn't returned to her until we'd left the magician far behind. Maybe it was the same with Arif.

Thank God for at least that.

CHAPTER 26

The Voyage over the Sea

I rubbed my still-aching neck as I watched the Victoria Island skyline disappear. I couldn't help but think that I was moving away from what remained of my normal life. We *were* leaving the land altogether, now. I hadn't left Africa since going to Ginen with Ejii. The boat creaked and bobbed. Thankfully, I felt no sign of seasickness. I wish I could say the same for Fadio. He'd started to feel ill as soon as we moved away from the land.

The magician, who sat at the front of the boat in an elaborately carved throne-like ebony chair with a pink cushion, only snickered to himself. I tapped Fadio on the shoulder. He slowly turned to me. "What?" he said, breathing heavily as he tried not to vomit.

"Here," I said, holding out a kola nut. I always carried a few with me. "Eat it."

"What is it?"

"Kola nut. It's bitter and full of caffeine, but it'll get rid of your seasickness, too."

He took it and popped the whole thing in his mouth. I smiled and waited. His eyes got wide as he worked hard not to spit it out.

"Ugh! Awful!"

"It's an acquired taste," I said, popping half of one in my mouth. I'd be jumping off the walls for eating even that much, but with all that was going on, this was probably a good thing.

"May you be stewed and boiled by a high fever, you son of a dog," Fadio mumbled.

I patted him on the back. "And may the fleas of a thousand camels lodge in your armpit." No one out-curses me.

━━━━━

Three hours later, it was Ejii and Arif who were having problems. Not from seasickness but from something far worse. Fadio was sitting near the magician as he nibbled at another kola nut. The magician was belting out a song that I recognized from one of Tumaki's few books by European authors called *Treasure Island*.

> *"Fifteen men on a dead man's chest*
> *Yo ho ho and a bottle of rum*
> *Drink and the devil had done for the rest*
> *Yo ho ho and a bottle of rum!"*

"My head's pounding like crazy," Arif growled. They'd both sat down on the floor. I sat down with them.

"Mine, too," Ejii whispered, her eyes shut tight. Ejii touched her nose and her hand came away with a droplet of blood. "Don't touch me," she hissed at me, though I hadn't. But I was about to. I got up and moved away from both of them.

"What's wrong with them?" Lifted asked.

"Don't know," I said. Though I thought I did. And what I thought scared me, so I didn't speak of it aloud. When we'd entered Ginen, Ejii had been in a similar state. Then she'd fallen over and died. I gazed over the side of the boat. The water just looked like water. Really deep water. I looked at the horizon and saw nothing. I looked back at Lagos and could still see the coastline. Just barely. Were we traveling into a different place by water? I hadn't felt a change. But Ejii and Arif certainly felt something.

"Do you see it?" Arif asked. He was on his knees looking out toward the horizon. Ejii rolled over and dragged herself to the side of the boat and looked.

"Yeah," she said. "I see it."

They both stared. I moved closer. Lifted held my arm. "Don't," she whispered. "Arif's shadows."

"They can't do anything on the magician's boat," I said, moving closer. If either of them so much as looked at me, I planned to jump away.

"It's a forest," Ejii whispered, staring. "Under the water." She paused. "Oh Allah, that is so strange."

"Describe it," I carefully said. She turned to me and I stepped back. Her eyes were bleeding. So were Arif's.

"Stop the ship!" I shouted at the magician.

"No can do, rainmaker," he said, pausing in his song. "This is a one-way trip."

"Something's killing them!" I said. Beside me, Lifted increased her glow. As if that would do anything to the magician. Fadio came stumbling over.

"What's going on?" he asked, his voice cracking.

"Shadow-speaker's delirium," the magician said, with a laugh. "The Island is part of your Earth, but it is special, as was that plant tower in Ginen that almost blew out Ejii's brain when it spoke to her. Ejii and Arif either live or die now. Ain't no turning back, baby."

I knelt beside them and used my shirt to wipe their bloody tears. Ejii turned back to the horizon. "We've got about a half hour," she said, her voice raspy. "The trees don't stay under water. I . . . I see palm, iroko, monkey bread, eke, and other kinds of trees . . . bushes I can't name."

"She can see farther than I," Arif said. "But I can see that the island is big, very big." He squinted, blood oozing from his eyes. I wiped them. "Behind the trees are stone structures, like a skeleton, plants and bushes for muscle." Blood began to drip from his nose.

"Jesus," Lifted said.

"Lie down," I said. Lifted helped Arif, I helped Ejii.

Fadio held out bottles of water.

"What's the pain like?" I asked.

"In my ears," Arif said. "Pressure. A whooshing sound. And . . . I can hear my shadows singing."

"I hear it . . . too," Ejii said, meeting my eyes. "I hear something."

"Just Arif's shadows," I assured her.

But Arif's shadows singing could only mean something bad. What must it have sounded like? Cicadas? A group of women ululating? Songbirds? Arif's shadows were violent things with a thirst for blood similar to that of the Adze. Definitely not songbirds.

Lifted, Fadio, and I could only huddle there with Ejii and Arif and hope.

Within fifteen minutes, both of them had passed out, and we could all hear the soft whispered singing of Arif's shadows. The magician sang his sea shanty louder, this time in Igbo, easily drowning the shadow song out. Still, the sun shined bright. There was a peak of something green on the horizon and a hint of greenness in the water. Another fifteen minutes later, we could see the island. But I didn't want to look at it. I only wanted to stare into Ejii's bright, revived eyes. Arif had come to minutes after her. I almost cried. Almost. All I could think of were Jaa's words. I hoped that this was the death Jaa had spoken to Ejii about in her vision.

"No," Ejii said, answering my question. "I've died before. That wasn't death."

Why wouldn't she and Arif look each other in the eye? And why the giddy smiles?

"No, that wasn't death," Arif said.

"Well, what was it, then?" I asked.

They met eyes and then looked away, smiling.

I frowned.

"Hard to say," Ejii said as she got up. When Arif got up, he was standing too close to Ejii. And he didn't move away.

I frowned more deeply. I turned to the water.

Within an hour, we were about a mile from the island. We all gathered behind the magician. I scanned the island, looking for dragons, evil masquerades, and slathering bloodthirsty beasts. The magician was the magician. For all I knew, he had brought us to the precipice of Dante's Inferno or maybe his own backyard. All I could see were a lone eagle, what looked like a group of tiny furry black monkeys, and a tree heavy with frolicking green parrots.

You could smell the place, too. Soil, mulch, mud, leaves, stems, it rose from the land like fog. The air was many degrees warmer. You could hear thousands of various beasts singing, chattering, grunting, calling. When we got within a few feet of the bank, I could see hundreds of robust green frogs cavorting at a place where the trees began to emerge from the water. The place was so alive. And healthy. This was still the Earth and this place at least was still okay. Some place was.

CHAPTER 27

Love

The magician brought us up a channel that was free of underwater trees. We stopped about ten yards from the island. I frowned. The water looked deep enough for him to bring us all the way to the land, where we could have just jumped off, nice and dry. Dieuri had landed and was waiting there for us and Kola sat in the tree just above his head. She was pleased and had a full belly. She told me that where we were going was safe.

"You arrive here wet," the magician said. "It'll have you no other way."

"What will?" Lifted asked. She was already taking off her shoes.

"The island," he said.

"Oh, come on," I said. "What'll happen if you just bring us to the land? Or can't Dieuri carry us one by one to dry land?"

The magician wriggled his fingers at me and shook his long long hair. "Ooh, terrible terrible things will happen if you don't arrive baptized in the ocean's fluid, my boy. You really want to find out what those bad things are?" He laughed really hard, stumbling backward. It didn't take much for him to amuse himself. That's how it is when you're nuts, I guess. No point in pressing the issue. The magician wouldn't move the boat. It was hot and humid. If we got wet now, we wouldn't be cold when we got out, but we wouldn't dry either.

"Safe journey," the magician said, suddenly very serious. "The plot thickens. This is the heart of darkness. There is darkness between trees, beneath breasts, under beasts. No light reaches our beating hearts, or any of those things surrounded by our flesh, will, hopes, and strengths. Terrible things will happen here, but remember there is darkness too."

He took Lifted's hand. She froze, looking as if she was trying hard not to snatch her hand from him and bolt. "I am sorry," the magician said.

There was a pause as she stared at him. Then tears pooled in her eyes and she gasped.

"Yet, somehow, you were able to become what you are," he said. "Well done. Your lover, she will live *forever* in your heart." He grasped both of her hands tightly as Lifted's glow flared for just a moment. Lifted reached up, hesitated, and then touched one of his locks. I gasped. But the magician did nothing. He actually allowed it. Wow. I did not know much about Lifted, not more than she'd fleetingly told us, but this moment told me that I wanted to eventually find out.

"Thank you," Lifted whispered.

He stepped over to Ejii, who stepped away from him. "I won't touch you," the magician said, with a chuckle. "Your man, Ahmed, flew into Ginen in search of the chief. He has wanted to kill him since you told him about his words to you and his intent. Yes, an act of stupidity for the sake of love.

Too bad he won't find the chief in Ginen." He paused. "And he'll never make it to the Ooni Palace, either, because in a small market in the town of Kirki he'll be emotionally disarmed by a young windseeker woman named Zahrah."

"H . . . his chi?" Ejii asked, quietly.

Why did she care if he found his chi or not?? What should she have cared? He'd left her.

"Indeed," the magician said. "Time for you all to jump in the water."

I took one last look at him, but he had no words for me. Lifted was the first to dive in. She swam like a fish.

"Can you guys swim?" I asked Ejii, Arif, and Fadio. They were desert people. The only places they had to practice might have been in temporary spontaneous forests, maybe. Arif responded by diving and swimming for land. Ejii hopped in and did a pathetic yet effective doggy paddle. I'd forgotten that these two had spent plenty of time in strange places. Arif had even traveled over oceans.

"Can't swim," Fadio mumbled.

I nodded. "Are you afraid?"

He narrowed his eyes at me.

"Take my arm, then," I said. "I'm a good swimmer. Just don't get all spooked and grab my head and drag me down or anything. Just let yourself float."

The others were too busy swimming to see him take my arm. We jumped in. The water was warm. Fadio didn't panic, thank goodness. He allowed himself to float quite well. When we got to land, neither of us spoke of his inability. Kola flew to my shoulder as we joined the others at a small house made of heavy white stone. It looked ancient and there was dried seaweed stuck to its walls. Kola touched my cheek with her beak as she hooted softly.

"So . . . this . . . is . . . Atlantis," Ejii asked, out of breath and sitting on a stone bench. She tried to pull her soaked clothes around her. It had no effect on what she was trying to hide. It was the same for Lifted, though she didn't seem bothered by the transparency of her wet clothes. Lifted wasn't from an Islamic-influenced culture, and she wasn't timid about her body.

I averted my eyes. I had to kick Arif to get him to do the same.

"Have some respect," I whispered. "Fadio!" He'd been practically leering at Lifted. As if they'd never seen naked women before! Honestly, I think cultures that make the strongest rules of modesty are the ones where people freak out when someone is naked or near naked in some way. Because they aren't *used* to it. Even Arif and Fadio, whom I know have both been with plenty of women.

"Is everyone okay?" Dieuri asked, but he was looking at Ejii and Arif.

"Now we are," Ejii said, her arms wrapped around her chest.

He nodded. "This place attracts the Changed and their families and friends. For the last two years, it's been happening."

"Like Kwàmfà," Ejii said. "That's my town. Where Jaa was from."

"I've heard of Jaa." When Ejii said nothing else, he said, "The Ginenians would hate this place."

We all nodded. We knew. And we knew what was in store for this place if it was discovered by them.

"But something about this place is potent," he said. "It is Earth, but . . ." He glanced at Ejii. "The waters around this place are heavy with the bodies of suicidal shadow speakers."

"Why didn't you say something before we traveled?!" I nearly shouted.

"Because, at this point, *mon garçon*, it is sink or swim," he said. "The Desert Magician says that Ejii needs to be here. We all know what is at stake. I am prepared to sacrifice. I assume you are too. Plus, you five . . . strong, strong kids. This girl, Ejii, amazing." He made eye contact with Arif. Neither looked away. "*You* are scary."

"So are you," Arif retorted, his freshly returned shadows darting threateningly at Dieuri.

He nodded and grinned. "Granted." He paused as he looked at the sky. "I'll take you each to my home. You first," he said to Ejii.

CHAPTER 28

Hang On

I swear, I wasn't sure if he'd return after he took Ejii. We'd all looked at each other when he said she should go first. After all, he'd said that she specifically had something important to do on Atlantis. Maybe he needed her to complete something he was working on. Who knew? But sometimes you just have to put faith in the hands of what will be.

"Hang on tightly," he said after Ejii climbed on his back. He laughed. "But I still need to breathe." She loosened her arms around his neck a bit and they took off. It was about a half hour before he returned. Then he took Fadio. Then he took Lifted.

"When he comes back," Arif said as we watched them fly off, "he'll take you. Then you'll never see me again."

"Huh?" I said, looking at him. "What do . . . ?"

He shook his head as he looked at his hands. "Or maybe the magician is making trouble again."

"I don't follow you," I said, confused.

"The Desert Magician, he told me that Dieuri doesn't want me on this island . . . because of my shadows and the way they behave. He thinks I'm corrupted."

I opened my mouth and then closed it. Arif's shadows had their issues and sometimes they behaved just plain evilly. But then again, sometimes they saved one's life, as they saved mine from the Adze at the arena.

"Then I'll make sure he takes you first," I said.

"So he can drop me when we get high enough?"

He had a point.

"Sometimes . . ." he started to say. Then the air around us grew darker as his shadows pressed in.

Several moments passed with him just standing there, looking down, his shadows looming over us like that. I grew apprehensive. "Arif," I said. "What are they doing?"

He suddenly looked me dead in the eye with a naked expression of shock. "You're cursed, too," he whispered.

"What?!" I said, stepping away from him.

But Arif was listening to his shadows. "They tell me . . ." He gasped. "I know what you did."

He spoke those words slowly, deliberately, coaxingly. My belly sank, though I had no idea what he was talking about. Not consciously. There was a flash in the back of my head. I saw a boy. Brown-skinned, but I couldn't quite see his face. Then it was gone.

Arif was staring at me with his deep violet eyes. Another image. Again, the boy whose face I couldn't see, and there was wind, too. I was remembering. A memory from the blank year. A memory I'd buried very very deep. For a reason. It was a terrible memory. It seeped back into my consciousness like bitter rancid water. I sank to my knees.

Here's how it came to me. *There was a hill with a dead tree at its top. I was wearing new clothes and new leather sandals. I came up this hill and stood beside the dead tree. I knocked on its dry wood and picked and crumpled a long dry leaf that still clung*

*to a dry branch. I savored the crackle that reminded me of fire,
static, or a tendril of lightning. There was noise from nearby. A
small dry town, just down the hill. I'd come to see what it was all
about.*

Arif was watching me as it began to come faster and
faster, and I gazed back at him, lost in his eyes. Glowing violet and around him whispering darkness. His shadows were
heavy upon us both.

"This is what they tell me," Arif said.

"I don't want to know," I gasped. But I already knew. I'd
known all this time. He brought forth my memories faster. It
was like freeing a ghost or a demon.

*There was a crowd gathered around another dead tree. Hang-
ing limply from a rope tied to a tree was a boy in blue. They were
throwing stones at him. A little boy. Maybe he was about six years
old. He had long clumps of hair, dreadlocks. I knew there were
seven of them. I knew why there seemed to be a distraught wind
hovering around the tree and the angry people. He was a windseeker.*

A horrible rage flew through me.

It filled me with heat and destruction.

It blew away all rational thought.

I called up a terrible tornado.

*I should have done this to the town of Timia where Tumaki had
been killed.*

But I would do it now, this time.

*I swept away **all** those people.*

I didn't even know what that boy had done.

But what could he have done that would warrant being hung?

I swept them away.

"I couldn't see his face," I whispered. I swallowed this truth about myself. It was something Gambo had taught me and that I should have used when Tumaki was killed. It was something I'd been doing since I'd returned to myself after the lost year. Haven't you wondered how I was able to keep going as bad thing after bad thing happened?

"Swallow grief, swallow pain, swallow anguish," Gambo had said. "Then hold it deep inside you as you keep it still and examine it. Then you make it a part of you. If you do not do this immediately, you will be consumed by it."

So I swallowed it. But this memory, this grief, didn't sit so well. I felt it deep within myself. Everything shuddered for a moment as I fought to hold together. Slavery, death, Tumaki, the lost year, Kwàmfà, my parents. Something unfastened deep within me. But I held strong. We were all damaged. Dangerous even. I stood up and straightened my shoulders and looked Arif in the eye. "We are good people," I said. I believed this.

Arif's eyebrows creased and a look of such vulnerability passed over his face. "Are we?" he asked.

I swear, if I had said he was not, right then and there, he'd have picked up a stick and plunged it through his heart or found some other way to instantly kill himself. He'd reached the end of his rope.

"We are," I assured him. "We make him take us both."

Dieuri arrived a few minutes later. "I'll take you next," he said to me.

"You'll take Arif and then me," I said.

He shot a look at Arif and then at me. Neither Arif nor I said a word, but we spoke with the way we held our shoulders straight and stood close to each other.

"If you don't take him, I won't go," I said. "Then you can explain to Ejii what happened to Arif and me and watch her not believe you." As I spoke, I could feel my memory of wiping out an entire town nagging at me, trying to push all else out of its way and force me to dwell only on it. I took a deep breath, as Dieuri scrutinized us both with his gaze.

"Come, then."

As he flew off with Arif, I prayed that I understood the man's body language well enough. Otherwise I'd never see Arif again.

CHAPTER 29

The Cloud Forest

"**I know what my old** mind tells me," Dieuri said. "Your co-husband is only trouble."

"Stop calling him that," I snapped. We flew high above the trees, though there was no reason to. I wondered if Dieuri was trying to scare me. Little did he know I had no fear of heights. My time with Gambo took care of that. I looked down at the dense forest. We'd recently passed over a large town of skeletal stone buildings and some newer wooden houses. The material for the stone buildings had to have already been there. How else would they have gotten it in the middle of jungle like this? Dieuri said it was a community of humans and Changed, similar to Kwàmfà.

"You stuck your neck out for him, even though you both love the same woman," he said. "What else is he to you if not a co-husband?"

I sucked my teeth. Some conversations weren't worth having.

We passed over another town. This one was even larger. Dieuri flew a little lower. More stone buildings. The architecture of Atlantis, or whatever this place was called, was like water. The thick stone structures weaved and looped into triangles and peaks. The houses and larger buildings that looked to be at least two floors were solid white-gray stone. But they looked like they'd been molded with large yet expert hands.

The skeleton-like stone was decorated with foliage. Vines, grasses, and air plants like orchids grew on the backs, tops, and sides of buildings. Dieuri was right; the people of Ginen would have hated this city of Changed and stone homes, the opposite of their vegetable homes.

Some of the buildings still had dry seaweed and other sea plants on them. Dried and crumbling. It had all obviously been underwater at one time. I wondered what made it rise up.

We came to the end of the city, where the trees grew higher and thicker.

"Look at all those frogs!" I said. The tree top, and probably everything below it, was covered with very large, nearly transparent creatures. Even as we soared past it, I could see so many large haunting yellow eyes.

"Frogs mean healthy land," he said. "You will see many of them here."

"Are they poisonous?" I asked.

"Yes," he said.

It started to rain. The sound of the drops on broad leaves was deafening. I didn't care about getting wet, though it was a little cooler above the trees.

Dieuri flew faster, and below, the forest changed again. A thick cloud seemed to have descended on it, and even after the rain stopped, the air remained humid. The trees seemed to grow shorter. Below, I glimpsed moss and large ferns filling in the gaps between trees and what looked like brightly

colored orchids hanging from tree branches. With the cling-
ing clouds and the closeness of the forest, it felt claustro-
phobic.

We arrived at our destination ten minutes later. The place
was at the top of a sort of high hill. A hill not high enough to
peak above the damn clouds. We circled around it slowly,
three times. I guess he wanted me to get the lay of the land.

The stone structure was shaped like a large mound, the
stone gradually sloping upward and then downward. Like
the back of a scarab beetle. The top of it was smoothest. The
water current must have made it to the shape it was now.

It was also full of large holes, windows with no glass.
Creeping vines with blue bulbous flowers crisscrossed its walls
and moss grew on the north side of the building. There was
something brown and long legged crawling up the mossy
side. It would occasionally stop, pull off some moss and eat
it. Some sort of monkey-type creature. All around the house
was garden. Not a tame garden but a garden nonetheless. You
could tell its growth was guided by human hands. The earth
rose here and there to support various fruit trees and bushes.
Flowers grew in formations too ordered to be a coincidence.
Chaotic but definitely a garden.

When we landed, without giving warning, Kola immediately flew onto my shoulder, her head turning this way and
that, as if she expected something to pounce on us. She let
me know that the place was full of birds. In the trees, on the
ground. We were being watched. I looked up into the cloudy
sky. Indeed, I saw several hawks, eagles, and vultures now
riding the wind in circles.

You could hear all sorts of jungle noises—clicks, creaks,

chirps, whistles, hisses, shrill calls. The winding path that took us from one side of the "garden" to the other finally came to an end right in front of the bone-white stone building. There was a large doorway in the center with no door. A tall brown-skinned woman with short dreadlocks was waiting at the entrance with Ejii, Lifted, Fadio, and Arif. I breathed a sigh of relief. Arif was alive. Dieuri could be trusted, maybe.

I walked up to them. The woman seemed about seventy. I looked past her. More plants and couches, stone floor; something lizard-like ran by.

"Good afternoon," the woman said in Yoruba. Like so many of the Lagosian women, she wore western attire. The knees of her jeans, however, were dirty, and her blue T-shirt looked as if it had been washed many times. Her fingernails had dirt under them. This had to be the gardener.

"Good afternoon," I replied in Yoruba.

"My name is Makeda. I'm Dieuri's wife."

━━━━━━

We spent the night here. I slept outside in the garden. Everyone else slept inside. There were more than enough rooms in there. The place was like a giant beehive made of stone.

It was strange. We had no plan. Dieuri told us nothing. But we all knew that the chief and his soldiers and his Adze and whomever he could muster were on their way to Atlantis. It only took us about an hour or two to cross the water to Atlantis. It couldn't take more than a day to get to Dieuri's home by foot. And maybe they'd be able to fly, too.

It was obvious what was next. Yet we all went to bed that

night without discussing this. Without Dieuri saying what it was Ejii had to do. It was an unspoken plan, I guess. We were going to make a final stand here at his home. I just hoped that whatever he had up his sleeve was enough to get us all through this. So we all went to bed. I think we all carried the chilling thought that this was the last time we'd ever sleep again. We all went to bed . . . except for Ejii and me.

"Dikéogu."

I was lying on my back staring at the stars and wondering what Kola was up to. She'd taken off with an eagle and a hawk and hadn't been back for two hours. I knew she was okay, but her dealings were otherwise hidden from me. "Bird business," was all she told me.

I sat up, all thoughts of Kola moving to the back of my mind. I frowned. "Ejii?" I knew it was her, but why was she wearing her burka?

She came and sat across from me, a glow lily in hand like a peace offering. I couldn't help but think of Tumaki and how she sometimes felt the need to put the damn thing on when she didn't want to be seen. Tumaki's burkas were all navy blue or black. Ejii's was bright yellow. She sat across from me. "Hi," she said.

I kissed my teeth. "Take that thing off," I grumbled. "I really hate those."

Reluctantly, she did so. In the glow of her lily, I could see her puffy eyes. She'd been crying. Oddly, this relieved me. At least now I knew that Ejii still knew *how* to cry. She looked down. "Was thinking about my . . . mother," she said. "After a while . . ." She shook her head. "No amount of training . . ." She pounded a fist on the earth and took a deep breath.

"I know," I said. I reached forward and took her hand. She smiled at me, a tear slipping down her cheek, but that was all.

"You have any idea what he thinks I'm supposed to do?" she asked.

"Nope. And don't ask me about tomorrow, either."

"Doom and gloom," Ejii said. She laughed.

"Whatever it is, I think you're prepared for it," I said.

"Prepared to die?" she asked.

"No."

I took her hand and pulled her over to me.

"Ejii will never die," I said.

We both laughed. She leaned her head on my shoulder. We sat like that for a long time. Listening to the forest. Hearing the breeze. This time she kissed me first. The rest, well, that's for our memories only. As if I'd share that with anyone else.

CHAPTER 30

Defend Yourself

He **started it. I swear** he did. I'd have never gotten into it when there was so much at stake. After the night before, after Ejii and then my dream about Tumaki and then what I knew was coming, I was confused as hell. I didn't have the time or the need or the energy to consider Arif. But he was considering me.

The early morning found Ejii and me in the garden on my mat. She'd gotten up before me, wrapped herself with her wrapper and was sitting straight up, her eyes wide as if she were hearing something loud. When I sat up and found her like this, I frowned and listened. I didn't hear anything. Kola landed beside me and clicked her beak. I immediately knew what she knew.

"Ginen soldiers," I said.

"Now," Ejii asked, grasping the ground and digging her nails into it.

"Yeah," I said, glad that she'd spoken. "What's your problem? What are you hearing?"

She looked to the left. I followed her eyes. Arif stood in the doorway. He turned and left. I cursed, getting up to get Dieuri. But before I went two steps, he landed feet away with Makeda on his back. Lifted came out after hearing all the commotion. Arif eventually came out to the garden, too. He glared at me.

"I'll go down the path," Lifted said. "At least I can hold them off."

"Not without killing all the plants," Makeda snapped.

Lifted shrugged. "Any better course of action?"

"How many?" Makeda asked me.

I looked at Kola. About thirty, she told me. "A lot. Thirty maybe." But I sensed a hesitation in Kola. Not now, she said.

"I'll bring a storm," I said. There was so much moisture in the air and a rainstorm happening not far away. It was easy to ask it to become a storm. "That will slow them down." I stepped away and concentrated. Kola took to the sky. No matter what, my storm would never touch her.

"I will go see, too," Dieuri said. He took off.

"I'm going," Lifted said.

"As I am, too," Makeda said firmly, following her.

"I can control my light," I heard Lifted snap at her. "You don't have to—"

"Not well enough," Makeda said.

Now it was Ejii, me, and Arif. Ejii broke the silence by sitting down and sighing. "I won't have you two fighting while I'm busy dying," she said.

But Arif's shadows were starting to billow from behind him like two giant bat wings. Thunder rumbled from above and I felt the noise deep in my body. If Arif wanted a fight, he would get one. It had been a long time coming. And if he thought I was weaker than him, he was sorely mistaken. I watched his eyes go from violet to glowing violet to a heated black.

I glanced at Ejii and felt a rush of emotion for her. She was the center of my world. Not Arif and his jealousy. Ejii was staring straight ahead again, her shadow-speaker eyes so wide that her pupils were black. The plants and flowers around her leaned in, as if she were some kind of organic magnet. She was swaying. A flash of green came from down the path. Lifted's light. Then I saw the trees undulate and bend forward. This was Makeda's doing. She was sending an attack. The Ginenians were already here.

Then Arif's shadows enveloped me with angry darkness. I fought for my life. I fought for my honor. I fought like hell.

I remembered the living storm. I had met Ejii in the middle of it. The Aejej. It had been full of rage. It swallowed everything. It was wind, sand, heat, anger, and murder. I remembered that well as I took the wind, lightning, and rain from above me and twisted it down to me. I didn't ask its permission. I didn't care about permission. I didn't remember a thing Gambo had taught me. I brought it down on both Arif and me as his shadows raised us both into the air. Away from Ejii, I guess. Maybe he *was* considering her life, even in his madness.

I was angry. I remember little of this. It was like my lost year, except I was aware of what was going on throughout most of this. In a fuzzy way. An offhanded way. In a way where I could do nothing about it. We rose high into the air in a whipping funnel of rain, uprooted trees, debris, soil, black clouds and even blacker roaring shadows.

His shadows pressed in on me as he wrapped his hands around my neck and squeezed. I did the same to him, sending bursts of electricity into him as I did so. I sent my worst. I was like a threatened, irrational electric eel. Burst after burst. His shadows pressed closer to me, rubbing at my skin. The noise was deafening, but it was also fading as I suffered from a lack of oxygen. I squeezed his neck harder. He began coughing. I gagged.

Then she was calling. And calling. Shouting. I don't know what, but it was loud. It was clear through all the noise. I blinked. "Come," I heard Ejii say as if right beside my ear. Her voice was angry, hard and powerful. The voice of a witch. "If I die, you'll die, too," she added.

Then something snatched at my ankle and yanked me toward the ground. I saw Arif falling, too. I was too shocked and terrified to scream. We'd been about thirty feet in the air. I flailed my arms out. I called the wind to catch me. It didn't. I slammed to the ground. I don't remember which part of me hit first, it was so fast. All the air was smashed from my body. I heard something snap as my head whipped back.

Then I was hearing the voice of another, someone very very old and female. "You're a 'shadow speaker,'" she said. "At its core, this means you speak to the shadows. Sight, communication, spirits. You, Ejii, you please me."

"*The Old Woman*," I croaked. I could hear my voice, but I could not feel my body. All was dark. But I knew I wasn't alone. Ejii and Arif were there too. And we were all realizing the very same thing at the same moment. The Old Woman

Ejii had spent a year with wasn't a woman at all. She was the soul of Ginen. Ejii pulled us both deeper into her vision . . .

. . . Ginen's soul was kind. It had let Ejii live with it for a year. It had cured her. And then it had prepared Ejii for this moment without Ejii knowing it. It had not exploded her brain or taken her mind. But it was healthy and old. The Earth's soul was sick and new.

We were all going to die.

Now, bear with my descriptions here, because I don't exactly understand what happened. It doesn't quite make sense. There are gaps. And a lot of this shit was just plain impossible. I will tell it as it was.

Suddenly, it came and Ejii took Arif and me with it. Sights, sounds, smells, touches, and tastes. The fragrance of forests and deserts. Colors and textures swirled. The smoothness of oil and the sharpness of jagged stones and the burn of flames. The taste of sugar and salt. Pleasure and pain. We weren't dead yet.

But it was beautiful like the Whole.

"Allah," Ejii said. Her voice sounded pure as seawater. She was answered with pain.

We all felt it.

The pressure to her head, to her skin, to her mind was practically unbearable.

We all felt it.

She had brought us along. What happened to her happened to Arif and me.

It met her mind.

She willed it as she'd willed the small life out of the

mango seed three years ago. She'd never told me about that. But now I knew. She'd done that. She could do that.

"Come," Ejii said. "Defend yourself."

A burst of rage and a roar of heat.

There was a moment.

Ejii opened her eyes and met Fadio's. "Brother," she whispered. He frowned and his hand tightened around hers. She saw what was about to happen, clear as day, murky as mud. She looked to the side and saw Arif and me. Arif didn't look as bad as me. He just looked like he was sleeping. Maybe his shadows caught him. Most likely. But me? I lay in a shallow ditch. That was how hard I'd fallen. Hard enough to make a ditch in the ground. Why didn't my wind catch me? Punishment? Was this what Gambo had warned me about when he said not to exploit the wind, rain, storms? That it controlled me as much as I controlled it?

You cannot understand how it feels to see your own body, several feet away, looking like camelshit. Looking dead. My nose was bleeding, my body was twisted. I wanted to keep staring, but Ejii turned her head away. Ejii was controlling things. She grabbed Fadio's other hand. A futile attempt to stop what happened next. The ground beneath her trembled. It undulated. It pulled her under. Ripping her from her brother's grasp.

═══════

It did not happen across the Earth. But it happened only on Earth. In those parts that were the Sahara region and parts of West Africa.

Ejii was a witness.

I was a witness.

Arif was a witness.

The Earth made choices.

In some towns, everything crumbled. Things fell apart. The mosque gutted by a group of women from Ginen in a Chadian town called Dinguel instantly crumbled to the ground. It killed five seed-shooter-toting Ginen women inside it, all of whom were responsible for the deaths of many locals. An entire Nigérien town named Zoo Baba sank into the ground, the Sahara sands covering the spot where it used to be. The town had been occupied by ghosts, angry violent men and women willing to sell their souls. Not one child lived here.

There were several places like this. And all were dealt with in a similar fashion.

In many places, a mere person disappeared into the ground. Sometimes a man, sometimes a woman, sometimes neither, sometimes both, only once a child. We saw that this child had been born with an ability to vomit black holes. This child's home was full of them, though they were tiny as the heads of a pin, the biggest being the size of a basketball. The child was five years old and parentless. Her father was dead and, the day before, the basketball-sized hole had swallowed her mother.

In other places, entire Ginenian armies disappeared. Yes, there were armies already claiming parts of Africa. Some were engaged in battle with Earthly folk. Parrots from Agonia, allies of the chief, were swallowed up. And those that were in midair were free to fly home in defeat.

Strange foreign people with silver skin jingled as they sensed what was happening. These people the earth also swallowed. And in these places, the deposits of silver would give the land a strange sheen. And when the air settled, and the breeze blew, the jingle of these people could still be heard. But it was a pleasant sound, not one of war.

Indeed Earth had taken control of itself and its destiny, shrugging off and swallowing the trouble spots that had become like cancers on its being. At the places where it connected to the other places, the Earth imposed its own plants and trees and bushes. It took hold of these places as one would use their hand to take hold of a hand that was roughly grasping their shoulder.

Then it was as if a great eye turned to look at Arif and me. I could feel my body now, though all I could see was black, a swirling vortex. Dancing and zooming shadows. Arif's shadows. No wind. No lightning. All that Ejii had shown me had knocked the fight from my heart. The world was shifting. Right at this moment. The soul of the Earth was gazing upon us. How was Arif still intent on harming me?

Then I knew. I was positive. I tried to scream. But I had no voice. I grabbed at Arif. Pain burst through my left wrist. We locked eyes. The shadows zoomed around us, yet his eyes were violet, no glow illuminating them. He'd lost control of his shadows. He'd lost control of himself. Blackness opened beneath him and he started to sink. He started to sink, o! I felt something already broken in me completely fall apart.

It was enough. Just enough. My parents letting me go, my uncle selling me into slavery, watching Adam die, nearly dying over and over, burning Big Blokkus to death, killing that town, Tumaki, oh my Tumaki, the death of Kwàmfà, Jollof; Ejii and Arif, damaged and powerful. I couldn't let this happen.

My left wrist was broken. But I grabbed him with my right, my stronger arm. But the ground beneath him was opening wide, taking him from the waist up. He shoved me away. Without a word. His face was unreadable. Resolve? Surrender? Sacrifice? Helplessness? Dammit! He didn't speak! He left me with nothing.

Then the shadows were gone. He was gone. The ground was wet. Ejii was pushing herself to her feet. And in front of her, a few yards away, stood a lean, muscular, black-skinned man of about seventeen. He clicked and clacked, his purple short pants and shirt embroidered with what looked like thousands of tiny white cowry shells and black beads arranged in intricate designs. He wore thick white bangles on his wrists.

Chief Ette. I could have wept.

CHAPTER 31

The Chief

The chief's new young face, the face of the son whose body he'd stolen, hardened. His stolen blood still ran hot. He carried two large seed shooters; a machete and a pouch of something hung from his hip. His hands looked as if they had been dipped in yellow-orange curry powder.

I scrambled to my feet and stumbled to join Ejii. She looked at me. I was so tired.

"He's gone," she said. Her face started to crack with grief.

My wrist throbbed, but I could still move it. *Maybe it's not broken*, I thought. *Where are the others?* I grasped her shoulder. "Not now," I said. "Hold, Ejii, hold."

"Not long to go?" she asked, her voice shaking.

"All else has been handled," I said. As we spoke, the chief approached us. He looked only at me.

I met his gaze. I was still seeing through Ejii's eyes a bit, and when my eyes hit the leaf of a nearby palm tree, I saw cells green with circular beads of chloroplasts. Nucleus, vacuole, mitochondria, Golgi complex. I shuddered. Was this what it was like for Ejii? I shut my eyes and took a deep breath. When I opened them, my eyesight was normal.

It wasn't an even match. Ejii was already nearly finished. I weep for her even now as I think about all she suffered. All we all suffered on this adventure to save the Earth from other worlds.

"I don't care what you've done," the chief said to me. He pointed at Ejii but didn't move his eyes toward her. "She must die. If my kingdom is to be safe, her death especially is essential."

"Why me?" Ejii asked.

I was watching his strange hands. His skin was dark dark gleaming brown, except for his hands, which were marigold yellow and looked dry as chalk. *What is that stuff?* I wondered. *And why do my eyes hurt to look at it?* One thing I knew, I wasn't going to let him touch me or Ejii.

"Slave boy, push her over here and let me finish her quietly," he said, ignoring Ejii.

"Ignore her again," I sneered. Suddenly, my wrist didn't seem to hurt at all. Suddenly, I felt fine, full of energy and fire. Everything that had happened retreated, at least for the moment. All I wanted was to take this man's head off. For all he'd caused, all he'd killed. For disrespecting Ejii yet again. For calling me a slave. I was no slave.

He laughed. "Both of you, filthy . . ."

I blasted him with the strongest lightning I could muster. It could kill a dozen elephants, fifty whales. No matter how terrible it was to see Big Blokkus burned to a crisp. This was different. The chief needed to die, and this time even my rational mind agreed. My lightning pushed him back a step or two. That was all. He straightened up, a disgusted angry look on his face. Then a beam of light came from beside Ejii and me. On instinct, Ejii and I ran back.

The chief shielded his face with his arms as he grimaced

with pain . . . but did not die. Lifted walked within feet of him, shining her light at full blast. Her face looked skeletal in the sick green glow. Even from where I was, I felt slightly ill. Quickly, the chief snatched Lifted's arm. But she was ready for him. She slapped his hand away and landed a kick in his belly. He stumbled back, surprised. He quickly recovered and took a fighting stance.

But Lifted was looking at the arm he'd grabbed. She looked up at him, angry. She swayed. At the same moment, Ejii ran forward, before I could grab her.

"No!" I shouted, moving forward.

"Stay back," she screamed, thrusting an open hand at me. "Help Lifted!"

Lifted was falling. Her light was out. Ejii threw herself at the chief. He seemed to welcome her with open arms. Their bodies smacked together in a most obscene type of embrace. Both his hands went around her waist. Her back was to me, so I couldn't see her face. But I heard her grunt with what could have only been pain. Then right before my eyes, they disappeared.

———

It was like three years ago, when Ejii died as we crossed into Ginen. But this time, she didn't even leave her body. She was just *gone*.

Lifted's skin went a sickly brown-yellow. I held her in my arms as I grew angrier and angrier, not caring about the possibility of Lifted suddenly awakening and accidentally killing me with her light. Not wondering where Dieuri, Makeda, or Fadio were.

I heard the forest around us churn and groan and I saw Dieuri sweep by above. I still didn't care. Kola flapped down beside me, her beak red with blood. A few of her feathers were missing. The blood wasn't her own. I didn't care. The air around me was heavy, though. That's what kept me alert. Heavy and humid. It smelled like curry. The chief was near.

Storm, I thought, flatly. I barely had to ask. The sky both perfectly understood and agreed with me. The clouds above me gathered tightly, dark gray, circulating in a three-mile-long diameter. I could feel and see this with complete clarity. As could Kola. She showed me flashes from minutes ago when Arif and I had fought each other. Makeda had watched Chief Ette come up the path with what was left of his men. About ten of them. Some men, some women, all had seed shooters. And all of them Changed. But not in the same way as those from Earth. These people were what they were not because of a human-made accident but because the land said so. They were "natural" Changed.

One could become like oil and slide nearly invisible on the surface of the earth. She would reemerge seed shooter in hand and shooting. Another could become a great black fast-moving elephant-like beast. And another could fly like a windseeker, except he was silent like the dead and brought no wind with him. Still, Lifted's deathly light took five of them down. Dieuri plucked two of them off like an eagle snatching up mice. And Makeda, who I now realized was a Changed One who could manipulate plants, dragged the earthbound ones to the ground with her vines.

When Fadio spotted the chief, he was smart enough not to try to fight him, but his yells for the others to come were unheeded, as Ejii, Arif, and I were . . . preoccupied. Kola witnessed all of this. She'd have witnessed more if a large white owl hadn't rammed into her from her left. The force of the blow sent her crashing to the ground.

This owl had once been an ally. Why had the owl changed? Betrayed the group? *No* bird was for the chief. Kola recovered, moments before hitting a tree branch. Then she'd attacked the giant owl, who was four times her size. But Kola was older and Kola was stronger. It was this owl's blood that was on her beak.

I didn't care. Kola didn't care. All we cared about now was the weight of the air around us. The smell of curry sitting in it. I showed Kola what I had seen and done. Her distress increased. And my distress escalated with hers. There was a ringing in my ears, sweat tumbled down my face, and my chest felt tight. She puffed her feathers, increasing to twice her size as she grasped my shoulder so tightly that she drew blood. I welcomed the pain. There was more of it from my tattoos. They burned and felt like tiny metal balls rolling around my face. I didn't need a mirror to know my tattoos were changing again. I felt the balls roll down my lips, chin, neck. They separated and rolled over my collarbone, shoulders, arms, and all ten of my fingers. I looked at my hands. The white lines and red dots ran up each finger. I clenched my hands into fists. I needed something to do with my hands.

Lifted was breathing and struggling to regain consciousness. We laid her down, Kola and me. We stood up, Kola and me. Somewhere deep in the sky, I could feel that goddess I'd seen during my training. The woman god who was also a bony fish. And I could feel the other, too, brooding and cavernous. They watched. And somewhere, I knew the Desert Magician was watching, too. We could feel every ripple of wind in the atmosphere. Every crackle of lightning. Every droplet. The vapor. The air pressure. It all wrapped itself around me like our skin and tissue.

That's what made us so sure. We could feel the change, smell it, taste it, hear it. We turned around. Then we could see it. He wasn't far. Just between. When he reappeared, he was right before us. Without Ejii.

"Where is she?" we, Kola and me, asked. Our voice was low and full of thunder.

The stupid chief didn't bat an eye. He could not see what was right before him. This was the chief's fundamental problem. He could never see past himself. Even in the body of his son, he was too enormous and expansive to see around his girth.

"I fed her to what waited for her there," he said, triumphantly. "Darkness. Shadows deeper than the universe." He pointed at me. "You should have been smart enough to flee."

"I've never been smart," we said.

"I can see that," he said, cocking his head. Was he seeing my changed tattoos? Sensing something else? Didn't matter. But he must have sensed something.

He held up his hands. "This is strong medicine. Ground-up demons, elgort teeth, and a curry whose ingredients can be found only in the Greeny Jungle. Taint only the hands and you can slip into time and space. A touch and you will see your destiny. A slap will end your life."

We didn't care for his babbling. Only one thing was on our mind.

"Your Earth will come to ruin," he said. "It must."

The gust was above us. It blew in a sideways spiral.

"A warrior never knows when the fight's over," the chief said.

We made it a funnel. We whipped it faster and faster. Gambo had tried to teach us how to do this, but it was beyond our capabilities. Or so we thought. But Gambo had said this back when Kola and I had been split. When Kola had been in Ginen and Dikéogu had been in the Aïr Mountains. We were together now.

As we whirled it faster, the chief stepped away from us. We pulled it from the sky and caught it in our left hand. Black-gray, it blasted everything around us with wind. Still unconscious, Lifted was blown into a tree. Plants, trees bent back. Everything moved away but the chief. The chief and his damn hands.

We held it like a spear, a great funnel of concentrated wind fifteen feet long, two inches in diameter. The chief turned and, finally, tried to run. Arrogance had made him wait too long. We threw. The true aim of a warrior. It was like a spear. Right into the left side of his back. Through his heart. The heart of his son. He slumped forward. Dead.

═══════

Kola flew from my shoulder.

The palm of my left hand burned. Both my ears were plugged. In my mind, the wind blew. I could still feel the sky. Certain Changed Ones must always pay a price to be what they are.

CHAPTER 32

From the Anthills

At some point, they all returned. Those who were left. Fadio, muddy but unscathed. He wandered off to the other side of the garden when he learned Ejii was gone. Dieuri with his sad sad knowing eyes. He knew he'd started this whole mess when he'd mixed sorcery and science so many decades ago. He deserved the guilt for not thinking his plan through. But then again, he still had accidently saved the world with his Peace Bombs. Makeda, blank-faced from her first taste of divvying out death instead of life. Lifted sat up, composed. I guess the glimpse of her destiny the chief had given her wasn't much of a surprise.

We'd just saved the world. Or helped the world save itself. It was over. All I could do was stand there and weep. I'll say no more of that.

At some point, I looked up and noticed the ground before a palm tree looked strange. A small mound puckered up. Like there were termites or ants below working their way to the surface. I stared at it. It gave my eyes and mind something to focus on. The soil was red, but hard. Only insects and trees could work their way through it like that. The mound grew; more dirt pushed out. A finger poked through. I ran to the mound and started digging. The dirt bit at the underside of my nails. I kept digging and scraping. Dieuri landed behind me.

"What is that?" he asked, looking around me. He gasped when he saw the searching finger.

"Help us," was all I said.

Fadio came running over.

"Help us!" I shouted.

"Is that Ejii?!" Lifted said. I didn't look at her, but I heard her try to stand up and then fall. She crawled over to us.

We had a hole dug around her arm. Ejii's arm. But the dirt was so hard that it was slow going. Even with the three of us digging.

"Stand back!" Makeda screamed. She dropped to her knees and dug her fingers right into the hard earth like it was pudding. She pushed Ejii out with such force that I had to catch her. Ejii coughed up and gagged on dirt. She was filthy with it. I held her tight. She was warm. Ejii was alive.

CHAPTER 33

Ejii won't talk about it much. All she'll say was that he took her to a place of light, darkness, vegetation, and death. She doesn't know if she was alive or dead. "After a while, does that even matter anymore?" she asked. I think it does. Even if you're Ejii Ugabe, she who keeps dying and being reborn, life isn't the same as death.

It was Arif who saved Ejii. While in the place the chief had taken them, the astral plane, spirit world, the wilderness, hell, whatever you want to call it, the stupid chief made a grand error. Still bloated on his arrogance, he "fed" her to the only one who could save her. The great shadow that was Arif. Allah bless Arif. God save me, now.

We've left Atlantis. Dieuri and Makeda remained there. Dieuri said he had other experiments to do. I didn't like the sound of that, but who am I to stop him? The Earth may be better off—the chief and his people had been able to do some good, putting out fires, encouraging forests, and so on—but it still suffers in places. It is still warming. We still have spontaneous forests and Aejejs. There may be more truly corrupted Changed Ones. All is not solved. But for the time, we left.

After talking that night, me, Ejii, Lifted, and Fadio, we

decided on one thing. To find Gambo. I think it had some-thing to do with me, but as I've told this story, I'm not so sure anymore. Was this when they decided to instead take me prisoner? Is this when Kola turned on me? I cannot remember now. It's been about a month. That I know. I know that I am seventeen years old. I know that I feel that the longer they keep me in captivity, the stronger the wind in my mind gets.

Only I know where Gambo is. I don't know what they think they will gain from holding me prisoner.

End of Dikéogu Audio File Series

Dikéogu Audio File Series
ended April 28, 2074
Current Location: *Unknown Region, Niger*
Weather: *39° C (101° F), N.I.U.F. (Not Including Unpredictable Factors)*

Aejej

Dikéogu's dreadlocks were growing wild. Ejii hadn't seen him wash them once since they'd left Atlantis. They were stiff and stuck out in all directions even though his locks were several inches long. Sometimes they sparked with static. The brilliant Nigérien sun had turned them a bright reddish orange, whereas his skin had only grown blacker. Though he sniffed incessantly at his food before eating it, he still ate heartily, so he was still broad shouldered and muscular.

His clothes were dust swept from the wind that he refused to calm. And his face and arms were covered with the strange alive artwork of what used to be his tattoos. It looked as if Shango himself had drawn the intricate red lines and perfect white dots that covered his arms and face like the branches of some strange tree.

They couldn't bind him. He could burn through rope and rust any metal. Even trying to grab him was impossible, for he could blast them with lightning. The only reason he hadn't run off was because they kept a constant eye on him. And because he wanted to find Gambo, too, and he knew he couldn't do it alone. *Or maybe Dikéogu's drawn to him*, Ejii thought.

"*Dikéogu's illness is Gambo's. As is the cure*," Jaa had said to Ejii in a vision just after Jaa was killed. It seemed so long ago, though it had only been a few weeks. But it *was* long ago, in a way. *Back then I wasn't an orphan,* she thought. *None of us were.*

Dikéogu started showing signs of unraveling hours after killing the chief. No, it didn't start with killing the chief, it was when he was battling Arif. Arif's shadows had done something to him.

As they traveled north, deeper into Niger now, Dikéogu began to grow suspicious of everyone. He'd allowed Ejii to sleep beside him that night, but he'd clasped her to him like he was sure someone would snatch her away again. And by morning, he didn't even want to stand close to her. "I just need some time," he said. But a wind had picked up and a storm kept rumbling from nearby but never coming. Threatening but never revealing the threat. The most disturbing thing was when he wouldn't even let Kola near him. Upset, she took to the sky. And though she followed, she refused to come near him.

Dikéogu stopped his camel and glanced at Ejii with distrust. She bit her lip and sighed. They'd fought enough. He wasn't rational. They all stopped as he climbed off his camel and walked some yards away. He stood looking out at the desert horizon. Ejii could see a spontaneous forest some miles east. Its palm trees were peopled with green parrots. Agonians. Ejii sucked her teeth. Who knew who they allied with now? To the west, she saw a line of desert foxes heading in the opposite direction.

"Come here," Dikéogu said, looking at Ejii. "Only you," he said, when he saw Fadio and Lifted step toward him.

Ejii slowly walked to him. He eyed her with his usual frown. Even without reading him, she could sense his mind was mostly clouded with dust, wind, and thunder. And rage. This was what was causing his distrust and memory loss the most, his rage.

"I feel him strongly now," he said. He looked at Ejii and smirked. "You have to let me go," he said. "Gambo knows we are out here."

Ejii sighed loudly. "For the millionth time, Dikéogu, we are not holding you prisoner. We're in this together for . . ." She trailed off as he turned from her. She sighed. "How much farther?"

"We travel another day and that should be enough," he said.

"Okay," she said. She wanted to take his hand. But he'd probably kill her. That night with Dikéogu in Atlantis, just before they'd faced the chief and his elite Changed soldiers, had healed her. The pain from everything had remained, but she was healed of its destruction. She no longer even heard the murmur of the Whole's song. Love really could heal even the worst wounds. Oh, Arif. But now what?

What was going to happen when they found Gambo? She'd been through too much to not admit the obvious. Dikéogu was slowly becoming an Aejej. Bit by bit, he was blowing away. Soon all that would be left would be his rage. Then he'd kill them all. He'd become like Gambo. All of them would fade into history. All but the rage of the storms Dikéogu and Gambo had become.

They traveled until Dikéogu said it was enough. A day and a half had passed. They were exhausted. He'd stopped them at a fat baobab tree. For the first time since they'd left Atlantis, Dikéogu's wind stopped. Ejii was afraid he'd leave them in the darkness of the night. She decided to leave that up to Allah.

In the early morning, Dikéogu joined them at the smoldering fire, sitting beside Ejii, close enough for their shoulders to touch. No one knew what to say.

"None of you can hurt me here," he said. "So tonight, we speak as friends."

Fadio spit into the fire. "Do you even know what our names are?" he asked.

He gazed at Fadio for more than a few moments. Long enough for Fadio to feel uncomfortable and look away. Lifted narrowed her eyes, but only shook her head. She didn't speak much to Dikéogu these days.

"Dikéogu?" Ejii asked.

Dikéogu looked at her with what Ejii realized was complete and total confusion. And then blooming shock.

"What . . . ? What the . . ." He frowned deeply and rubbed his forehead. Then he looked at Ejii. And Ejii saw within him. She saw him seeing that night on Atlantis. He was remembering. She took his hands but he snatched them from her and shook his head. He stood up, still staring at Ejii.

"Where is Kola?"

Kola hooted loudly from the top of a palm tree. But she didn't fly down.

Ejii saw it in his eyes. He glanced up at his owl, his chi. Then he looked back at Ejii. He recognized them both. He loved them. So dearly. He'd die for them. He couldn't understand how he'd forgotten. *Guilt. Shame. His goddamn parents. The chief had taken Ejii away from him.*

The blast of wind sent Ejii tumbling into Fadio. Lifted

was smacked against the baobab tree. Kola took to the air. The smoldering coals and their tents were whisked into the desert. The camels took off.

Dikéogu stood in the middle of the maelstrom unmoved by its wind. Then Ejii could see it. Coming from the west. An Aejej. Gambo. Dikéogu turned and ran toward it.

"No!!" Ejii screamed, her voice cracking. "Wait!!" She sobbed, watching him run. She took off after him. She felt the breath in her chest burning. Sand stinging her eyes. She saw him disappear as the whirlwind grew twice its size. The sound of thousands of women screaming deafened her ears. She shielded her face with her arms. Then she stopped, head down, trying to calm herself. Every breath was part sand.

As she'd been trained by the soul of Ginen to call on the Earth's soul to save itself, she'd been trained for this, too. How to concentrate while in terror. She'd once saved the baby of an idiok baboon by staring down an elgort. She could do this, too. *Calm,* she thought. The opposite of Gambo and Dikéogu. *Peace. Love. Pride. Life.*

Suddenly, the winds around her stopped. She could hear them churning feet away. But for the moment, she was safe. She looked up. Two pairs of gigantic red eyes. The size of truck tires. One pair was narrow. The other was sorrowful.

"Gambo," Ejii said. "We've come . . ."

A black cavern deep as the universe, the size of a bus, opened before her. "RAHHHHHHHHHHHHHHHHHHHHH-HHHHHHHHHHHHHHHHHHHHHHHHHH!" it screamed. Every cell in Ejii's body vibrated with terror. She fought hard to keep in control. If she fled, the winds would shred her to nothing but bone.

"Dikéogu," she said, her voice shaking. But she stood tall. "My love." Tears came into her eyes. "My decorated warrior. Stormbringer! Let him go. Come back to me! You have other storms to rain down. Good storms. Come back to me!" She fell to her knees. "We are needed. You and I."

She looked up, staring at the sorrowful pair and ignoring the narrow one. Willing them to look into her stinging eyes. The cavernous mouth opened again and screamed rage at her in Arabic. Gambo had been an Aejej for centuries. Now here he was again. It pained Ejii's heart. Gambo was lost this time. All that had been of him had died with Jaa and Buji. But Dikéogu . . . she held his gaze.

Her visions of the future were rare and unpredictable. The one she had now, she shared with Dikéogu. It shocked them both. Then there was a great gust of wind, as one storm pushed another storm away. It began to rain sand. Marvelous soft sand. Ejii lifted her head, her eyes closed, her breath held. Then she stood up, her head down as she waited. When it stopped, the sand was to her waist. And there Dikéogu stood, wearing only a bright white caftan. Ejii dug herself out and walked up to him just as it started raining . . . water.

"Not my asking," he said.

"Okay," Ejii said.

"I'm sorry."

"Shut up," she said, taking his hand.

Behind them, Lifted and Fadio came running, rare smiles of relief on their faces.

Dikéogu pulled Ejii to him and drew her into a glorious kiss as they stood in the middle of the Sahara Desert in the middle of nowhere showered with rain.

Desert Magician Water

So there it is.

My duology. An African future. Sight seen. Sound heard. Scent smelled. Land touched. Now it exists in you, too.

The fire has dwindled to a lone ember. Now it is a fart of smoke. We've burned down a lot of wood, no? It had to be done; where would the story be without fire? What do you think? I could not bring you water without bringing you close to the fire. I hope you have witnessed, gathered, and processed much from all these pages, from these words, these worlds, these ideas, these *characters*. Not generated, but homegrown.

As for me, I'm tired of you. And that means it's time to move on. I like my space to think, to do, to rest, to dance. Space is good. It keeps you stable and, even when you're not stable, when you have space to wobble, being unstable does not matter. Come back when I have had some rest. When I have soaked up alone time. I won't be here, though. You know me, the desert magician can make water appear where there is none, and I also can make it dry up and leave nothing but dust. It all depends.

For now, leave me.